THE VAMPIRE OF

MAPLE TOWN

Congratulations Dianna
on winning the LibraryThing
giveaway for The Vampire of
Maple Town! I hope you
have a happy holiday and
enjoy the magic of Maple
Town and all its inhabitants!

Kane Mobzller

THE VAMPIRE OF MAPLE TOWN

By Kane McLoughlin

EverAfterPress

An Imprint of EverAfterPress

To my family, friends, my darling Elizabeth, and the promise I made on Navy Pier all those years ago for which none of this would have been possible

The Vampire of Maple Town

ISBN-13: 978-0-578-409-733

www.kanemcloughlin.com

Give feedback on the book at:
kanemcloughlin@outlook.com

Twitter: @withachippedcup

First Edition

Printed in the U.S.A

CONTENTS

CHAPTER ONE

THE BOY ON THE ROAD

The carriage had golden vines that snaked and interlaced like elaborate shoelaces. They hung over the doors and behind the wheels. They beat against the carriage, following the steady rhythm of the two black horses that led the way. In daylight, it would have been garish. At night, it was beautiful—that is, it would be if there were anyone to see it. Beautiful, but strange. The carriage was like a shooting star pulled by horses. However, it was much too fast for anyone to make a wish on.

Just ask the driver. He clutched his broken overcoat and shivered as the cold autumn air nipped at his exposed flesh. His shouts cracked through the air. His four horses sprinted faster.

The woman in the carriage sat with her legs crossed. She wore a sleek black dress and jostled with every minor bump the carriage took, making her feel unbearably light and untethered. However, her eyes remained fixed on the dark countryside as they watched everything and nothing at all.

"We're almost there, miss," the driver called.

The woman's eyes narrowed.

Just silhouetted in the distance, she could see it. It was faint, but she'd recognize its shape anywhere. She traced the outline of the odd mansion on the windowpane, her memory filling in the gaps where the edges seemed to blur into the night. The mansion slipped beyond the horizon and she felt, for a split second, a feeling of brazen warmth, one that had remained dormant for so long she had forgotten it was there. And with it came a dull ache that made her want to jump through the window and run home.

Whatever reverie she experienced, though, was short-lived. Bit by bit, her left arm began to glow with ethereal blue markings that snaked up the limb in a mysterious pattern. The woman winced. She dropped the arm to her lap, the satin from her dress doing its best to cover the marks. Her forehead hit the window with a muffled thud, and her hair fell across her face. She absentmindedly mused at how the moonlight turned her brown locks bronze.

"Of course it wouldn't be this easy," she muttered. Her teeth grated. She struggled to raise her right hand. She breathed heavily until the final traces of the blue markings faded away.

The woman glared at the large black cat across from her. Despite her best efforts to compose herself, she knew the damage was done. She had been foolish to let him see her moment of weakness. He beamed at her with his large amethyst eyes, looking almost amused at her pain. Because like the woman, the cat knew that the two of them had no business going to a town where she was declaratively dead.

"It's almost as if everything has been frozen in time, no?" the cat said. His eyes glinted as his mouth curled into a wide smile.

The woman slid her eyes over the cat before returning her gaze to the window.

The cat purred. "You could have declined, you know. People fall under the weather all the time."

The woman shot the cat another look. She flicked her wrists. A thin silver piece of paper with black lettering materialized out of the empty space. It was no bigger than the palm of her hand. It hovered in the air until she grasped it between her thin fingers, if only to check for what seemed to be the hundredth time if this was all worth it.

Your presence is requested at the Autumn Ball. A gold carriage will arrive at your residence on the next full moon. If come midnight the carriage remains vacant, we will assume your absence.
Lord Autaine

"What's the matter?" The cat beamed. "Cat got your tongue?"

"There's a girl at this party," the woman said. "She needs a teacher."

"But you can't be it. At least, not anymore." The cat smirked. "And might I add I'm very impressed you've made it this far. Those runes can't be very comfortable." His eyes peered at the arm on which the glowing blue marks had appeared.

The woman winced as the marks again ripped into her skin. However, this time she was faster to regain her composure. She readjusted so that the runes were once again concealed, gripped her left arm, and gave the cat a cheeky smile.

"I'll be fine," she said. "Anyway, this all has to do with a silly promise that I made to an equally silly woman. The point is you're going to have to take my place. So be on your best behavior. You're going to teach her as you did me."

"Strong words coming from a witch losing her magic," the cat said. He gave another wide smile and turned away to stretch against the velvet seat, disregarding the heated glares aimed at

him. He gave a sigh before continuing. "But suit yourself. I was getting bored anyway. She's not going to be a brat like you were, is she?"

"I wouldn't know." There was a slight pause. It was brief, but it was enough to make the cat's large eyes narrow. "But her father says that she shows a lot of potential in becoming a great witch."

"I see. So, some protégée bitch, is she?" The cat laughed, his eyes rolling back in their sockets.

"Watch your mouth."

"Easy," the cat said. He loosened his shoulders before giving the woman a surprisingly sober look. "I'll be on my best behavior."

The woman gave a small, tired smile. "Thank you." She sighed. "Give her this too, will you?" She waved her hand in a circular motion, creating a hole in the air. Her hand disappeared inside it and then reappeared with an old deck of playing cards that she set down beside her. "It's a gift for her. They were her mother's."

The cat leapt over to the woman's side and circled the deck of cards. He pawed at it as if it were going to explode. His attention shifted toward the woman. "I never pinned you as the sentimental type."

"I'm not."

"You and your secrets."

The cat began swallowing the deck whole when suddenly the carriage came to an abrupt stop. The force threw the woman and her feline companion with such force that the cat nearly choked on the deck.

The woman nursed her throbbing head and glanced over at the cat. He cursed and coughed profusely, but overall was fine, with no stray cards out of his mouth.

The woman rushed to the window. "What happened? Why have we stopped?"

"We hit a snag in the road," the driver said, already out of his seat and looking at the patch of ground in front of the carriage.

"Well, can you get rid of it? Or at least move the damn thing? You nearly killed my cat!"

"It's not that simple, miss," the driver said. "I didn't see him. He was just there. Luckily, I didn't hit him, but I almost did. Sorry about your cat."

"Wait, what did you almost hit?"

The driver was silent. He seemed to struggle with the words, cocking his head and blinking at the front of the carriage until finally confirming what he saw.

"A boy," he said. "But it can't be. This out of the way?"

The woman tore out of the carriage and joined the driver outside in the hopes of demystifying his unusual claim. However, it was just as he had said. There lying on the road was an unconscious and filthy young boy. Not quite a child, but lacking the subtle touch of adolescence. It was hard to put an age on him. She pinned him for maybe twelve or thirteen. It was his face—his face still held a few delicate features that made him look young, while his body was awkward, as if his limbs and his joints had yet to decide whether to stop growing or not.

Though by the looks of things, it didn't appear as if he were going to get any older. She parted his bangs to see, hidden behind a few wet locks of dark hair, splatters of mud and hints of something red: blood. Her heart raced and she quickly leaned an ear against his chest. She felt a long-held breath tumble out of her.

He was alive.

"Driver! Quickly, get him into the carriage!"

The driver hastily lifted the boy inside while the woman followed shortly behind. She excused the driver before returning her attention to the boy that sat across from her. The woman

began searching for the source of the blood and stopped when she discovered a large gash under his neckline. She fell back in her seat.

"Well, isn't this interesting," the cat said.

The woman whipped her head.

The cat hopped over to the boy's left side and pawed at his collar. "You know what this is. We can't have it here. Tell the driver to stop."

The woman ignored him. She raised a hand only to lay it down by her side. She knew the cat was right. She should've left the boy behind, let him out of her carriage right then and there, but she didn't. Perhaps it was her motherly instinct that drove her to reach out and finally lay a healing hand on the boy's neck; whatever it was, it made him suddenly wake with a shudder.

"Who are you?" he asked. His voice was weak and scratched, much like the rest of him.

The woman pulled her hand back in alarm. His eyes were startlingly blue, briefly reminding her of the sky at midday. They looked so delicate—like little pools of glass that reflected all that they saw but would shatter with even the slightest show of force.

"It's okay. You're safe now," she said in a low voice so as not to startle him. "You were barely hanging on when we found you."

The boy propped himself up on his elbows and surveyed the scratches and marks that marred his body. "Thank you," he said. Suddenly, his eyes took on a distant look as he shot up from his seat. He grimaced at the sudden movement, but that didn't stop the words from flying out his mouth. "We were attacked. Please, we need to go back! Please!"

"There, there," the woman said in what she hoped to be a comforting manner. She took the young boy into her arms, her brief hesitation disappearing as he willingly leaned into her touch. "It's going to be okay."

She brushed a hand over his eyes. His eyes shut. His features smoothed out. He passed out in her arms with tears trickling down his cheeks. The sight made the woman's heart clench as she felt herself holding him tighter.

After a moment of deliberation, she raised a hand to his head.

"A memory charm?" the cat said. "Seems rather unnecessary, don't you think?"

"Temporary. Don't be so cold! I can only imagine what he's been through tonight. This will ease him until he's ready to remember. Memories can be cruel things."

Within moments, the boy woke up again and backed out of the woman's arms. He practically fell back in the seat across from her. He whipped his head wildly from side to side before an involuntary shudder ripped through him.

"Cold?" the woman asked with what could almost be described as affection.

"Just a little." The boy remained huddled in his damp clothes, trying his best to suppress his shivering.

"Here, let me help."

The woman's eyes widened a bit as the boy shrank away from her outstretched hand. Strange, when he was leaning into her just a second ago.

"I'm not going to hurt you," she said. "Just watch."

Suddenly, the damaged needlework of his clothing began to stitch itself together while bits of blood and dirt disappeared from the fabric. All the dirt and blood on his face seemed to evaporate as well, until there was no trace of anything other than a few strands of brown hair out of place. The boy sat puzzled for a moment, then turned toward the woman as the cat hissed at them. The woman rolled her eyes.

"Is he alright?" said the boy.

"Oh, don't worry about him," she said. "He's just a sourpuss."

"What's that?"

"An annoying cat that gets very fussy when I use magic so frivolously," she said, and gave a frustrated sigh. She gently ran a hand over the boy's neck. "There, now that nasty cut is gone. For now at least."

The boy didn't say anything at first, just stared at her with unblinking eyes. "So, you're a witch."

"Not the bad type," the woman said quickly.

"A good witch?"

"Exactly," she said. "However . . ."

"However?"

"No, I'm just messing with you." She ruffled his tangled brown hair. "Here, come look." She nodded toward the window. "Out of all the places I've been to, nothing compares to Maple Town."

The boy cautiously joined the woman by the window as the carriage entered a small provincial town. There were lots of trees and even a train passing by in the distance. Rows of wooden cottages with double-story windows populated the sides of the streets their carriage passed. They were still and lifeless, with only the faint wisps of smoke that came from their chimneys to indicate that anyone inhabited them.

The woman laughed to herself, watching as the boy's eyes jumped from cottage to cottage. For a moment, a memory escaped her of a young girl staring in awe out a similar window, laughing to her companion about the many adventures they'd have together.

She clutched her left arm tightly.

They passed an area where different shops and houses surrounded a large empty space, in the middle of which rested a beautiful fountain. The fountain was an abstract design that

both the boy and the woman couldn't decipher, yet they stared, mesmerized by the trickling water that echoed quietly through the marketplace.

Beyond the town square was the odd-looking mansion, up on its high hilltop. It wasn't very large, but it wasn't exactly small either. In fact, it seemed much too thin and tall. It sat awkwardly, like an oddly configured vulture surrounded by a tall black fence. Unlike the cottages, it was constructed out of many different rooms and walls, as if someone had taken bits and pieces of different houses and mashed them together to create it.

The woman saw the boy grimace at it.

"Despite its rough edges, it's a beautiful place," she said. "The man who lives there—at least, I think he still lives there—built that place from the ground up. I couldn't believe it when he told me he wanted to do that. Never picked up a hammer in his life and up and decided to build all this. All because I said he was nuts. Nuts! Can you believe it?"

"You know a lot about him."

"You could say that," the woman mused before abruptly turning away.

"Why's that?"

"You ask a lot of questions," the woman said sharply, causing the boy to wince. She smiled at him apologetically before continuing in a much gentler tone. "But I guess that's life, isn't it?" She sighed. "One big yarn of questions that continues to tangle itself up."

"Why don't you untangle it?"

"It isn't that easy." She paused. "You make choices that are tough and sometimes painful, yet you know you're doing the right thing, so you feel good about it, but then it eats you up because you don't know what would've happened had you done something else, you know?"

The boy only regarded the woman with a blank stare and a furrowed brow.

"Of course not," she said. "And then years later, you look in the mirror because you can't sleep, wondering if you made the right choices at all, but at that point you're stuck. The old options are gone. Does that make sense?"

"That sounds like a very tangled yarn."

"Doesn't it?" The woman gave a sad smile, shrugged her shoulders, and turned her eyes back to the window. "But that's life."

"So, are you going to see him?"

She turned back to him. "Who? The man in the mansion? Why do you say that?"

"Well, you're in that pretty dress." The boy meekly hid his face and kicked his legs over the edge of his seat upon realizing he'd told the woman she was pretty.

"No, no, no. He hates these sort of things," the woman said. "I won't. Though I might. Who knows? No, that can't happen. Absolutely not."

"You don't want to see him?"

"Of course I do!" she said, not realizing that she'd practically shouted it. Then, almost as an afterthought, she recoiled her hand to her chest. "Ah wait, no. Again, it's complicated."

"Everything's complicated!"

"You're telling me," the woman said. "Hang on!"

She looked out the window, half of her surprised that they'd long since passed by the vulture-like mansion, the other half worried, giddy, elated—and sick to her stomach. The mere thought of attending this party and by some chance seeing the man in the mansion set all these emotions aflutter. *Because what if*—? she thought, but quickly stopped herself from remembering

that which she'd locked away many years ago. She didn't deserve hope, as her body would remind her; the blue markings again snaked up her left arm underneath her sleeve. She slammed a fist against the side of the carriage and crumpled the hem of her dress. She wanted to scream but didn't, noticing the alarmed looks on both the boy and the cat. She composed herself, and came to the same conclusion she'd drawn all those many years ago. *I can't. I just can't anymore.* She bit her lip and peered up at the boy. She eyed him up and down before finally giving him a weak smile.

"You should go in my place."

"What?"

She took the boy's hand. "You heard me. Just take this invitation and show it to the man at the door. Say I'm sick. Say you're taking your mother's place. Say whatever you want." She looked back at the odd mansion in the distance. She bit her lip again before finally shaking her head. "If he's there . . . if there is a slight, even minuscule, chance that he will be at that party, I can't be."

"But—"

"No buts! I just . . . I just can't be there. Please, do this for me because life just isn't fair. Can you do this?"

The woman stared intently at the boy's unsure face until he lowered his head. She watched him give a reluctant nod. It was all she needed. She ruffled his hair again before thrusting the invitation into his hands.

The carriage came to a steady stop. The doors swung open. The woman eyed the boy for the last time that night. She wavered for a moment over making him go in her place. She felt almost guilty sending him. He looked so lost as he glanced at the invitation and the building in front of him. Then the pain returned. Her teeth grated against one another, but the pain this time was much

more intense. It seared through her blood. She almost fainted, but instead leaned against the boy, disguising the action as one last reassuring hug.

"You'll be fine. Take the cat with you. He's a gift for a young girl. He'll find her," she said. "You'll be fine."

Everything about the mansion screamed to be looked at. It appeared as if it'd take days to walk up the stairs that led into the white fortress. The bright lights illuminating the colossal building were so bright, the boy had to shield his eyes until they'd adjusted to the tacky decor.

And that was just the entryway. At the side of the grand house was a rose garden that extended behind the mansion, though it was impossible to tell how far. Even past where the entrance lights touched, the boy could see faint traces of green and red here and there by hanging lamps, which were filled with fireflies that would lazily traverse from one lamp to another, giving the illusion that the garden was illuminated by hundreds of low-hanging stars.

The boy followed the cat and many of the other guests up the marble stairs to where a thin, short man in a black suit stood like a gatekeeper, taking invitations almost robotically. He spoke with a monotonous voice, repeating something angrily that the boy couldn't understand at first.

"Invitation, sir."

"My mother couldn't make it. She sent my cat and me inst—"

Before he could finish, the thin man snatched the little silver invitation and gave a curt "Enjoy."

The doors creaked open. The boy and the cat walked with the group of guests down a gilded corridor. A long red carpet snaked along the floor like a tongue, inviting them deeper and

deeper into the mansion. They passed a fountain that oscillated between different colors. It was carved to resemble a stunning woman in a sundress holding a large sunhat. She stood with one hand raised to her forehead as if she were looking at something in the distance.

Whatever the statue woman was looking toward, the boy noticed it was where he and the procession of guests were heading. The boy poked his head just barely out of line to notice that the guests were all heading toward a large white wall. But still, the line kept moving. Each guest seemed to disappear into the wall. Suddenly, the boy and the cat were face-to-face with the white wall.

The boy gave a hesitant look at it, not knowing what to do next.

"Go on," said a man behind him. "Don't keep us all waiting."

Someone gave the boy a shove.

The boy stumbled forward expecting pain, but instead was welcomed by silky fabric and dim lights. He watched as the guests before him confidently continued down the new hallway as if it were the most natural thing in the world. The boy quickly followed them through what seemed like twelve sheets of vanilla-scented fabric before reaching what he believed to be the most spectacular thing he would see throughout his eventful night.

Much like everything else in the mansion, the ballroom was gigantic. There were shimmering crystal chandeliers that lit the entire room. There was glitter falling from the second story and large ivory pillars draped with the same silky white fabric. The boy stood at the top of a large entryway staring down at what lay below.

Flower petals fell like raindrops. People laughed loudly to the clinking of champagne glasses that echoed like a chorus to the party. Women were dressed in the most exotic colors, dancing to

the music that came from the balcony directly opposite the boy. There was an eating corner, where a line of chefs stood nodding, cutting, and serving the most delicious meats and pastries that did nothing short of make the boy's stomach growl. Waiters skillfully dodged people dancing and dipping, all the while handing out drinks and taking empty glasses away on their trays.

Everyone around the boy sprinted down to join the festivities below. Some would dance, occasionally lifting one another off the ground. One woman twirled so fast that she seemed to float like a kite before stepping in time with her lover for the night. Other times, women and men disappeared and reappeared on different sides of the ballroom. Little spiderlike sparklers occasionally fell from the ceiling before suddenly bursting into small clouds. The boy watched children and adults alike chase those little bits of sparkle dust. It all seemed like a dream, a fantastic dream that the boy didn't want to wake up from.

Then, suddenly, the lights in the ballroom dimmed and refocused on a single figure that stood at the heart of the dance floor. He was a tall and extremely thin man in a white suit. He held a large purple masquerade mask. He tipped his head slightly, letting the large purple mask hang in a weird limbo between his chest and the bridge of his nose. He took a dramatic pause before looking upon his guests, whom he left breathless. He let the anticipation mount just enough before finally clearing his throat. In a single fluid motion, the mask and his left arm disappeared behind his back, while his posture straightened. He stood there for a brief moment, letting the ballroom grow so quiet that nothing but the bated breath of one's neighbor could be heard.

"Welcome, one and all," the man said. "I'm so very glad you have all arrived. As for those who don't know me, I am Lord

Autaine. Welcome to my humble abode!" He gave another low and elegant bow. "This year marks the eleventh anniversary of the Autumn Ball. To think how you've all put up with me for so long is beyond me." He paused again, letting the low murmur of laughter subside. Then for a moment, his face grimaced. "Eleven long years," he began, letting the words linger. Then his face softened and the grimace returned to a warm smile. "Eleven years of festivities and celebration. This year is the white year, if you haven't noticed." He gestured toward the white pillars and drapery. A few in the crowd laughed. "White for the upcoming winter. White for a new year, and, most of all, white for a new beginning and a newer and better Autumn Ball than I hope you all have experienced thus far!" There was a roar of applause. Lord Autaine brought the purple mask up and bowed once more to his guests. "And with that all said, I am the author of tonight, and I say eat, be merry, and let's dance the night away!" He ended enthusiastically, laughing at the sounds of applause that followed.

The boy clapped along with all the other guests until realizing that the cat was gone. He managed to catch a glimpse of it as it darted toward the dance floor. He scurried down the stairs, going underneath and ducking past a large man whose conversation with a rather plump lady had turned them both an equally bright shade of rose.

"You saw Vincent?" said the large man.

The boy stopped. For a moment, he thought the man was talking to him instead of his date for the night.

"No, I didn't. Is he here?" the plump woman said. "That's very rare of him to attend such things."

"He was filthy! He was out of breath. He caused such a scene! Pity, he always seems to be so put together."

"Oh really? I wish I could see that! Is he still here?"

"I wouldn't know. Ah, I think I see him now. Don't look at him! Here, have another drink, my dear."

The large man and the plump lady turned, unintentionally pushing the boy forward into the crowd. The boy was bumped and tossed by the throng of people until he found himself knocked to the ground.

"I'm sorry," a voice said. The boy looked up to see a girl with long brown hair. She wore a silver dress with little ocean-blue flowers embroidering the edges, but he found himself most struck by her different-colored eyes—her left eye was green, while her right was turquoise. She smiled and blushed a deep beet red before hastily adjusting her flower hairpin. The flower on the hairpin had an intricate design made entirely out of miniature playing cards, all hearts. The boy bolted to his feet. The two stood at equal height and were both unmistakably uncomfortable in front of each other, not once daring to meet the other's gaze—as all kids are wont to do when they meet someone that makes them discover that the other gender isn't so icky after all.

"It was my fault," the boy said quickly. "I'm sorry."

"Oh no, really, it was me," she said. "Is this your cat?"

The boy turned his head slightly to see that there by the girl's leg was the large black cat.

"No, but he seems to like you."

"He does," the girl said. "He's very friendly."

"It's probably because you look so nice tonight," the boy blurted out. He immediately lost his nerve and turned his attention toward his shoes.

The boy peeked up just enough to catch a flicker of a smile.

"Thank you. Papa dressed me tonight. But, well, can you keep a secret?" she said in a hushed voice.

The boy must have nodded because his body froze as the girl leaned close to whisper something into his ear.

"I kind of hate it!"

"It can't be that bad," the boy said.

"But it is!" She crumpled up her face. "I can barely move in this thing! It's no wonder I crashed into you. In fact, I should be thanking you because you might have saved me from falling over myself."

The two of them laughed.

"Do you have a name?" she asked.

The boy could see her blue slippers clicking together nervously. He began to open his mouth, but the words wouldn't come out.

"I don't know," he said, scratching his head.

"How do you forget your name?" she began but was interrupted when another girl commandeered her by the arm, almost knocking them both down in the process.

"There you are!" the second girl shouted. "I've been looking all over for you!" She tossed her blonde hair and laughed. She wore a similar dress with white stripes and red roses embroidering the fringe. She was also taller and had an air about her that made her seem older, or at least more confident, than the first girl. "Who's your friend?"

Before the boy could say anything, the blonde girl extended her hand.

"I'm Sally Maple. I don't think I've seen you before," she said. "And I know everyone. Are you new in town?"

"I don't know," he replied, blushing less than he had with Sally's friend. For some reason, he couldn't recall anything prior to meeting the woman in the carriage. He didn't have much time to think about it, though, because the second after he spoke, Sally covered her mouth, trying her best to hide the fit of laughter that threatened to erupt.

"He's so precious. Where did you find him?"

Sally grabbed the boy's arm with her other arm and beamed at him. He stood frozen, and he glanced over at the brunette girl, who looked equally uncomfortable underneath Sally's grasp. Then came another shout from the crowd.

"I've been looking all over for you two!"

"Atticus!" Sally said. "I didn't know you were looking for us."

"That's because we're trying to get away," the brunette girl whispered.

Atticus looked the same age as Sally, or maybe a year or so older. It was hard to tell as he looked so neat, with his chestnut hair parted to the side and his immaculate white suit. It painfully reminded the nameless boy that he was still in a simple white shirt and brown trousers.

Just as Sally had, Atticus noticed the boy as an afterthought. "And you are?" he asked, turning his head slightly.

"He doesn't remember," interjected the brunette girl.

"What are you talking about? How do you forget your name?" Atticus said.

The boy's head began throbbing more and more as he tried his best to remember his name. He glanced over at the brunette girl as if she had the answer, but to no avail.

A jolt of pain struck his neck.

The boy fell to the ground. He clutched his neck tightly, but it throbbed stronger and faster with each second. It sent waves of pain all over his body. He felt the two girls and boy hover over him, heard the bits and piece of their concern, before he managed to get to his feet.

"Sorry, I'm not feeling well," he said, and turned away.

"Hey, where you going?" Atticus yelled after him. "Weirdo."

The boy broke into a dash. He felt his neck ooze blood. He pressed his hand over it, but it wouldn't stop bleeding. He needed

to get away. He needed to get outside. He ran past the dancers and bumped into a few people, but he didn't care. He needed to get away from everything. It was getting too loud. It was getting too bright. Everything needed to dim down.

He managed to make it outside, where a cool autumn breeze brushed against his face. It was calming. It wasn't loud out here. He looked up at the night sky, which slowly grew hazier. Stars became faint specks, and the pain in his neck grew utterly unbearable. It seared his throat as if someone were making him swallow lava. He let out a muffled scream before everything turned black and he fell to the ground.

At the last second, he felt a pair of arms catch him. He lost consciousness for the third time that evening, but not before hearing a man's voice.

"I got you, Charlie."

CHAPTER TWO

THE MAN IN THE MANSION

"I wonder what goes on in that mansion," Maurice the baker said, setting down a tray of rolls on his market cart.

His wife emerged from their bakery carrying a basket of those same rolls in one hand and pastries in the other. She shook her head upon dropping the baskets into the cart that they'd take to the market along with the other vendors that morning.

The baker's wife had a thin face and piercing brown eyes, while her husband sported a fiery-red beard and had a large belly that was always in competition with his wild imagination concerning which one was fatter. Both wore aprons speckled with flour, though hers had fewer splotches of oil. Her sleeves were rolled up, exposing her thin milky-white skin to the unforgiving sun, while her auburn hair was tied back in a ponytail that bobbed as she reluctantly joined her husband, who remained planted outside their shop staring up at number thirteen Chiaroscuro Lane.

The mansion sat ominously just beyond the marketplace, situated atop a hill and surrounded by a tall black gate. Although, it was hard to call the structure a mansion at all. It was as if a tornado had picked up a whole village that then put itself back

together in the form of a structure that looked as if it were going to fall apart at any moment.

But it never collapsed.

Vincent Prowl had lived in that vulture-like mansion for as long as anyone could remember. There were tales of people waiting in anticipation on a windy day to see the whole thing fall apart. There were stories of Vincent building his massive black gate in a single night. However, what became painfully clear over the years was that no one really knew the man in the mansion.

There were just three facts that people knew for sure. The first was that Vincent was a doctor. The second was that the tall black gates would open every morning at a quarter to nine and then again at six in the evening, when Vincent returned from work. The third was that Vincent never had visitors.

What made that day so peculiar was that Vincent Prowl had broken two of his three known facts: one, the tall black gates didn't open at a quarter to nine that morning; and two, just barely visible in the shadow of the mansion was a black carriage.

"You see that? The shadow in the window," Maurice the baker said. "He's pacing. What do you suppose happened?"

"Oh, don't worry about Vincent. He's always been mysterious like that," his wife said, waving her hand. She went back inside, then brought out another basket of rolls to the cart. "He probably has a lot on his mind."

"How do you explain the carriage, then? Way over there. It's hard to see. It's black. I almost thought it was my eyes playing tricks on me again, but I swear it's a carriage. You can see it, can't you?"

"Maybe your eyes aren't as shot as I thought," she said. Whether she wanted to believe it or not, her husband was right. There in the shadows of the mansion rested a black carriage, which she had to admit was odd, even for Vincent.

"See, what did I tell you? Makes you wonder, doesn't it? They say no one's been up there for years, except for Vincent of course. I wonder who they are."

"Let the man be. Yes, I guess I am a bit curious, but his business isn't our business." She proceeded to carry more baskets of bread while staring, perplexed, at her husband, who merely continued to stroke the hairs of his fiery-red beard as if this particular carriage were some sort of magical creature that had sprouted wings and begun throwing up rainbows.

"Must be weirdos." Maurice the baker began pushing the cart while his face contorted as if he were recalling some far-off memory. "Have to be." He nodded in affirmation. "I always told you that man was too odd for this town. I mean, who can they be? Have you ever heard him say more than two words to anyone? Not to mention he's a coldhearted—"

"Maurice! Maurice! Did you see? The pacing!" the chimney sweep called.

"And the black carriage!" the baker shouted back. "Aye, we did."

"Yes! The carriage!" the chimney sweep said. He looked like the soot-covered broom that he carried, even down to the slick black of his hair. He hopped down the rooftop, carrying his long black broom over his shoulder, then skillfully slid down the drainpipe to join the baker and his wife. "Who do you think they are? I mean, this is Vincent we're talking about."

"Trying to figure that out myself."

"I'm perplexed at how one man's sick day could mean so much more than that he's actually sick," the baker's wife said.

"Oh! Don't tell me. Marie doesn't know, does she?" spoke a woman passing by with her husband.

"No, I don't think she does," said the grocer as he added a few pears to the stack on his fruit stand. He, too, joined the small crowd that had gathered around the baker and his wife.

"That man hasn't had a sick day since his wife was around," the woman's husband said.

"I heard that too!" the chimney sweep said. "I couldn't believe it when I found out. I even lost my best coat because of it. But it's strange to think that heartless man used to be married."

"What? Married? Him? With that frozen heart of his?" a laborer interjected.

"That's what I said at first," the chimney sweep replied.

"That I heard," the baker's wife said. "I personally find it lovely that a man like him could have found love."

"She's dead I heard," the sorrowful fabric woman said, passing by with her trademark frown.

"Not just dead!" another man shouted. "I heard he killed her!"

"He killed his wife?" the butcher said.

"Are you talking about Vincent?" A regal man wearing a monocle approached the growing crowd after exiting the clockmaker's shop. "No, no, what you need to understand is that she left him. This is the real truth. Heard it from my friend's brother's uncle. A very reliable source."

"You don't say," Maurice the baker said. He gave a shrug. "I don't blame her."

The group of people whose ears had pricked at the sound of "Vincent" all laughed at Maurice's last comment. For talk of Vincent Prowl was not uncommon in Maple Town. Every morning, the tall black gate would open and out would walk Vincent carrying his black medicine bag in hand, glaring at every man, woman, and child that was unlucky to meet his gaze. It was only after years of mystery that people began to regard him as some urban myth. To the townspeople of Maple Town, Vincent was an oddity, and his mysterious nature fueled the fire for even more gossip regarding the man in the mansion.

"Vincent, I take it?" a man coming out of his shop said. He was an elderly man with little strands of white hair clinging to his head. He began polishing his half-moon spectacles against his teal apron, before joining the crowd that had gathered outside his shop.

"Aye, we are. What do you think of the man, Oscar?"

"What do I think?" The tailor was now holding his glasses to the sun to make sure the lenses were clean. "For one, he never used to be so cold."

"That's what happens when your wife leaves you!" a man shouted.

"Whatever it may be," Oscar said, "I hope that man will find peace. In all my years, I've never understood Vincent. In fact, he made an unusual request just the other day."

"What was it?" multiple voices shouted.

"Well," the old man stuttered. In the crowd's enthusiasm, he had fallen backward. "He requested I tailor him a long black tail coat, for a five-foot-eight male if I recall correctly. He then asked for a blue marble-style vest, a gray-blue button-down with similar measurements, and a mustard tie. He's coming to pick it up later today."

"Anyone know how tall Vincent is?" one man asked.

"He is much taller than five foot eight," another woman said.

"No, no, he is exactly five foot eight. I've seen it with my own eyes," Maurice the baker said.

"Well, you may need a new set of eyes, my friend," Oscar said.

"Then who could it—"

"He's coming!"

Just as quickly as the people had gathered, they dispersed at the sound of the tall black gate creaking open. The townspeople proceeded to work diligently as out of the gate came the tall black-haired man with his signature scowl. He wore his hair in

a long ponytail. He had his spectacles, which he donned only when addressing a patient, neatly placed in the left breast pocket of his black suit jacket, and wore a crisp white button-down. It was all in all the appearance that everyone had grown to expect of Vincent Prowl. However, that day he was without his black medicine bag, and continued to walk, ignoring the constant eyes following him, until he reached the tailor's shop.

Maurice the baker began setting up his stand with his wife. He took one last look at the tall black-haired man before shaking his head. He returned to his work unaware that he was right; something was indeed happening at number thirteen Chiaroscuro Lane.

At that exact moment, in a small study up in the mansion, two young girls sat by the fireside with teacups and saucers in hand. If it weren't for their incessant chatter, they would've easily been mistaken for two porcelain dolls. The sun glazed their matte skin, and their gray eyes glinted in the light.

The two girls continued their exchange of pleasantries, with only brief pauses between to stare at the young man passed out on a long burgundy couch across from them. Their gray eyes stared in anticipation, focusing on every frayed hole in his pants, every strand of silvery hair that covered his eyes and shoulders, and every rip and tear of a shirt that seemed undecided whether or not to be white or meringue. When nothing happened, they'd take another sip from their teacups and resume their conversation.

The study gradually filled up with light, illuminating the shadowy outlines of the girls' white-blonde hair and their identical faces. The young man on the long burgundy couch gave a stir as the sun grazed his skin. For a moment, it seemed he couldn't comprehend the light, but he soon accepted its warmth as his cerulean-blue eyes flickered open.

The young man stretched his arms and rubbed his eyes. Everything was so hazy. He shook his head in the hope his vision would focus. His head was throbbing. He nearly fell over but managed to catch himself with his hand, then blinked fast, trying to recall a pleasant dream he had had about carriages, white mansions, and magical balls.

"Looks like he's coming around," one of the girls said.

"You said that the last time," the other girl said.

"Charlie. That's your name, right?"

The young man didn't see who'd spoken. He scanned the room until his vision finally focused on the two identical girls sitting by the fireplace. However, though the two girls looked identical, they couldn't have been any more different. One was smiling brightly at him and even waved, while the other sat hunched over and glared at him in between sips from her cup.

What did they ask him? The young man couldn't remember. His name? Charlie?

"I think so." He began rubbing his forehead again. He had a lot more hair than he remembered. "Who are you two?"

"I am Vera," the smiling girl said. "And this disagreeable one over here is my sister, Mira. It's a pleasure!"

"Not really. I can't believe Vincent did this. He's so young," Mira said. Her frown never wavered as she looked Charlie up and down before shaking her head. "I don't accept this. What was he thinking?"

"He's not as young as us," Vera sang. The phrase had a particular effect on Mira that made her give her cheery sister a pained look.

"Anyway," Mira said. She took another sip from her teacup of what Charlie then noticed was something red. "What now?"

"What are you talking about?" Vera said.

"He's awake," Mira said. "So do we wait for Vincent or just go on with it?"

"Oh, I see your point." Vera laid her teacup down on a small end table. She continued to grin widely before returning her gaze to Charlie. "I don't know."

"We have to do something," Mira said.

"I know, but you know how Vincent gets when he's angry," Vera said.

"Grow a spine, will you?" Mira reached into her bag while Charlie continued to stare at the two girls with a mixture of confusion and fear.

"Fine, I will!" Vera snatched the scroll from her sister's hand. She unclasped its seal and gave it a quick shake before it started unraveling, unraveling, and unraveling, until it trailed all the way from where Mira and Vera sat to Charlie's burgundy sofa.

"Ahem," Vera said. "As a vampire, you have certain obligations."

"A what?" Charlie asked.

Mira and Vera only glanced at each other, then slowly peered over at Charlie.

"You. Don't. Know," Vera said. She lifted her teacup and took a sip. Charlie could see that she was shaking. "Of course, he didn't tell you. You've been dead for two years, and he did what he did. He didn't say anything, did he? I knew Vincent is who he is, but to do something so vile . . . You're so young! You were what, thirteen when he turned you? And even with dying, you only age to fifteen! But that's it! Fifteen! What was Vincent thinking?" Vera stopped and took a deep breath before regaining her cheery disposition. "What are we going to do, Mira?"

"Dead?" Charlie said.

It was as if the twins hadn't heard him.

"Well, I'm not going to tell him," Mira said.

"Why do I have to?" Vera said, lowering her teacup.

"You started it," Mira spat. "Obviously, the cat's out of the bag now."

"I'd rather not, though."

"Don't look at me like that. You always make me do stuff with that look."

"What look? I don't know what you're talking about," Vera said. "Please, Mira."

"No. Besides, you owe me for that one time," Mira said.

"I owe you nothing!" Vera said. "That's a lie and you know it!"

"I'll handle it!" growled a voice entering the study. The tall black-haired vampire rubbed his forehead. He muttered a string of swears before finally composing himself. He held a parcel in his left hand and threw it on a small desk nearby. The twins eyed Vincent quietly, sipping away at their teacups. Their eyes would innocently go from Charlie to Vincent, then back to Charlie. Vincent opened his mouth but closed it. He ran a hand over his forehead again. He began pacing from the doorway to the window and back again. He'd occasionally stop and open his mouth, but always returned to his pacing until he finally stopped at the window.

"Mira, your mirror," Vincent said.

Mira cringed as she reached into her handbag. She pulled out a silver and emerald hand mirror with little ruby thorns along the edges of the glass. She walked over to join Charlie on the couch, trying her best not to look at him, while Vera held her hands to her mouth, shaking her head in anticipation. Mira handed Charlie the mirror.

The stranger that stared back at him had long white hairs that trailed down to his shoulders, limbs that looked starved of any food for years, and deep-red veins running through cerulean-blue eyes.

The mirror fell with a loud crack.

Charlie frantically felt his face. He stared at his bone-thin limbs, unable to vocalize what he'd seen in the looking glass. It wasn't a boy, it wasn't a man—it wasn't even human. He kept regarding his hands. They were so thin and frail that they looked as if they would break if Charlie weren't careful. His shoulders were broader. There was such a vast expanse between them—a stark contrast to the size of his bony shoulders at the ball. He felt a small hand on one of them now. He looked up to see Vera's concerned eyes.

"Welcome to the damned," she said, raising her teacup.

"Vera, why don't get him cleaned up," Vincent said, rubbing a hand over his eyes. "I think the contract can wait."

Vera nodded and walked arm in arm with the skeleton man beside her, who had begun to shed tears. Vincent and Mira watched them leave, hearing Vera's comforting words grow fainter as the two ascended the large staircase. When they were finally gone, Mira let out a sigh and began picking up the pieces of her in cleaning up the broken glass shards. The two worked in silence while Mira continued to shake her head.

"You did know what you were doing when you did that to him, right?" she said at last.

Vincent was silent.

"Vincent! He doesn't even know what he is!"

"Clean the boy up, get his signature or whatever it is you two need, and get out of my house!" Vincent said. "Join your sister. The sooner you two finish your business with him, the better. I'll clean this myself."

"You know, we aren't the bad guys here," Mira said. "You were the one who practically begged us to raise him. This is your deal he's signing. You should be ashamed."

Vincent never raised his head, but instead continued to work on cleaning up the glass shards. He heard Mira's footsteps echo away and up the staircase.

Now, given all the rumors and tall tales concerning vampires, it should be made clear to those who haven't actually met a vampire that the truth among all the fiction is quite underwhelming. Vampires don't fear garlic, burn in the sun, have magical powers, nor go around seducing women. They just have the unfortunate curse of living off human blood. So what Vincent did next was very unlike anything a normal vampire could ever do.

When Vincent was sure Mira had gone, he waved a hand over the glass shards. Suddenly, all the broken fragments moved on their own, scuttling about like puzzle pieces trying to find one another on the mirror's frame. Within moments, the emerald hand mirror had repaired itself, leaving no trace of its ever being broken.

Vincent reached down and picked up the mended mirror. He looked at his reflection and saw, for a moment, kind eyes underneath a piercing glare. His scowl that he'd worked so hard on cementing on his face relaxed into a frown while he pocketed the mirror in his suit jacket.

Because the truth behind this ability to perform such feats is that it can only be described as the remnants of magic from a wife who loved the man in the mansion dearly. And had anyone known this—other than his wife, who did already know this—they'd believe the man in the mansion wasn't so scary after all.

CHAPTER THREE

ARIA

Now, not many people knew Vincent well, but the very few who did would all agree that living alone and taking care of only himself for decades had made him inept at looking after anyone else.

And nothing made this more apparent than the weeks following Mira and Vera's visit. Vincent spent one day drenched from head to toe in black ink because he wanted to dye Charlie's hair black to match his. Another day, he haphazardly cut Charlie's hair with a razor blade, and took half of the second-floor curtains along with it. And the week after that, upon realizing Charlie was still dressed in rags, Vincent grabbed the parcel and dressed Charlie in clothes that, all in all, made him look like he'd grown up with the type of wealth and status that one would expect of Vincent's son.

Vincent had given him three identical suits consisting of a midnight-black jacket with matching black pants, a dress shirt, and a vest. At first, Charlie couldn't get used to dressing in the light blue-gray button-down, blue marble-patterned vest, and mustard tie, but the ensemble soon grew on him as Vincent left him little else to wear.

By the end of his first month, what became brutally clear to Charlie—and anyone else who had the pleasure of living with Vincent—was that Vincent Prowl had no business taking care of another life, even if that life was undead. And no one knew this more intimately than Charlie.

Because the aforementioned mishaps were but a few things Charlie noticed about Vincent and his new life. Another observation was that every morning, Vincent would leave the mansion at a quarter to nine, and would return only at six in the evening. Then promptly at a quarter to nine in the evening, he would call Charlie to the mansion's library to do mandatory studies until midnight. At midnight, Vincent would then disappear into his private quarters, which Charlie was forbidden to enter, only to repeat the cycle at a quarter to nine the next morning.

This morning was no different. Charlie heard the bronze double doors slam shut, then immediately rushed to one of the tower windows to watch Vincent march through the tall black gates with his black medicine bag in hand. Charlie could barely see the faint furrow of the vampire's brow and the movement of his mouth as a long string of swears spewed like venom from his lips. Charlie snickered, knowing exactly what swears the vampire uttered.

Vincent always left muttering some variety of oaths about the townspeople. In Charlie's mind, this made no sense at all. On the one hand, Vincent was the doctor who helped them, and on the other, he despised them all. He openly complained about them during Charlie's lessons, but that's where it would end. Vincent never alluded to why he hated them so much. Whenever Charlie asked why, he'd get a solemn nod and a curt "Don't worry about it. Just know you are safe in the mansion. It's better this way."

Now, what that meant, Charlie had no idea. All Charlie knew was that it was reason enough to keep him locked up in their mansion on the hilltop. For that was another fact about Charlie's

new life that quickly became apparent: he was not allowed to leave the mansion. Vincent absolutely forbade it and had gone to great lengths to bar and lock every window and door to make sure his rule was enforced.

It was not like Vincent gave Charlie any reason to run away, though. The mansion seemed to have an endless supply of rooms. In them, Charlie discovered bright hallways with tall windows; rooms with chandeliers of different colors and sizes that sparkled, making the rooms seem filled with shimmering starlight; and rooms containing maps of oceans, countries, and constellations that boggled his mind to no end. One day, Charlie discovered a white room with art supplies and unfinished paintings that, sadly, were beginning to collect dust. Another week, he found rooms full of broken machine parts of different shapes and sizes—little gizmos, whatsits, and whatchamacallits that sprang, rang, and lit up before finally dying in Charlie's hands.

Charlie jumped down from the window ledge when Vincent was nothing more than a speck in the distance. He regarded the library around him and how quiet it was.

He could almost hear the echoes of his thoughts. He contemplated exploring to find new rooms. He could've read some of the many books Vincent's library had to offer. He could have done a number of different things, but instead he found himself walking back to his room.

This wasn't the first time this had happened. At first, Charlie thought he was just tired. But then, the feeling kept coming back more frequently as the weeks dragged on. It only happened when Vincent left for work. Charlie became bored of even the new rooms he discovered. They just seemed less grand. Then the hallways seemed not as bright. The curtains started to look dustier, and all the gizmos and gadgets that Charlie found interesting gradually stopped making him smile.

It was a feeling that made Charlie want to give up exploring altogether. Instead, he spent his days in bed, waiting for Vincent to come home—because the oddest thing about this weird phenomenon was that this feeling would disappear as soon as Vincent returned.

Charlie made the final turn toward his room.

His room, once bare, was now a menagerie of exotic items and finds. Knickknacks and salvaged pieces of furniture sat sporadically around the room, little things he'd collected as he'd explored the mansion. But not even these trinkets interested him now, and he simply plopped down onto the queen-sized mattress and looked up at his many dream catchers and perplexing charms that changed shape in the light.

"Why do I feel like this?" he whispered.

The room remained silent and lifeless, unable to reply to the boy. And as the minutes ticked by, the silence grew more permanent and real. It seemed to constrict him like some giant snake that would, unknowing to him, gradually eat away at him until he eventually found the whole mansion repulsive. For what the young vampire didn't realize was, much like any lonely boy in his situation, what he longed for was something that all the things in the mansion could never give him.

He then noticed something on the pillow beside him. Neatly folded shut was a white envelope. It was addressed to him in Vincent's script. He reached out to pick it up and realized it was heavier than he expected it to be.

Dear Charlie,

I have noticed that you have been very inactive during my absence, so I have taken the liberty of giving you this list of assignments that you must do while I'm gone.

Your guardian,

Vincent Prowl

The letter ended and out of the envelope came a twenty-page list of chores specifically made to make the mansion not just clean but absolutely spotless. Charlie could imagine Vincent sardonically laughing as he scribbled down each mundane chore.

Another note followed, and as if Vincent were reading Charlie's mind, it read:

PS – Charlie, don't think of these tasks as a punishment, but as a learning experience.

Charlie crumpled the letter and marched to his first "learning experience."

The first item on the list was to clean the attic of cobwebs. Charlie didn't even know that the mansion had an attic. However, thanks to Vincent's heavily detailed instructions, he managed to find it at the very end of the east-wing hallway. The hall was dimly lit and less cheerful than that of the other hallways that Charlie had explored.

The entry to the attic itself was a carved cherry door with an enormous brass knob. It took Charlie a few pushes before he managed to swing open the door, sending a cloud of mothballs into the air. Charlie coughed and made his way up the attic, half-curious and half-frightened of what he might find.

Shadows snaked across the creaking floorboards. Charlie maneuvered carefully around the attic. He took note how layers of dust had made their home on a variety of objects. He saw what must have been furniture covered with sheets. The only light in the dark room came from a single beam pouring through a high-up window.

Charlie could only wonder why Vincent wanted such a creepy attic cleaned. He brushed away cobweb after cobweb until he saw, silhouetted in the light of the high window, the outline of a woman. Charlie retreated, frightened at first, but the figure didn't move. He gradually stepped closer to find that it wasn't a woman at all, but a beautiful white wedding dress draped over a mannequin.

The dress had intricate designs that covered its ivory material like wispy spiderwebs. He reached out to touch it. It was smoother than he'd expected, cool to the touch, and so thin and delicate that he had to be very careful not to rip it.

"Why is this here?" he said. He circled the dress and stopped when he saw something on the shoulder of the mannequin.

It was nothing more than a piece of paper made to look like a swallow, but it made Charlie smile. He was reaching out to touch it when it suddenly came to life. It fluttered and danced in the air. Charlie fell back in shock. It flew gleefully over and under Charlie as a real swallow would. At times, Charlie even had to remind himself that it was made of paper.

"Hello there," Charlie said. He cocked his head at his paper friend.

No response came from the paper swallow. It just continued to flutter around Charlie before finally resting on his shoulder affectionately.

"Can you understand me?" Charlie asked.

The paper swallow jumped off his shoulder and flew up and down frantically.

"You can, can you?" he said. "Do you have a name?"

The paper swallow rested on the mannequin's shoulder again, looking blankly at Charlie.

"How 'bout Aria?"

Charlie didn't know why he chose that name. It was almost as if the wind had whispered it in his ears. It seemed like the right name for some reason. The little paper swallow thought so too as its small paper head perked up at the sound of its name. It flew about, doing more flips, and flapped gleefully around the attic.

"I'm glad you like it," Charlie said. "Now, what are you doing up here?"

Aria began flying frantically from side to side before crumpling up into a ball and falling onto the floor.

"Wait!" Charlie shouted.

It was too late. The crumpled remains of Aria fell to the ground with a light thud. Charlie continued to stare at the scrunched-up piece of paper, frowning that his new friend was gone. Then, all of a sudden, the paper began to move. It shifted, unfolded, and refolded until it flew into the air again as the same paper swallow.

Charlie could have sworn it was laughing at him.

"Don't do that to me!" Charlie said. "I was really worried about you, you know?"

Aria flew up to Charlie until she was eye level and dropped her head sadly.

"It's alright," Charlie said. "Just don't leave me again, okay?"

Aria did a few flips before contently perching herself on Charlie's shoulder. Charlie petted her tiny paper head because he didn't care if she was real or not. She was at least someone to talk to.

"But really, do you know why you are up here?"

Aria lifted her head and remained perfectly still before finally shooting from his shoulder, down the attic stairs. Charlie raced to catch up as she maneuvered her way through the mansion.

She eventually stopped outside a room Charlie didn't recognize. She fluttered happily in front of the door before unfolding into a square sheet of paper and sliding through the door crack. Charlie opened the door and followed her inside.

The first thing he noticed was how the room sparkled. The whole thing was made of reflective crystal, and the walls shone light from every angle like a mirror. There were little stained-glass paintings hung here and there, a single glass end table with two matching crystal chairs in the middle, and a wide window. The window illuminated the room so much that Charlie had to cover his eyes until he adjusted to the brightness. Eventually, little fixtures in the room slowly came into focus. He saw what looked to be a dead flower in a vase on top of the crystal table. There was a small cot in the corner and a nightstand full of dusty books.

Charlie hesitated before joining his paper friend.

Aria flew around the room a couple of times before finally resting her drooping head on the crystal end table. She had a sad look on her face, and if paper could cry, Charlie could very well imagine Aria would be weeping a pool of tears over the dried-up rose.

"Is this what you wanted to show me?" Charlie said.

It was as if Aria hadn't heard him. Her gaze remained fixed on the dead flower, not moving for anything, like a living statue recalling whatever memories the flower reminded her of. It was at that moment that Charlie realized that Aria had not flown into this room for his benefit, but for another reason altogether. This place was significant to Aria in a way Charlie knew he would never understand.

"Whoever lived here was important to you," Charlie said.

Aria looked up at Charlie. It was a look of recognition, of understanding. In the silence of the paper swallow, Charlie heard volumes.

Aria flew up again, circling Charlie before dancing around the wide window. She would occasionally ram herself against the window with a loud thud, but never break through.

"Hey now, be careful," Charlie said. "You're going to get hurt."

His voice left him. What he saw out the window was a world that he'd only ever imagined.

It was the only window that gave a complete view of the town below. In the middle of the busy marketplace, there was a fountain that kids played around. There were businesses and vendors everywhere offering their latest catch or freshest produce. Charlie took note of a boy whose mother wouldn't allow him to jump in the fountain and a woman dumping some water out of an apartment window over an unsuspecting man below.

Charlie spent the rest of the day with Aria, watching the town square, until the dark shadows of twilight fell over the town like a magic spell. In a flash, the busy streets of Maple Town became bare and empty, and with the light, whatever trance that had captured Charlie for that whole afternoon faded too.

"Would you tell that thing to settle down and stop flying around me?" Vincent said. They were both in the study. Vincent was reading a book while Charlie worked on his penmanship.

"She likes you." Charlie chuckled at the sight of Aria resting affectionately on Vincent's shoulder. Why Aria liked Vincent, Charlie didn't understand. But when Vincent came home, Aria had shot toward him and hadn't left his side since.

"Well, she's annoying." Vincent had given up shooing the paper bird away and now turned another page of his book. "You found her in the attic—that's what you said, right?"

"Yeah, she was on a mannequin," Charlie said. He then bolted to his feet. "Please, don't take her away! Can we please keep her?"

"On a mannequin?" Vincent said.

"Yes."

"I see." Vincent took another look at Aria. He extended a finger to the bird, which she gratefully hopped onto. Though Vincent didn't seem to be looking at Aria. Charlie could tell by the way he stared at her. He seemed to be looking through her and on toward whatever memory Charlie's words had taken him to. "Interesting. I never thought any of them would have survived."

"Survived? There were more Arias?"

"Something like that," Vincent said. "There's a legend about a terrifying witch whose specialty was bringing paper to life. She used to make things like this all the time." Vincent paused, and Charlie watched as Vincent's face contorted. Then the black-haired vampire shook his head. "That was a long time ago."

"Makes you wonder what else I'll find once I actually start making a dent on that list of yours," Charlie said with a smirk.

Charlie could have sworn Vincent grinned, but thought better of it.

"It gives you something to do," Vincent said. "A whole eternity to make this place spotless!"

Charlie looked over as Vincent went back to reading his book. He returned to his studies, but something about all he'd seen that day compelled him to ask the one question he'd thought about every day since he began living with Vincent.

"Vincent, why can't I leave the mansion?"

"Don't worry about it. Just know you are safe here. It's just better this way." Vincent gave a solemn nod, then turned to the next page of his book. He raised his head and paused. "Are you going to keep asking this?"

"No," Charlie said. He began looking at his studies more seriously.

"Good." Vincent reached into his pocket to check the time. "Don't bother yourself with it. Besides, it'd be trouble because no

one knows you exist, to be honest."

"What?"

"Yes, you're a ghost from what I've been hearing. The people in town think I have acquired some curse. Childish nonsense," Vincent said.

"Why don't you tell people?"

"Because people are dangerous, and the less they know about you, the better. They wouldn't hesitate to kill you if they knew what you are. Remember that."

Charlie could feel Vincent's anger rising and decided to drop the topic.

"I think that's enough for tonight, don't you think?" Vincent said. "Get your mind off those humans. It will do you a lot of good because you still have that list to do in the morning, boy."

Charlie closed his books, and Aria flew over to his shoulder. He made his usual march up to his room to lie on the bed. Aria fluttered around the room and eventually rested by the windowsill. However, Charlie couldn't sleep that night. He continued to lie on his bed looking up at Aria. Well, not necessary at Aria, but at the window behind her. He'd look up at that window all night until a quarter to nine the next morning.

CHAPTER FOUR

MAPLE TOWN

"I wonder what they're like down there," Charlie said.

He and Aria were in his bedroom. They had formed a sort of routine since discovering the wide window in the crystal room. Charlie would rush every morning to finish at least one chore on the list, and then hurry to the wide window. He wondered whether the apple vendor knew kids stole from his cart. He wondered how the baker was able to make such delicious-looking pastries. And he wondered if the vendors would still set up shop in the rain. His mind was afire with thoughts that persisted long after the townspeople went home for the evening. So much so that Charlie would search the library for books about the most obscure things, from cookbooks to an encyclopedia of fabric, to possibly answer some of the many questions that he didn't dare ask Vincent.

"And the fabric lady—you know, with the frown all the time?—I wonder why she's so sad. She makes the most beautiful carpets. I wonder if any of the carpets here were made by her. She must spend hours and hours sewing and weaving. Then there's the baker! What do you think he's going to make today? Croissants? No, he made those yesterday. Maybe it's a pastry day today."

Aria, of course, never responded. However, her company alone was comfort enough for Charlie.

Their talks ceased once a quarter to nine rolled around. Charlie watched Vincent leave for the day and then went to put on a clean outfit.

That morning, he scrubbed the floors—all the floors. At first, Charlie shook his head, checking again to make sure he hadn't read Vincent's list wrong. Even Aria checked. Then after reading, she flew in backflips as if laughing her head off.

The scrubbing seemed endless.

Charlie polished and scrubbed until his hands were so pruned up that they were barely distinguishable from the sponge he used. From time to time, Aria would flutter by his shoulder for moral support, but she could only do so much as he'd eventually have to return to the scrubbing.

"I read that in some far-off places, servants do all the cleaning," Charlie said, wiping his forehead with a dry sleeve. Soap and water had sloshed all over various parts of his clothes. "Not just one, though. There'd be a whole bunch of them to keep the home looking nice. So why is it that it's just me here?"

Aria flew over and dropped a dry rag for Charlie to wipe the spots of water that had gotten on his face.

"Thanks." Charlie gave Aria an appreciative smile before looking down the rest of the long hallway that remained unwashed. "Vincent is crazy if he thinks doing all these chores is possible. It's enough to—"

Aria crumpled herself into a ball and fell to the ground.

"Exactly!" Charlie said. "I need a break. What do you think?"

Aria uncrumpled herself and danced around him, tugging at his shirt collar.

"Alright, alright, give me second." Charlie jumped to his feet, and the two rushed down the hallway that led to the crystal room.

Charlie pulled one of the crystal chairs up to the wide window and leaned against the glass. Aria flew around the window, ramming into it as she always did. The vendors had already gathered. They called out to whoever would listen. Children and their parents walked to and fro completely unaware that a young vampire watched them longingly.

Charlie sighed and pressed a hand against the glass.

Then something happened. The latch gave way. Charlie felt himself fly out the window. He gasped for air as he fell to the grassy hillside below. He landed with a heavy thud, though with surprisingly the same impact as if he'd tripped over himself down a flight of stairs. He nursed his throbbing head and looked up at Aria, who still remained in the crystal room.

"Aria, you coming?" Charlie asked.

Aria darted out the window to Charlie's side. The two felt a gust shut the window above them. He frowned, letting Aria dance around his fingertips in the open air.

"I guess our way back in is gone. Maybe we should find a different way inside before Vincent finds out."

Aria cocked her head and tugged at Charlie's collar. He looked out into the distance at the town. It looked so much more real now that he was finally outside. A broad smile lit his face. "Well, maybe it wouldn't hurt just to explore a bit. At least before Vincent gets back, right?"

Aria danced in the air. All it took was one greedy gaze. Charlie jumped up with Aria at his heels and ran out the gate.

Everything from tailor shops, to butcher shops, to post offices and anything else offering goods that could fit into a cart stood at various ends of the marketplace.

Charlie and Aria passed many vendors carting their wares. He laughed at the way a pair of boys stole melons from under the fruit vendor's cart. He watched playful children running around the oddly shaped fountain.

The obscure monument trickled water out of its spouts while kids and pets would occasionally jump and race around, relishing every splash that graced their smiling cheeks.

Charlie accidentally bumped into many angry people. They would shout the most vulgar things at him, some of which Charlie had only heard Vincent say before going to work. A man tried pressuring Charlie to buy his extremely cheap pears, while another forced upon him some silver watches. Charlie laughed at all this and politely denied their requests. He had read a book about street vendors once, and these people were exactly how the book portrayed them. Many tried to grab at Aria as they walked. They whispered and pointed until Charlie felt Aria fold herself up in his pocket.

However, as she hid away, Charlie suddenly found himself on the ground. Aria flew away in the commotion, while Charlie felt a body fall beside him. Charlie staggered to his feet, glancing around for his paper companion, but only saw the young man who'd stumbled next to him. The young man had faded brown overalls and a newsboy hat that he'd hastily put back on his shaggy brown hair.

"Thief! Thief! Get back here, you swine!" a voice shouted.

Charlie looked back to see a large man running toward him, shaking an apple and cursing wildly at whoever he was chasing.

The stranger shot to his feet. He was tall and lanky, a few years older than Charlie. He looked ready to run, but it was too late. The large man stared down at both Charlie and the stranger.

"Now I've caught you! Pay for that apple you stole, boy, or it'll be your head!"

"You got the wrong man. It wasn't I who stole your apples. Check my pockets," the stranger said. "See, no apples. Now, my greedy friend here, he has sticky fingers, you know?"

Charlie remained frozen. He glanced over at the stranger next to him and then was snapped back to attention by the large man's booming words.

"Empty. Your. Pockets," he said.

Charlie began to empty his own pockets, and his cold, dead heart sank. Out of one of them he pulled a ripe red apple. Charlie's eyes bulged at the sight of it. "What?"

"I'll murder you!" The man shook his hand threateningly.

"See, what did I tell you? Now, if you don't mind, I'll be on my way." The stranger turned and began to make his leave, but not before whispering to Charlie, "Thanks, I owe you one."

The young man with the newsboy cap broke into a dash, and Charlie immediately followed, with the angry apple vendor behind him. Charlie ran past merchants and skittered through crowds. He and the lanky stranger jumped over various stands and ran through shops, doing their best not to look at the vendor behind them. They kept running until they reached a shack in a much quieter part of town.

"Here, come 'ere," the overall-clad stranger shouted. Charlie reluctantly obliged and joined him inside.

The shack had metals and hammers of different sizes all hung on the walls, and huge piles of hay and stacks of coal ready to be shoveled into the large furnace. It roared and crackled as the two boys waited quietly at the door in the hope that the vendor had given up.

But before long, there was a loud knocking on the shack door.

"Blacksmith, open up! You are holding two fugitives in your shop! Let them out so I can murder 'em!" the apple vendor shouted between knocks.

"He's just not quitting," the young man said. He was doing his best to hold the door closed.

"Are all vendors like this?" Charlie whispered.

"Nah, this guy's just a loon," the young man said. "I'm Skat by the way."

"I'm Charlie. Need some help?"

"That'd be peachy," Skat said. "Besides, we only need to do this until—"

"What've you gotten into now?" a tired voice said. A long-haired man dressed in all black came over and pushed the two boys aside. He wore a black bandana over his forehead and across his right eye.

Suddenly the door burst open, knocking Charlie and Skat to the floor. The angry vendor came storming in, waving the apple, his eyes crazy with rage.

"About time! Let me at those two," the vendor shouted.

The blacksmith held a hand up to stop him. "Fancy seeing you again, William. May I ask what the problem is?" he said.

"What's the problem? WHAT IS THE PROBLEM? I'll tell you! These, these criminals stole apples from my cart," he said, spitting and pointing at Charlie and Skat.

"How many apples was it?" the blacksmith said. "I'll cover it. But only this time," he added, staring directly at Skat.

"How many apples? To hell with the apples!"

The blacksmith's eyes widened. "Well, what do you suppose we do, then, master vendor?"

"I want punishment," he said in a low voice. "I want to see these boys hanged!"

"Over a matter of a few apples."

"Yes!" replied the vendor.

"Well, I'll take care of that for you, then. Streamline it a bit. No sense getting the town involved." The blacksmith proceeded to drag Charlie by the arm to the furnace. He lowered Charlie's head just barely over the anvil. Charlie's eyes widened as he felt the heat protruding from the furnace. "Now, how would you want them punished? A hammer to the head, burned alive? I'm impartial to whatever. Let's just get this over with. I got work to do."

"A hammer—no, burning. Make him suffer," the vendor said gleefully.

"Good choice." The blacksmith then pushed Charlie's head over the stone that sat directly in front of the flames. The blacksmith readied to shove Charlie into the furnace, but stopped when he saw the vendor turn his head away. "Where are my manners? Please, watch! It's been quite boring around here. We're working men. I'm sure we could both use a little bit of excitement!"

The vendor cringed at the blacksmith and slowly edged his way toward the door. "I think I'll just leave it to you. I'll hear the screams as I leave."

"Your choice." The blacksmith shrugged. "Now, if you don't mind, I have some work to do."

"Great, I'll just be on my way," the vendor said. "This will teach you to steal from my cart!"

The vendor left, and the shack was quiet. Charlie closed his eyes, expecting the worst, but nothing came. The blacksmith held a finger up to his mouth when Charlie opened his eyes and looked up at him.

"Now scream," the blacksmith whispered.

Charlie grinned and let out the loudest, most ear-piercing scream he could muster.

The three of them kept quiet, listening to make sure that the vendor was gone. When it was clear, the blacksmith released Charlie and began making his way toward Skat.

"Thanks, Sam," Skat said. "I thought me and Charlie over there were done for." He laughed.

"Skat." The blacksmith paused. "I can't keep sticking my neck out for you like this."

"But it was just an apple. I mean, if anything, I need to pick better targets."

"The poor man's always your target. I swear, another stunt like this and I'll personally hang you myself. Are we clear?"

With that one statement, Skat clammed up, and the two finally noticed Charlie still catching his breath in the corner. His tail coat was dusty with soot, and his vest held pockets of hay.

"Now, who is Charlie?" Sam said, raising an eyebrow.

"Dunno. He's someone I met on the street. Seems nice enough, though." Skat offered a hand to help Charlie up. "You new in town?"

"Kind of," Charlie said. "Who are you people?"

"Ah, well, you can call me Sam, and this is my blacksmith hut. Not the flashiest place, but we do things the old-fashioned way here, and for that, the place has character," Sam said, giving an approving nod at the hut. "And I don't think I need to introduce this idiot over here."

"Hey, this 'idiot' saved him from that crazy vendor."

"You mean I saved him. Hell, if we're keeping tabs, I'd say you owe me your life and then some. I swear, it's a downright miracle as to how you've managed to not get yourself killed yet."

Skat readied to talk again, but the blacksmith shot him a glare before instructing him to add more coal to the furnace.

"Anyway, you seem like a nice enough lad," the blacksmith said to Charlie.

"Aria!" Charlie blurted out.

Both Skat and Sam stared at him.

"My bird. She flew away when we started running. I need to find her!"

Charlie was already on his feet when Skat stopped him.

"Hey, Sam, mind if I end things for today? It's my fault he lost his bird. I think I should make amends for it, don't you think?"

Sam laid his hands on his waist and looked over at the metal clock that hung over the furnace. He wiped his brow, then proceeded to take a small key and begin hammering away at it. "You would do that from the kindness of your own heart?" he said without looking up.

"I'm insulted that you'd doubt me!" Skat gradually walked Charlie to the door of the hut. "I mean, we both know how dangerous it is out there. Imagine where this birdy friend of his is without his owner, and all because of me."

Sam rolled his eyes before giving a long sigh. "Fine. Besides, I'd rather be alone with the customer that's coming in today. He asked for a very unusual key to be made. You're missing a great learning experience here. You know that, right?"

"I'll live!"

Sam looked up and smiled at how fast the boys left his hut, then picked up the key with his tongs to inspect.

The autumn sun beamed over the boys' shoulders as they searched the town. In between shouting Aria's name, Charlie caught the heavy scent of warm beer that emanated from the brewery. He closed his eyes as he imagined the golden liquid filling his mouth. Though they were looking for Aria, he wanted to experience everything the town had to offer.

Scarlet leaves drifted lightly to the ground on a gentle breeze, creating an inviting crimson carpet for the constant flow of horses and carriages to meander across. Horses' whinnies mingled in the air with the sounds of children laughing mischievously.

"Not over here either!" Skat called.

Charlie noticed that his new friend had moved several paces ahead of him and was now standing at the base of the obscure fountain. Charlie recognized it as the same fountain he'd admired from the mansion. The closer Charlie got to the fountain, the more he saw it for more than what it seemed to be—he felt as though it were the heart of the little town itself.

In the center of a large pool there gurgled three circles of water, each gradually getting smaller until, from the center of the uppermost and smallest circle, there sprang a steady stream of the clearest, most sparkling water Charlie had ever seen. The stream shot straight upward before thundering back down into the pool, sending tiny droplets of glittering water into the air as it collided with the surface below. The reflection of the sun in the water was almost enough to blind Charlie as he stood transfixed by the structure.

By the end of the day, the two of them had crisscrossed the town a hundred times over before finally reaching a patch of trees that stretched past the town. Charlie could just make out the faded wooden sign that said "Maple Orchard."

"Last place," said Skat. "If she's not here, then you might want to consider getting a new bird."

"Hopefully she's around here," Charlie said. He stared at the wooden sign. "So, who are the Maples?"

"Well, they only think they own this town. They're rich and I hate how they feel like they are royalty because of their name." Skat shook his head. "But they do have the best trees around. I'll give them that. They grow some pretty amazing things with this lot of theirs."

"Are they really that bad?" Charlie asked.

"Eh, well, I guess it depends on how much money you have."

Before Charlie could ask Skat what he meant, he saw a flicker of paper wings flying toward him. Aria did backflips around Charlie before finally landing on his fingertips.

"I've been looking all over for you!"

"That's Aria?"

Charlie looked up from Aria to see Skat's eyes go wide. He ran a hand through his hair. Charlie couldn't place it, but something about Skat's tone was off. It was as if Aria were some sort of ghost.

"Charlie! Hide her now!"

"Why, what's wrong?"

Before he could finish, Skat grabbed Aria and shoved him into Charlie's pocket before looking around the two of them.

"What's the matter with you?"

"You didn't mention Aria was magic!" Skat said in a harsh whisper. "Are you"—he paused, and his eyes narrowed—"a wizard or something?"

"No!" Charlie said. Immediately, Vincent's warnings echoed in his head. They'd kill you if they knew what you are. "I'm just like you. I didn't even know Aria was magic. I swear. Is that so wrong?"

"You didn't know?" Skat spat. "How . . . ? Doesn't matter. Just hide her, and don't go around showing her to anyone. No one! You got it? People talk. You could find yourself dead if they think you're a wizard or something. Promise me you'll never show anyone in town Aria. I mean it. I'm just looking out for you."

Charlie stood, stunned. He blinked occasionally as Skat stared at him. It was the first time that Charlie had seen fear in Skat's eyes.

"I promise," Charlie managed to voice.

Skat backed off and sighed. "Good. Now let's get out of here. This place gives me the creeps."

Skat began pulling Charlie by the arm. However, he was yanked back when Charlie's feet stopped moving. It was like Charlie was cemented to that single spot. It was so sudden that it almost made Aria creep from his breast pocket.

Leaving the orchard was a young woman with a red bow tied in her long golden locks. She wore a modest red-and-white striped dress. hummed a lovely tune as she skipped past them, apparently unaware of their existence. She carried with her a small brown basket, and as she passed, Charlie caught the intoxicating floral scent that came from her hair.

"Who is she?"

"Ah, don't tell me you too," Skat said. He ran a hand through his shaggy, greasy brown hair. "She's Sally Maple, the pride and joy of Maple Town. Every man, except for me, seems to fall under her spell, but I'll tell you now, she's nothing but trouble."

"She seems wonderful."

"Key word, seems, my friend," Skat said, but quickly realized all too well that Sally had captivated another victim. "Let's go, lover boy."

"Wait," Charlie said, pulling back from Skat's tug. "Where's she going? Do you think we can see her again?"

"Sure, sure, why not." Skat rolled his eyes. "Let's go already. We've just scratched the surface of what this town has to offer."

"But what's wrong with finding out where she's going?"

"Fine, I'll tell you! She's going to her grandparents' home. Now, let's get you out of here before you declare your undying love for her, please!"

Charlie reluctantly followed Skat, but turned back occasionally to watch Sally's image grow smaller and smaller. Seeing her made him happy. She seemed so familiar, but he couldn't quite put his finger on how. Far in the distance, he saw her laughing with the driver of a hay cart before jumping in the back. And for a brief moment, Charlie could swear she was smiling at him.

CHAPTER FIVE

DOLLS AND DEALS

Vincent was no fool. He knew about Charlie's fascination with the townspeople. He knew Charlie visited his late wife's study every day. He also knew that no amount of chores would sate the curiosity that possessed his adopted son to spend hours on end just watching the townspeople below during his absence. He knew all this because nothing happened inside the mansion without him knowing it.

However, even despite knowing all that, none of that knowledge could have prepared him for what happened that afternoon. He'd felt as if he couldn't breathe for the last few hours. He was exhausted from searching for the source of Charlie's escape. His stomach was in perpetual knots, and by three in the afternoon, he'd broken all the furniture in his private quarters. By the end of the day, Vincent had little energy to do anything but watch the window in his room. He leaned against the glass playing with a small iron key in his hand. He sat for some time with his eyes fixed on the tall black gate until finally a warm breath tumbled out of him. He leaned back against his chair and felt the knot subside. He pocketed the key and rose to his feet. He held his head in his hands upon seeing Charlie struggle to open the tall

black gates, then he waved a hand at the gate as he watched his son climb the hill, full of smiles.

Vincent massaged his brow and slammed a fist against the window's edge. The punch reverberated throughout the dark room, shaking the little trinkets that sat on a single bookshelf. Only a small decorated box fell. It dropped with a gentle thud, playing a melody that echoed softly throughout the room. It was a haunting, wistful tune that caused the vampire to turn toward it and stare. He looked intently at the fallen wooden box before finally walking over and closing the lid, then returning the box carefully to its spot on the shelf.

Vera stood in the background with a perplexed look on her face. Vincent's private quarters were almost as broken as he was. Everywhere, there were shredded bits of fabric, scattered splits of wood from ruined pieces of furniture, and clouds of dust. The maroon carpet had so many rips and gashes through it that it looked like Swiss cheese. Yet among all this debris there was a single bookshelf that remained untouched. In fact, there wasn't a speck of dust on it. It wasn't like there was anything valuable on this bookshelf either—a shriveled-up wreath of daffodils, a silver pocket watch, a stained black ribbon, and a couple other bits of useless-looking junk that sat next to the wooden box Vincent had just picked up.

"He was always going to come back," Vera said. "You did know that, right? Vincent, you knew he was going to come back."

Vincent was quiet. He glanced at Vera, but returned his gaze to the window. Charlie had just reached the bronze double doors and realized they too were locked. The vampire cringed as he gave another quick wave of his hand. To Charlie's surprise, the door unlocked, and he raced inside. Even with the boy at his quietest, the vampire could hear the faint awkward little footsteps his son took up the stairs.

"You don't know that," Vincent said.

"Is this why you wrote to me today?" Vera turned her head before blinking wildly at the vampire in front of her. Feeling bold, she approached him. She even dared to place one of her small childlike hands on his shoulder. "You sent a paper bird with a scrap piece of paper strapped to her leg to find me."

"Her name is Aria," Vincent said. He tried to shrug off Vera's hand, but she kept it firm on his shoulder.

"Even with your illegible script, I could tell something was wrong," Vera continued.

"Well, how do you expect I reacted when I found Aria of all things flying toward me after I finished meeting with one of my patients?" Vincent said. "She's magic. It's amazing no one burned her, let alone noticed her! And she was alone! God only knows where my idiot son was at the time."

"You practically begged me to come over immediately," Vera said. She continued to regard Vincent with a calm smile.

"Of course!" Vincent rose to his feet and began pacing the room. "What if they found out that he wasn't like them? What if they hurt him? What if they killed him? What if—"

"What if he didn't want to come home?" Vera interjected.

"Yes!"

Vera gave Vincent a pained smile before taking a seat on the edge of his tattered bed.

"You know he can't run away from his contract," Vera said. "He's bound to this town whether he likes it or not."

"But not to here!" Vincent said. He waved his arms at the whole mansion. He finally composed himself and plopped back down in his chair by the window. "If he were smart, he would've left this place and never come back."

"You mean if he hated you, he wouldn't come back," Vera corrected.

"Yes," Vincent said. "I'm not blind, Vera! He hates it here. I know he can't live in isolation forever. He's suffocating in boredom living here, but it's the only way to keep him safe! Why didn't he listen? I told him how dangerous those people are!"

"It's because he's young," Vera said. "You should've known that when you turned him into a vampire! He doesn't know how dangerous they are yet."

"I know."

"Then why did you do it, Vincent?" Vera shook her head. "Seriously. And then you asked us to raise him! A vampire raising another vampire is unheard of. You bite them and then leave them to become what they want after consent! Charlie had none of that!"

"He was dying. His mother begged me," Vincent said.

"Still!" Vera rose to her feet. "That doesn't mean you should have done it. Vincent, he's in this mess because of you!"

Vera could have continued, but she stopped. She hung her head, for she wasn't heartless. Her words had already done far more than she'd expected them to. Underneath Vincent's heavy layer of scowls and bitterness, Vera saw the thing she hated the most: self-pity. The utter powerlessness the individual feels when they realize there is nothing to be done to undo their mistake.

"He's met them, Vera," Vincent said, his voice weak. "How is he supposed to kill any of them now? He's not going to be able to."

"That was the deal, Vincent. Their blood is on your hands," Vera quipped. "Once a deal is struck, there is no going back. I'm sorry. He will kill someone from Maple Town of our choosing. Those were the conditions for you raising him."

"Please, he shouldn't have to kill one of them. Anything but that."

"Vincent, don't do this. Begging doesn't suit you," Vera said. "You knew what was to be expected when you signed a deal with us. Do you know how many deals Mira and I contract? No one ever wants to pay the piper. This. Was. Our. Deal."

"I can do all the killing for the both of us!"

"You don't get it, do you?" Vera snapped. "No one ever does. I can't change this! No one can. This is on you. His fate, his life—that is all your doing! Does he realize what you've taken away from him? He's going to be like this forever because of you. You realize that, right? I don't care how many times you say his mother begged you to save him. It's your fault you are here now, you cruel beast of a man! Like I said, begging doesn't suit you, Vincent." Vera pointed at the window. "Stop groveling and find a way to remind that son of yours what he is."

"I need to protect my boy," Vincent said quietly.

"Like I said." She held a hand to her chest. "Remind him what he is. It doesn't matter how. Just do it. It will make it easier for him when the time comes. He's a monster. We all are in some way. Make him realize that, and maybe he'll distance himself from them."

"Leave me," the vampire said.

Vera turned to take her leave. Vincent rested his head against the window again, and for a moment, Vera contemplated walking over to give him one more reassuring hand. She wanted to remind him that he shouldn't feel bad, that he was doing everything to keep his son safe. She wanted to remind him that Charlie would make it through all this and that she and Mira were cheering for them despite their unfair role in all of it. But she stopped midstep. She took one last look at the dark and battered room of

Vincent's private quarters. It was then she noticed, at the bottom of the bookshelf, something that didn't belong to Vincent. It was an emerald hand mirror with barely a scratch on it. Vera gave Vincent a sad look and left.

Deals alter the natural order. They form an intricate web that, for better for worse, connects all those who agree to them. No one knew this better than Mira and Vera.

Mira and Vera acted as the fibers within this web of deals. It should be made clear that the twins were not vampires. They weren't human. They weren't witches. They were the result of a tragedy involving a doll maker and his two daughters. Neither living nor dead, but simply existing on, ironically, a deal made with a great and powerful demon, who then bestowed his deal-making powers on the twins.

And in time, Mira and Vera learned the three common threads of all deals. The first was that everyone ignored the cost of their deal until it was time to pay up. The second was that there was always a bargain to strike.

Vera made her way down the hill and out through the tall black gate to where her sister sat by the obscure-looking fountain, waiting for her and kicking her feet impatiently in the white dress that matched Vera's.

"There you are," Mira said. "You sure took your time with Vincent."

"Is what we do wrong?" Vera said.

Mira's face softened. She looked down at her own white shoes and clicked them before popping off her seat to join her sister.

"Sometimes it does feel like that. But once a deal is made, there isn't any way to change it."

"I know, but sometimes just watching like this . . ."

"It's the price for our own deal," Mira said quietly.

"I know," Vera said. The two walked in silence until they reached the edge of Maple Town. "So, what did Lord Autaine want?"

"He managed to find a loophole in our deal."

"How?" Vera stopped. "That's impossible. He has to give up his sight."

"No, Vera. We said he'd never see another ball again. He and I made a counterdeal. He's a lot cleverer than he looks."

"I see."

Mira and Vera continued to walk, but not before turning around just in time to see someone leaving number thirteen Chiaroscuro Lane. He was just a speck from where Mira and Vera stood, but still, Vera gave Vincent a sad smile and turned to walk away, knowing that he would take her advice to remind his son what he was—in whatever way that was. Yet she knew, as did Mira, that it wouldn't be enough.

Because this was the final common thread of all deals: nothing that people got in return for their deal would make them happy forever. All deals become undone with time. It was an unspoken rule that Mira and Vera were bound to never tell, but always knew. So as much as Vera knew Vincent would give his life in pursuit of becoming a good father to Charlie, what hurt her the most was that she knew that too would be undone eventually.

CHAPTER SIX

THE GIRL LOCKED AWAY

Now, there's one more character that matters in this tale. Among Charlie, Vincent, Aria, Skat, and Sally, there is one other girl. In fact, if it weren't for the insistence of a certain witch, she wouldn't be mentioned at all. But not because she isn't important.

What makes her so interesting is that despite existing—and there is enough proof to suggest she did—she would have curiously vanished from our tale if it weren't for the few people that knew she was visited every morning around ten o'clock by a tall black-haired vampire with a black medicine bag.

Alice Autaine's eyes remained fixed on the pack of cards in her hand. She sat cross-legged on the mangled sheets of her bed, her loose brown hair falling over her shoulders as she closed her eyes in preparation for her most ambitious trick yet. Just before she opened her eyes, she muttered three words under her breath:

"Pose, prestige, prestidigitation."

With that, her one turquoise and one green eye flickered open. She placed a hand on the deck and began to press down. Steam erupted from the pack as fifty-two became four in her hand. Finally, when the smoke had cleared, she fanned out the four

cards to reveal to her imaginary audience. They were all blank. She paused, then blew on the cards until their red and black ink returned in the unmistakable form of the letter A on each card.

In her mind, the crowd went wild and she took her bow. In reality, she smiled the same smile that she'd be giving her adoring fans. It was a smile that few but those who spent hours honing their craft would understand. In that smile was a decade and a half of solitude. It was years of lovelorn labor, working toward the one thing that helped her get through the day, every day, all days she could think of. She smiled because it was one of the few moments when the abyssal hours of practice smiled back at her in acknowledgment of her achievement.

"A for Alice. Cute," said a voice next to her. "Though I fear all my teaching is going to waste if you're just going to do card tricks all day."

The voice had come from a large black cat. He scratched at the cards, unimpressed, before walking away with his fluffy tail waving back at Alice.

"I've been working on that trick for weeks," Alice said. "Least you can do is clap."

"Like that ego of yours needs any more stroking," the cat scoffed. "You'll get my applause when you've earned it. Now, if you're done, practice some real magic."

"What's the point? It's just pricking my finger with a needle and healing it. That's not magic. That's boring," Alice said.

"Boring, perhaps," the cat said. "But you never know when it might come in handy. Besides, it isn't like you've got anything else to do."

The cat turned toward her and rested his paw against his chin. He eyed Alice, challenging her. She turned away, but not before throwing the ace of spades with lightning speed at where the cat would have been if he'd hadn't moved at the last second.

The ace pierced the floorboard like a metal blade, leaving behind a small trail of smoke.

"Temper, temper," the cat said. "No rush, though. The world isn't going anywhere."

What the cat referred to was the fact that, despite possessing unfathomable magic, Alice was someone who would remain hidden from the world. Years without sunlight had made her look more docile than she was, while many lessons from various teachers had taught her the proper poise, manners, and grace that none would ever see or hear, because as far as the world was concerned, Alice was a very sick girl.

Similar to Charlie, she lived in a mansion that contained every single thing imaginable to cater to whatever interest captured her father's imagination. She used to adore it, but then she discovered books about far-off places and wondrous maps that made her long for the world outside the mansion walls.

Unfortunately, her father had other plans for her. He'd declared to the world when she was five years old that she was sick, and she hadn't recovered since. Her father had tried to supplement her time with many lessons of all sorts. However, these did nothing to sate her desire to go outside. She used to throw the biggest tantrums growing up, in the hope of leaving the confines of her luxurious prison. Eventually, her father became so weary of her attempts that he put magic locks on every door and window—because metal bars would just look gaudy, and quite frankly would clash too much with the ivory white of the mansion. In the end, she spent most of her time practicing her magic in secret. She'd taught herself the basics and later used most of the novels she read as inspiration, which led to her obsession with card tricks. It was only within the last few years that Alice had received a formal teacher for her magic.

"So how long do I have until he gets here?" Alice asked.

The cat didn't have time to answer as there came a knock on the door. She turned over and eyed it, contemplating just not answering. She stared at the door as another knock rapped at her door. She didn't move. She didn't want to. Then came a rapid succession of knocks.

She gave her best fake smile.

"Come in," she sang, and the door swung open. "Sorry, I was just getting up."

"You're lying," Vincent said. "Not like it matters. Because you're. Not. Really. Sick."

"We know that, but Papa doesn't believe that," Alice said.

She palmed her hands together and conjured up the vanished deck of cards. She nodded her head at the ace of spades stuck in the floorboard. "Mind getting that for me? I could easily levitate it, but I figure since you're here, might as well have you do something, right?"

Vincent walked across the room and retrieved the stray ace. He then took a seat on the stool by Alice's bed. Alice liked to refer to that particular stool as "Vincent's stool" because he was the only one who'd ever occupied it. And it was only added to her crystal bedroom out of pure necessity.

Vincent had visited her every single morning since she was five. It didn't take long for the doctor to figure out that Alice wasn't sick, and it took an even shorter time for both of them to realize that his visits were nothing more than a formality to further convince the town that she was.

Most of the time, the two would sit in dead silence, glaring at each other. However, as the years drew on, Alice had taken it upon herself to use Vincent as an audience for her magic, though much like the cat, he was never impressed.

"Did you know that in some places, people perform magic for wide audiences?" Alice said.

"I've heard. But it's not real magic. They're only pretenders," Vincent said. "And anyway, we've been over this. Your father is adamant that everyone assume you're sick and that you never leave."

"Come on, Vincent. We've known each other for how long now? Do you really need to remind me of that?" Alice said. "Just pick a card."

Vincent sighed and took a card, stuck it in the deck. Alice proceeded to perform the same trick she'd mastered earlier, only to find her audience looking out the window instead.

"Do you hate your father for locking you up in here?"

Alice snorted. "Of course I do. If it weren't for these magical locks, I'd be so far gone from here. I'd be on the big stage. I'd perform far and wide. I'd be using this magic as it was intended to be used!"

"But you do know he keeps you here because he loves you, right?"

Alice's face contorted. She blinked rapidly, taken aback by his question. Vincent was certainly being very un-Vincent-like. He wasn't even scowling as much. He just kept staring out the window.

"I . . . I guess I do." Alice stammered as the words finally caught up with her mouth. "Though if this is how he shows his love, he has a weird way of doing it."

"I bet he means well, though," Vincent said quickly. "That must count for something."

"No. No, it doesn't."

Her eyes had grown cold and icy. She stared at the vampire with a look that contained years of resentment, a prisoner regarding her warden. It was so piercing that Vincent had to look away, back out the window.

"But I'm just trying to keep him safe!"

Suddenly, Vincent was on his feet, and the cards that Alice had been mindlessly shuffling slipped from her grasp. They scattered all over the floor. But that wasn't the weird part. Little streams of smoke were rising from the fallen cards. And none of it was because of Alice.

Alice's eyes widened, then narrowed as she gave Vincent a knowing look. She wouldn't be able to confirm her suspicions, though, because just then her door burst open to reveal a blonde-haired girl in a red-and-white dress fluttering her hands over her face.

"Alice! Alice! I have so much to tell you!"

She was flustered, and to Alice's benefit, didn't seem to notice the smoking deck of cards. Alice gave a small cough to put them out.

"Oh, sorry! I didn't . . . Sorry, is she contagious today?"

Vincent and Alice exchanged a look.

"No," Vincent said. He rose from his stool and made his way to the door. "She's not contagious today. I'll be back tomorrow."

"He's so strange!" whispered Sally. And then, as if a switch had flipped in her head, she began fluttering her hands again and jumping up and down. "I almost forgot! Alice, Alice, it's news!"

Sally twirled all around the room, the edges of her red-and-white dress lifting slightly off the ground. She opened every curtain and window in one elegant motion. Alice shielded her eyes, for with just a few pirouettes, the room sparkled. Alice's room shimmered because, at the cat's insistence, everything inside it, from the vanity table to the various fixtures, was made of some sort of crystal. The only exceptions were the large bookshelves that stood in the corner and Vincent's chair. The cat told her that crystal helped foster magic, but in the back of Alice's mind, she couldn't shake the feeling that it also had to do with the cat's odd obsession with it.

Alice smiled weakly at Sally. "So what is this news?"

"I don't know where to begin!" Sally said. "Well, for one, it's an amazing apple season at the orchard. But that's not what I wanted to tell you. A few weeks ago, I was walking over to Grandmother's house. Luckily, Grandfather was heading the same way, so I hopped onto the back of his wagon, and guess what I saw, Alice?"

"I could guess," Alice said. Sally Maple didn't get this excited unless a man was involved. Sally had this girlish excitement every time she met a man that interested her, which happened quite a lot. It was a slight character defect that Alice kept note to never succumb to. She knew all too well the various war stories that Sally Maple had accumulated over the years. Sally fell in and out of love so often, in fact, that the men she slighted had begun calling her "the queen of broken hearts" when she was out of earshot. However, despite the nickname, all the men still worshipped the ground Sally walked on. It was the strangest thing.

"Does this really happen that often?" Sally gave a pained look.

"Unfortunately," Alice said.

"It's not on purpose! You know that! It's been like this ever since I turned sixteen," Sally said.

"Oh, I'm sure. Though I'm not in any rush to be in your shoes, thank you very much. Not like anyone wants to marry a 'sick girl' anyway."

"But you're so beautiful, Alice. It's a shame that you're so ill! But you're right. Sometimes I wish I were still fifteen like you. Such a simpler time. Oh, how I miss it. All these suitors can be dizzying and exhausting."

It was clear she was looking to receive some sympathy, and Alice complied because she knew Sally meant well.

"Look, it can't be all bad," Alice said. "So who is he?"

"Yes, yes!" Sally stood up again, waving her hands frantically. "He looked new. I can't say I've ever seen him in town before. Well, no, that's a lie. I don't know, Alice." Sally sighed. "It's like I've seen him before, but I can't remember when, you know? Don't you hate that feeling?"

"Maybe you have." Alice walked over to her vanity table to brush her tangled locks. "Remember that guy—who was it again? Oh, yes, the laborer! Didn't you think you'd met him before and found out that he helped build your bed? Maybe it's similar to that. He could be another laborer."

"No, this one was wearing such nice clothes."

"Maybe he's visiting from another town. You never know these days with that train station. Because I'm pretty sure every nobleman around has tried his hand at wooing the elusive, teasing—"

"Alice!"

Sally struggled with the words before realizing she didn't know what the words were. No matter what, Sally could never find a way to explain that which she so desperately wanted to express. The truth was that the men who chased Sally would catch her attention for a time, but she'd always tire of them and let them go without anything more than a charming smile and a cute curtsy. Sally knew it was wrong, but they just weren't right. There was always something a little off about every man that fell for her, something that just didn't seem right. She didn't know why they were never right. It bothered her to no end. And she'd feel even worse after she rejected these men because they would still be so nice to her. Why that was the case was beyond her, but she smiled and curtsied away, accepting to be loved rather than hated for breaking their hearts.

"So what's the problem, then?" Alice said.

"Yes. Well, no. I think he likes me, but I don't know for sure. Ever since that day, every day when I'm walking over the bridge by the mill, he's there with this friend. Every day, at the exact time I'm crossing. Isn't that weird? Anyway, I was wondering if you'd like to accompany me today."

"Sally, my illness," Alice said.

"But, Alice!" Sally said. "Can't you make this one exception, please?"

"You know I can't go." She marched over to her dresser to pick out her outfit for the day. "Though what this 'illness' is perplexes even me! But Father insists I stay in the mansion for my health, and that's what I must do. In other words, my hands are tied here."

"Alice, please! I need you," Sally whined. "He hasn't said anything to me every time I've passed by. Yesterday, I walked so slowly over that bridge that the apple tarts got cold. They got cold, Alice! Maybe he hates me."

Alice rolled her eyes and stared at her best friend, collapsed on her bed. She, on the other hand, continued bustling around the room. Alice settled on her usual slightly baggy white blouse with a black sash to wear over her favorite gray-and-blue skirt. She disappeared behind her silver changing screen.

"No one hates you. That's impossible—trust me." Alice peered out from behind the screen to give a firm nod. "You just have to keep walking over that bridge until he says something. Guys can be so silly like that. He obviously likes you, but he's too nervous to say anything."

"I make him nervous?"

Alice emerged from the screens fixing her ponytail and adjusting her playing card flower hairpin. She glanced over at her mirror and smiled at herself, appreciating her handiwork.

"Yes, you do," Alice said. She pulled Sally up off her bed and held her at arm's length. "Now, go there and keep walking over that bridge. And don't come back until you do!" With this, Alice began guiding her friend to her bedroom door, despite Sally's many protestations.

"Alice, wait! That doesn't even make sense!"

Without another word on the matter, Alice gave her a friendly shove across the threshold, and with a loud slamming of the door behind her, Sally was gone.

Charlie and Skat stood leaning over the edge of a long stone bridge across from the blacksmith's hut. The chill of winter had crept into Maple Town. Charlie looked eagerly out into the distance while Skat clung tightly to his thin coat. The trees were slowly losing the last of their leaves but were too stubborn to let winter finish them off. Skat continued to glare at Charlie while they stood together, every now and then throwing little pebbles into a small hole in a log that lay on the other side of the quarry. It had become something of a game, seeing how many rocks each of them could shoot into the hole. The two of them played it religiously because they stood in that exact spot every day, at the exact same time, for the single reason that drove Skat crazy.

"Will you just talk to her already?"

"It's not that simple," Charlie said. "You know that."

"Oh yeah, and standing here every day chucking rocks into that hole while she passes by isn't weird at all," mocked Skat. "We're gonna fill that hole someday, Charlie. Then what?"

"Then . . . ," Charlie said. "Just shut up, okay? She's coming."

And sure enough, skipping toward them was Sally Maple. Charlie had figured out her routine. She walked to her grandmother's house at the other side of town at this exact time each day. For

what reason, he had no idea. But he was glad that, in these brief moments, he could see her. However, she could never know that he'd planned all of this out, because Skat was right—he was not making himself the most appealing gentleman by doing so.

Charlie tried to look busy chucking rocks in the hole. She passed by, and it was like he couldn't breathe. Like every day before, he became mesmerized by her floral scent, her golden locks shining in the sunlight, and the red shawl she wore over her red-and-white striped dress.

Skat rolled his eyes before making a quick pass, picking something out of Sally's basket. Charlie could only stare openmouthed as an apple tart stealthily appeared in Skat's undetected hand. Then, giving a quick wink to Charlie, he plopped the confectionery into Charlie's hands.

"You dropped an apple tart, miss." Skat nodded toward Charlie. "Luckily, my friend over here was able to pick it up."

"Oh my, thank you," Sally said. She held a hand over her mouth. "I'm very grateful to run into two charming men such as yourselves."

"Ah, it's all my friend here," Skat said, nudging the still-speechless Charlie. "He's the real hero, miss."

"Is he now? Well, can I have the name of my gallant apple hero?" She smiled at Charlie, and her eyes seemed to suck him in, like whirlpools of brown that glistened and didn't intend to let him go.

"I-I'm Charlie," he managed to stutter. "It's a pleasure, and really it's nothing."

Sally laughed a melodic laugh before answering. "Well, I don't think it's nothing. I think you saved me from searching all over town for my missing tart." She paused. "I hope you don't think me rude, but I'm afraid I haven't seen you or your evasive friend

anywhere in town. And may I add, I know everyone," she said, nodding at Skat. Charlie looked over to see Skat was now a good distance away from them, so far in fact that Charlie wouldn't even have recognized him. With his back turned to the two of them, he began shooting more rocks into the hole.

"You could say I'm new," Charlie said.

"And what brings Mr. New to our little town?"

"I wouldn't be able to tell you. I don't even know," Charlie said. Then he nervously continued. "Though, maybe you can say I found what I've been looking for."

"Oh, and what might that be?" Sally's eyes lit up.

"I don't know what I'm saying," Charlie said quickly. "It's getting cold these days, you know? Hay fever is catching me and all."

"Well, I'd hate for my gallant apple hero to become sick because of me," she said. "And I'm afraid you're right. It is getting chilly. I'm hoping to get to my grandmother's house before dinner. It was nice meeting you, Charlie. Tell your friend the same. Oh, and keep the apple tart. I make the best tarts in town, or so I've been told."

She curtsied and then she was gone. Charlie stood, shocked at what had just transpired. He held the apple tart in his hand as if it were the treasure of a sacred kingdom. He heard the faint sounds of footsteps behind him and then felt the apple tart escape his hands with quick and precise movements.

"If I didn't know better, I'd say you might've stolen the queen of broken hearts' heart," Skat said. Then he flashed his signature grin, took a bite, and winked. "Now this is interesting."

CHAPTER SEVEN

THE SECRET GARDEN

The first snow sprinkled down like powdered sugar onto the gingerbread houses of Maple Town. Almost overnight, the whole town seemed to transform, and come morning there were no merchants or vendors to be seen in the marketplace. Rather, in their place were children—running here and there, throwing snowballs at one another, or sliding down the hillside on thin sheets of wood. The sight of it all left Charlie sighing constantly, mesmerized by the sweet, sparkling powder that blanketed the town.

However, unlike everyone else in town, who blissfully played in the snow, Charlie spent the day sitting at a dining table that neither Vincent nor he ever used. In front of him was what seemed like an endless supply of silverware, sprawled out on the table. Because, similar to every other adult in town, Vincent had not left at a quarter to nine that morning. Instead, he had decided to drag Charlie to the dining room table and put him to work. At least the room had a window.

Whack! Whack!

"Pay attention!"

"I didn't even say anything that time!" Charlie protested.

"I know exactly what you were going to say," Vincent said. "And the answer is no! Now, let's try this again." Vincent shook his head and circled Charlie's chair at the head of the table with a wooden spoon. "Which is the soup spoon?"

Charlie bit his lip as the pain subsided. He wanted to kill the person who'd decided it was necessary to know twenty different forks, knives, and spoons. He stared cautiously at the silverware, for every time Charlie chose the wrong piece, Vincent would strike him with the wooden spoon.

Aria, of course, took great joy in watching this spectacle. She perched herself on the other end of the long dining table. Each time Charlie was struck, she would fall onto the table, gleefully laughing her silent laugh until she'd composed herself enough to fly again. Then there were the times when Charlie would complain, which were also greeted with another curt strike. Charlie could swear Aria was tearing up.

"But why does anyone have to know this?"

Whack!

"I told you. Manners and proper etiquette. Now, soup spoon."

"I never leave the mansion anyway!"

Whack!

"That's for talking back!" Vincent barked. "Soup spoon!"

Charlie rolled his eyes. They had been at it for hours now. Charlie's hand quivered as he carefully reached for another spoon.

Whack! Whack!

"This is ridiculous! Why does this even matter?" Charlie said. "I don't even eat anything!"

"It's proper etiquette. You'd learn a bit or two if you stopped staring outside," Vincent said. "I swear, sometimes I feel like I'm talking to a rock. How many times do I have to tell you that there's nothing worth finding out there?"

"Maybe you're wrong! I mean, how can that be bad?" Charlie said, motioning toward the window just in time to catch a group of children on their backs in the snow making circular motions.

"That's because they're children," Vincent seethed. "They'll grow up. They all do, and then they realize that there are more dangerous things out in the world than cold and frostbite. Don't be fooled! They all become ugly in the end!"

"Vincent! You can't possibly believe that?"

Whack! Whack! Whack!

"You're a vampire! You aren't human! Get that through your head, boy! We'll be at this all day if we have to."

Charlie winced as the wind from the wooden spoon came down once more, but he felt no pain. Charlie peeked up at Vincent who'd stopped midstrike.

Vincent turned his head. "Did you hear that?"

"Hear what?"

Before Charlie could get an answer, Vincent had rushed over to the bronze double doors. He wasn't gone for long. The doors opened and closed with a loud slam. Charlie glanced over from his chair, not daring to leave his spot, but noticed a faded blue fabric in Vincent's hand before he hastily shoved it into one of the pockets of his black suit.

Vincent reached for his silver pocket watch. This watch was something Charlie noticed Vincent always had on his person. It had become an indicator of sorts of when lessons were over and when Vincent would proceed to the next odd task in his routine. However, something was wrong today. Vincent's face grimaced when he glanced down at his watch.

"We're done for the day," he said as he reentered the room.

"But you just said—"

"I know what I said." Vincent sighed. "Just listen! Clean all the silverware up, and then . . ." Vincent rubbed the back of his neck. "You know the far room in the west wing of the mansion?"

"I do," Charlie said. "But what does that have to do with anything?"

"Meet me there tonight at a quarter to nine. I don't care what you do until then. Chores, whatever, just be there tonight. Don't be late."

"But that room is—"

"Don't be late!"

And with that, Vincent disappeared into the corridor and up the stairs. Charlie cleared the table and put the silverware in the cabinet in their unused kitchen.

He, like Aria, knew exactly which room Vincent was talking about.

The rest of the day was a daze until nightfall came. At a quarter to nine, Aria fluttered happily as she and Charlie made their way down the west wing corridor. She led the way to the only room that was explicitly off-limits—always.

This was not the first time Charlie had made his way to its battered white door. He'd tried multiple times to see what was inside Vincent's personal room, but never could get inside. Each time he knocked, he received the same response: silence. And the door was always locked. Charlie even tried to get Aria to spy for him and report back. She'd unfold and slip through the cracks, only to come back looking disheartened. And every time Charlie asked what was inside, she'd crumple up.

Again, like the many other times before, Charlie raised a hand to knock on the white door. This time, however, the door swung open.

"You're late," the vampire said. Then he sighed and nodded up the stairs just inside the doorway. "Come up here."

Aria fluttered as she always did when she was excited and shot up the stairs to Vincent's room. Charlie stared at Vincent's stony face. There was no way of telling what his intentions were, so Charlie followed the paper bird and the vampire, half-curious of what to expect and half-afraid of what he would find in the room that Vincent disappeared to every evening.

Vincent's room looked like an old sunroom that had gotten confused and found itself three stories off the ground. It had been constructed in such a way that the glass ceiling was in just the right spot for the moon to shine directly in and illuminate the whole room with a natural, ethereal light. However, everything inside it was covered with ripped fabrics and broken furniture. Only a few artifacts remained untouched. Charlie went over to an old bookshelf, noticing the little decorated vases, art projects, and dried-up daffodil crowns that sat on it. They were all worthless and didn't make any sense to Charlie, but he could tell that among the torn-apart bed and shredded curtains and canopies, these were what Vincent cared for the most.

Much like in the crystal room, there was a large window that overlooked the front of the mansion and the whole town beyond. There was also a small glass end table in the middle of the room. On the table was a small vase with a single blue rose.

Charlie had never seen a blue rose before. It cast a faint shadow in the moonlight, which made the ocean-blue flower seem almost mystical. Charlie couldn't help but walk toward the magical-looking rose. A single petal fell and landed on the familiar silver pocket watch that Charlie had just noticed was placed beside the vase. It lay basking in the moonlight, absorbing its light.

For the first time, Charlie noticed the intricate floral design

that decorated Vincent's signature silver pocket watch. Intrigued, he picked it up and opened it to see the time, but to Charlie's surprise, the clock was broken. The glass was cracked, and the thin hands looked as if they hadn't moved in years. They were stuck on a quarter to nine.

"Careful with that!" growled a cold voice behind him.

Charlie quickly turned to see Vincent glaring at him. He was so surprised that he dropped the pocket watch, which Vincent skillfully caught. Vincent let out a sigh of relief before slowly setting the pocket watch down.

"I told you to be careful with it," he said.

"I'm sorry," Charlie said nervously, walking away from the table. "This room is so sad."

Vincent ignored Charlie's comment and walked toward the tall mirror on which Aria perched, watching them.

"Come here." The vampire beckoned him. "Look in this mirror. What do you see?"

Charlie turned and joined Vincent in front of the mirror. It looked like a regular mirror. It reflected himself, Aria, and Vincent much like any other mirror would.

Charlie glanced up at Vincent and then back at the glass. "Just the three of us. Why?"

"This mirror is special," the vampire said slowly, running a hand over the side of the mirror. "Look carefully."

The contents of the mirror began to shift. They swirled, mixing all that the glass reflected in a silvery, shadowy vortex until Charlie felt a cool breeze coming out of it. The breeze was fresh, warm, and sweet. It smelled of flowers and other fresh things, and it sounded like birdsong. It was peculiar, feeling the wisp blow through and past him. Charlie couldn't see much of what was reflected in the mirror. All he saw were large, lush greens peppered with snow.

He looked up at Vincent, who didn't seem surprised by any of this. Vincent even took a step forward and walked into the mirror. Aria flew in after him. Charlie hesitated before following them.

The mirror led to a clearing within a forest of seafoam-green trees. In the clearing was a small cottage. The wind howled softly to the rhythm of the water mill that sat beside it. The roof of the cottage had a thin layer of snow, as did the tall weeping willow that hung overhead. Leading to the house was a gravel path fringed with bushes of the same blue roses as in Vincent's room, as well as other plants Charlie had never seen before.

There was a whole garden of flowers that hung like lamps and shone and flickered in different colors. Charlie stared at them as they oscillated between shades of fluorescent blues, greens, and yellows. Some plants smelled of chocolates, pastries, and mints. Some were as silver as the moon itself, and others were as dark as the night sky and had little stars sprinkled on their leaves. There were even plants that opened up to reveal a light so bright Charlie had to look away.

As Charlie walked the gravel path flanked by all this glowing, glittering, colorful foliage, he felt almost as if the plants themselves were waking up to greet him. Even the ivy that encased the cottage snaked playfully toward him, producing little ice flowers that, as soon as they got close enough to Charlie, shattered to reveal beautiful pink flowers, their buds bursting open and shaking any residual frost off their petals.

Charlie finally made it to the window of the cottage and peeked inside. He saw a small fireplace and what looked to be a very modest home, with a single stove, a large bookshelf, and a wooden table with two chairs pressed against the bed. There was a stain on the wood flooring, and a thick layer of dust occupied everything from the furniture to the floors.

"Where are we?" Charlie whispered. He turned when he felt a hand on his shoulder.

"This is where it all started," Vincent said. He turned toward the forest path and stared at the moon. "Elizabeth and I created everything you see here. Everything our imaginations could fathom became reality. We would step through the mirror to this spot and just create something only we could understand. This place is far removed from Maple Town. It was perfect for us to escape to. We came here when Elizabeth felt her magic growing dull. We came here on dates and anniversaries—it was our little getaway that was only a mirror away. I actually practiced building number thirteen Chiaroscuro Lane right by that tree stump. A dry run, if you will, before taking the actual lumber to build the mansion. It was perfect. This was our secret garden. I make it a point always to come here often."

Vincent shook his head and hurried down the path leading away from the cottage.

"Why are you telling me this?" Charlie called after him nervously.

"Come on!" Vincent pressed. "We should hurry. We don't have all night!"

"But where are we going?"

Vincent marched deeper into the forest. Charlie hurried behind him, watching as he navigated through the tall pine trees. Charlie tried several times to ask the mountain of questions he had, but Vincent's long strides made it so Charlie could barely make out a couple words before he had to start jogging to keep up with Vincent's pace.

Charlie felt the chill bite at his face the more they walked. A few gusts whistled past them, making it sometimes impossible for Charlie to see anything aside from Vincent's black cloak in front of him. Then the path ended in a loop around a single

dead tree. In the distance, Charlie could faintly make out a figure. It looked like a speck at first, but as the two got closer, Charlie saw that underneath the tree was a man, tied up. He was an older man with white hair. For some reason, Charlie felt like he'd seen him before, but he couldn't put his finger on it. The man was wearing a faded blue nightgown with large claw marks gashed on the front.

"I can't move. Who are you?" the man said, giving Charlie a pleading look. "Please, whatever it is I've done, I'm sorry! Just let me go! I beg you!"

"Who did this to you?" Charlie said, rushing over to the old man. Charlie tried tugging on the ropes, but they wouldn't budge. "Here, I'll run and find a sharp rock."

"Leave him," Vincent said.

Charlie winced and stopped moving.

"Who is that? Show yourself!" squealed the old man. Tears began streaming down his cheeks. "I'm sorry for whatever it is I've done. I'm sorry! Just please, let me go!"

"Do you remember the woman you burned?" Vincent said in a voice barely above a whisper. There was a silence between the three of them. The wind howled behind the vampire's words. Vincent took one step closer, and then another, until he loomed over Charlie and the old man, staring with his coal-black eyes.

The old man's face turned milk white when he saw Vincent. He began to squirm again, working himself up the side of the tree trunk. "No, it can't be. You can't be . . . ," the old man said. "I didn't know. We didn't know!"

"You burned her alive," Vincent said. He gradually came closer, like a lion easing toward its prey.

Charlie felt a sudden chill run through his spine. He closed his eyes when Vincent knelt down next to them.

"Vincent, we were afraid. She was a witch for God's sake!"

"Who," Vincent said, "told the town?"

"A young man I never met before. I-I never caught his name," the old man stuttered. "Vincent, please don't do this. It was a mistake."

Vincent smiled. He began playing with what little hair was left on the old man's head. He slowly brought his face to the man's neck. He whispered something in a low breath, something quiet and so full of hate and anguish. So raw. Charlie couldn't keep himself from watching.

"A mistake that I found out," Vincent said, "or a mistake you killed her?"

"We were just trying to protect our families! We couldn't let her keep teaching our children. She'd kill them. You know that!" The old man sobbed. "Please, you don't have to do this."

"She loved this town!

The next few seconds were filled with snarling and a scream that Charlie didn't even know men were capable of. He shut his eyes, and when he opened them next he saw Vincent and the man disappear behind the red liquid pouring out of the old man in thick streams. Bits of flesh and blood dribbled down the once-proper vampire's mouth.

"As if she'd kill anyone," Vincent whispered.

Vincent let out a few dry heaves. The man's body was still shaking. Vincent gripped it, then, almost as if just noticing him for the first time, he looked over at Charlie shivering in the snow. He let out a low growl.

"You see, this is what we are! Look at it! We are killers, boy!" the vampire shouted. "Nothing more than killers! It's kill them before they kill us. They don't care who you are. They only care what you are!"

"You're nothing more than a monster," the old man croaked. "We burned her to keep this town safe. I don't regret that."

Charlie remained frozen to the spot as something came over Vincent. The vampire began ripping the man apart with his nails and his teeth until the thing beneath him was barely recognizable as once being human. Vincent panted and screamed, "Die! JUST DIE!"

There was a pause. Charlie could see bits of clear liquid dripping from the vampire's face.

Vincent fell to his knees over the carcass. "We can never live with them! We can never love them! GET THAT THROUGH YOUR HEAD, BOY! They will only shun you for what you are. They. Are. Our. Prey! Never forget that! It's in their nature as this is in ours!"

Vincent pointed at the mangled body. He broke the neck with his teeth and lapped up every bit of the blood that dripped down his chin. The vampire gave a sigh of relief, as if his thirst had at last been quenched. Charlie began feeling his throat dry up just watching. It was an odd sensation. A part of Charlie longed for a taste of the red liquid that Vincent drank greedily, but the other prevented him from moving from his spot.

"This is who we are, boy. They will only hurt you in the end! Learn that if nothing else."

Vincent reached into his coat for a flask and filled it with the splashes of blood that fell from the old man's snapped neck. The sound of each drop filling the flask echoed throughout the forest. Once it was full and capped, he threw the container aside and stared at the ground, growling and cussing. Then the growling turned to silent seething. The moonlight grazed the vampire's bloody cloak with a comforting light, and eventually illuminated part of the proud vampire's face. Charlie could see trickles of moisture fall from the vampire's eyes and leave little holes in the snow.

Charlie remained quiet, watching. He didn't know what to say, if there was anything to say. He merely stood feeling the cold snapping at his face, realizing that winter was far colder than it appeared.

"People are dangerous," Vincent said finally. "We were happy. We thought we could live pretending to be human. We were wrong. We were so wrong! Because one day I came home to find Elizabeth not there. I searched around the mansion for her until I heard a mob forming in the marketplace. I scoured the streets looking for her until I saw in the distance a young woman being carried off. It wasn't until I heard what the mob was chanting that my heart sank."

Vincent closed his eyes and clenched his fists.

"They were chanting 'witch,'" he said. "They were carrying my wife to be burned alive. I rushed through the crowd, yelling out to her, but I received no reply. I was too late. I can still hear her screams some nights. And every time I close my eyes, I see her burning there, looking to me for help. But I couldn't help her. I was too late. I was a coward. I could've done something! Instead, I just hid away as they all went about their lives, forgetting about the woman they had burned. But how could they not care? How could they be so cold?"

He rubbed his eyes, then waved his hands at a nearby bush. It split in half, revealing a bed of violet flowers with petals that flapped like butterfly wings. It wasn't until Charlie stared at the gray stone behind the bed of purple butterfly flowers that Charlie realized what he was looking at.

"You see," Vincent said, "I tried it. Living with them doesn't work. You can't love something that's always going to be afraid of you. That fear . . . All it takes is just one piece of doubt, and it can transform people into monsters. I never want you to experience what I saw that day."

Vincent spoke in such a soft voice that Charlie could barely hear him. Charlie looked over at the vampire with sorrowful eyes. Vincent rested his hand longingly on the tombstone.

The two left the forest in silence. They eventually found their way to the clearing with the cottage. That was when Charlie almost bumped into Vincent, who'd stopped to look up—not exactly at the little house, but at a time that existed long before Charlie was born.

Without warning, Vincent broke the silence in a soft voice that sounded so unlike him.

"Here, drink up." He threw the flask at Charlie.

"I don't want it."

"Drink," Vincent pressed. "I need to start feeding you. I can't avoid it anymore. You can really hurt someone if you don't drink."

Charlie hesitated before finally taking a sip. He felt the cold red fluid trickle down his throat. It was the sweetest thing he'd ever drank, but he felt conflicted as he took in the sweet nectar. His mind told him he shouldn't drink anymore, yet his body yearned for it. He eventually emptied the flask's contents before throwing it back to Vincent.

"I do what I do to protect you. If they knew what you are, they'd kill you like they killed Elizabeth," Vincent said, giving the same pensive look he had worn their whole walk back. "When you were placed under my care, you signed a binding contract with those two blonde girls. Remember that? In that contract, you are required to kill someone from Maple Town. That's the deal. That is why you're alive at all. I've pled my case to them, but they will not bend their rules. I'm sorry. I've tried, but it's inevitable. So listen to me when I say don't get attached. Don't love them."

"What if I refuse?"

"They'll kill everyone."

Charlie and Vincent returned and retreated to their respective sides of the mansion. Charlie heard the door to Vincent's room slam shut in the distance. The next morning, he heard the bronze double doors slam shut again, and wondered where the night had gone. Charlie left his room and climbed out the wide window.

Charlie walked through the snow-covered marketplace with all the vendors and customers bundled up in their coats and scarves. He couldn't help but notice something had changed. Maple Town didn't look any different; it was still covered in snow, and the people looked the same. However, he now noticed things that he hadn't just a day before.

Charlie felt the cold, chilly wind bite at his skin. His eyes darted from person to person as he wondered who it was he'd have to kill. Would it be the sorrowful fabric woman? How about the kind baker and his wife? His eyes flickered around the throng of people. He skittishly escaped talking to anyone, then broke into a sprint to the blacksmith's hut and closed the door behind him.

In the hut, at least, he'd get some peace.

"About time you got here! I start making my blood blade today! I couldn't start without my number two, you know?" Skat put an arm around Charlie's shoulder. "You have no idea how long I've been waiting for this."

"What're you talking about?" Charlie said, trying his hardest not to imagine killing his best friend.

"A blood blade," Skat said in awe.

"A what?"

"They are the only things that can hurt a vampire," Sam replied, wiping his sweaty forehead. He'd been shoveling coals into the furnace. "Very complicated to make. The blade leaves a piercing mark on a vampire that they can never recover from. It's the bane

of their existence and an incredible sword."

"Is it?" Charlie said.

"You better believe it," Skat said. "I'll finally get revenge on them for killing my mother."

"What?"

"I told you, didn't I?" Skat spat. "Vampires killed my mother. I'll kill them all if I have to."

Charlie rubbed his neck and looked at his friend. In the corner of his eye, he saw the future for what it was. Someday, men like Skat would hunt his kind down and kill them, just as Vincent had killed the old man. Or he would have to kill them first. It was an endless struggle of who drew blood first.

"I've talked to Sam, and he said you can help me." Skat grinned. "Besides, I could use another set of eyes, you know? Don't want to mess this up."

"I don't know about that," Charlie said. "I barely know what I'm doing when I'm helping you."

"Nonsense," Sam said. "He's right. You never know what you might run into. Learning how to make one of these swords might do you some good. And I've seen what you can do with fire. You're more than qualified to help. You have a real talent. And this idiot over here could use all the help he can get."

Charlie turned, gave a weak smile, and looked between the blacksmith and his student, having their daily quarrel, before whispering, "When do we start?"

CHAPTER EIGHT

THE QUEEN OF BROKEN HEARTS

For weeks, the townspeople wondered where their beloved Warren Maple had disappeared to. Signs were posted at every corner of Maple Town. People told stories about how on some nights, they could see old Aggie Maple pacing back and forth at the Maple estate until she'd paced herself to sleep.

However, it should be noted that no one except for Aggie Maple seemed especially worried. This was because Warren had given up most of the responsibilities of the family business to his son and daughter-in-law and spent most of his days delivering the fruit that the orchard produced in his hay cart. He'd be gone for days on end sometimes, so it wasn't uncommon for people to not see him for some time. People came up with all kinds of explanations for his absence, from the old man losing his way during one of his trips, to forgetting to leave a note for his wife before leaving on his most recent journey (Warren was a very forgetful man). They all expected jolly old Warren Maple to come up the road in his beaten-up hay cart any minute, wearing his faded straw hat and sucking on the tails of a honeysuckle. He'd smile and laugh, completely unaware of the worry he'd caused his poor wife.

It wasn't until the Maple family was called to the graveyard one cold January night that all rumors were put to rest. However, what happened that night still remains a mystery to everyone except the grave keeper and Aggie Maple.

Everyone in Maple Town, from the laborers to the shopkeepers, came to the service, shivering in their coats. It was an excellent service, one that everyone thought Warren would have loved. The baker stood holding his baker's hat, his head down as he shyly wiped away his tears on his sleeve. The laborers all said a few words about how they would always look forward to seeing good ol' Warren coming up with his cart of fruit. He'd tip his hat, crack a few jokes about how lazy they were, and continue on his way.

At one point, everyone dropped something into the grave. The apple vendor dropped his finest apple; the sorrowful fabric woman dropped her best unused spool of silk; and Lord Autaine dropped an exotic orange feather the size of his arm. This continued until the grave was full of things from everyone in Maple Town.

Charlie had escaped the mansion that morning to attend the service. He stood next to Skat, who had his fists clenched and was whispering venomously under his breath about Warren's killer.

"They say it was a vampire," he whispered. "I swear I'll kill him. I swear it!"

Charlie rested a hand on Skat's shoulder, providing just enough cover for him to slip a small note into the grave without anyone noticing.

There was one young lady present who cried more tears than everyone combined. Her grandmother's eyes, too, were already red and puffy when it came to her turn to walk up to the grave.

If it weren't for the young lady that clung tightly to her hand, the old woman probably wouldn't have made it. The two of them walked, the eyes of the rest of the mourners following their backs, until they stared down at the coffin that contained the mangled body of the old man with the beaten-up hay cart.

The young lady pulled her signature red ribbon from her beautiful golden locks and was about to drop it in the grave, but the sight of the coffin was too much for her. She fell to her knees with tears streaming down her cheeks. Everyone who saw this came to her aid with small hugs and encouraging words, but nothing was enough. It was a sadness that only those who had lost someone could understand.

Alice knew such sorrow, which made it especially hard for her to accept that she wasn't at the funeral that morning. Despite her father's attendance, she was still forbidden to leave the white mansion. She begged, pleaded, and cried until her eyes were so red and her face was so blue from yelling that her father left, not wanting to hear any more of it. Then he doubled the number of magical locks on the doors.

Alice stared out at the funeral in the distance and drew little circles of ice on her window. She was still in her baby-blue nightgown with half her hair combed straight. She had been halfway done getting ready to go when she and her father began arguing.

At the very least, she wasn't alone. She turned and stared at Vincent with tired eyes, taking note that he'd proceeded with his day as if it were any other. It was as if the news of the funeral didn't faze the tall black-haired man at all. He just continued to take various medical objects out of his black medicine bag, and occasionally stared at the little circles of ice she'd created.

"If you keep glaring at me like that, your face will stay like that forever," Vincent said, putting away his stethoscope.

Alice blinked. "I wasn't glaring!" she snapped. "But if I was, I have every right to!"

"I'm sure your father means well," Vincent said, shaking his head. "He loves you very much." He paused for a moment. "Even if it doesn't always seem like it."

Alice groaned and collapsed on her bed. "Where's the cat? I need to hit something."

"Sit up," Vincent said. "I only took out my equipment because you insisted on sitting by the window. We need to make this look convincing, so stop moving or this empty syringe will actually stab you."

Alice reluctantly rose and allowed Vincent to play fake doctor with her. She glared out the window. It had started to snow. Alice watched how occasionally the snowflakes would blow toward her window and quickly liquefy, dripping down the panes as if the window were crying.

Vincent began putting away his equipment, eyeing Alice as tears welled up in her eyes. She had scrunched up her face to try to conceal them or maybe stop them—Vincent couldn't figure out which. Then Alice switched gears to ask the question she'd been bugging Vincent with for weeks. "So, are you going to tell me why you know magic?"

"I told you," Vincent said, nonchalant. "That smoke from your cards was you. You're becoming a better witch."

"But that wasn't me," Alice said. She pressed because she knew it bothered him. If she had to suffer, so did Vincent! "We both know that, so fess up! How do you know magic? It's the least you can do for a poor girl who can't even comfort her best friend."

Vincent rubbed his temples. "It was given to me by a witch," he said quickly. "There, now you know."

"No! Try again! I'm stuck here while Sally is crying her eyes out. You need to do better than that."

Vincent glared at the young girl, then cracked his neck before returning to his usual stoic position. "What do you want to know?"

"Well, if magic can be transferred, do you think I can do that?"

"Why on earth would you do that?"

"I don't want to be a witch if it means being locked up all the time," Alice said. "You know, I haven't been to the festival before."

"What?"

"The festival. The one the town throws each year. It looks so much fun," Alice said. "He never lets me go. He doesn't even let me visit Sally at the Maple Orchard. He doesn't let me go to anything but his stupid Autumn Ball. I can't believe Papa can be so cold! She's my best friend. I should be there."

"He has his reasons."

"What reasons? So what if I'm a witch? It doesn't give him the right to lock me up like a prisoner! It's not fair! I'm not going to hurt anyone."

"It's not you he's worried will hurt them." Vincent stopped. Then almost as an afterthought he added, "Also, you don't want to give away your magic. Giving away even half your magic means shortening your own life. Imagine magic as a kind of circular entity. It runs infinitely throughout your body. But if you give half of it away, the tank becomes finite, and you die once it runs out. I was given magic because I would have died otherwise."

Alice remained silent. "Fine, I won't do that."

"Promise you won't!" Vincent said, more serious now. "No matter how bad it gets living here, don't ever give up your magic."

"Fine, I won't," Alice said again.

"Good," Vincent said. He returned some of his equipment to his medicine bag. Alice could have sworn he smiled, but thought better of it. He reached inside his bag again and pulled out a small iron key. "You remind me of her, you know?"

"Who?"

"The witch who gave me half her magic," Vincent said. He played with the key in his hand.

"What is that?" Alice said, reaching out to grab it.

Vincent pulled his arm back. "You need to promise me that you will not use it today. Promise?" he said. "This key wasn't meant for you, but it's clear you deserve it more."

Alice hesitated, her hand quivering. She wondered what the key was and if she should make such a promise. "So why give it to me?"

"It doesn't matter," Vincent said. "Now promise me."

"I promise," she said, meeting Vincent's hand. "Now what does the key do?"

"It can open any locked door once," Vincent said. "Remember that. After you use it, it will break. However, it will grant you one free chance to go out through that door. You need to come back, though. If you don't, you'll be brought back by force, so you might as well come willingly. Don't you dare waste it. Skeleton keys are rarer than anything your father owns."

"How did you get it?"

"I made an underachieving blacksmith make it for me. Now, remember: you promised not to use it today. Use it wisely."

The sheer shock of hearing the icy man's not so icy words was more than Alice could comprehend. Vincent remained by the window, deep in thought about something. He began playing with the little ice circles that Alice had created, before finally turning back to her as if suddenly remembering she was in the room.

"What about me reminds you of her?"

"Who? The witch?" he said slowly.

"Well, does she have a name?"

"Elizabeth," Vincent said softly. "She was always in a hurry to become something. The type that leaped before looking, but somehow always landed on her feet."

"I guess that sounds like me," Alice said. "Thank you, Vincent."

For a moment, Alice could see some of the ice melting from the man in the mansion. He seemed genuinely happy when he talked about this woman.

"Anyway, don't waste it," Vincent said. He cleared his throat, and suddenly the ice had returned.

He turned and left.

Weeks passed, and gradually the snow dropped from the branches. Winter's cold embrace slowly loosened its grip on the world, while an array of yellow, orange, and green flowers started to raise their heads from the ashes of a bitter winter.

One day, a heavy rain poured into the town, washing away the remaining traces of winter. Charlie tried his hardest not to look out the window, but his eyes would always betray him as he worked away in the library, alphabetizing the stacks of books and returning them to their high shelves.

The people in the marketplace didn't seem to notice the heavy droplets that fell upon them. There were people still carting wares in every which direction, vendors yelling at other vendors, and women leading their children away from puddles while they indecisively chose between buying bread or fruit. Overall, life continued like a well-oiled machine. It continued to move, unaware that Charlie hadn't visited the town in weeks.

"I'm so stupid, Aria," Charlie said. He threw a couple of books onto the shelf.

Aria didn't move from her spot. She kept to her perch and watched Charlie with her head drooped. She'd tried for weeks

to cheer him up, but nothing would work. The only thing that seemed to remotely ease the young vampire's misery was to listen.

"What was I even thinking?" he said. He came down from the ladder he'd been standing on to get another stack of books to organize. "I'm a vampire. A vampire! There were only a few ways it could have ended. I was stupid for thinking I could live with them."

He closed his eyes and imagined the town; life had gone on as if he had never visited. The townspeople were better off without a monster among them anyway.

"He was her grandfather!" Charlie shook his head. "He begged for mercy, and I watched Vincent rip him apart. I drank his blood. It was—"

He couldn't bring himself to say he'd enjoyed it. It was always at this point that he'd begin focusing back on his chores. Every time his thoughts returned to Sally, all he could think about was her crying at the funeral. Every tear she shed was a reminder of the pain he'd caused her. It was all his fault.

For this reason, Charlie had drowned himself in chores in the weeks that followed the funeral. He'd practically finished everything on the list just trying to keep his mind off the town. Not only was everything spotless but he had even taken the time to shine all the fixtures.

"You've been busy," said a voice below.

Charlie finished stacking a few more books before peering down the ladder. Vincent stood at the bottom with an eyebrow raised at him.

"Well, I wanted to be alone. Besides, I need to get my chores done, right? That's exactly what I'm doing," Charlie said. He refused to look at Vincent more than he had to. Talking to him was the last thing he wanted right now.

"I see that," Vincent said. "This is the last of the chores, is it not?"

"Yes, after this I'm all done."

"I'm impressed," Vincent said. He took a book and helped Charlie shelve it. "I didn't expect you to actually complete the list."

"Well, I did."

There was a pause between them, which soon ended with Vincent cutting to the one question Charlie knew was coming.

"Why don't you come down?"

"I have work to do. Besides, aren't you supposed to be at work? It's long after a quarter to nine." Charlie nodded toward the big bronze grandfather clock he'd finished polishing several hours ago.

"It's night," Vincent said flatly. "I've gone to work and come back already."

"Really. Well, welcome home, then," Charlie said, throwing more books onto the shelf.

"Would you come down already?"

"Why should I?"

"Just come down, boy!" Vincent shouted.

Charlie silently climbed down the ladder and glared at Vincent. It was in staring at the tall vampire's coal-black eyes that Charlie noticed things he had neglected in his isolation. Vincent's hair was frazzled, and he hadn't changed his clothes since who knew when. His white sleeves were both rolled up and were stained with a strong soap that burned Charlie's nostrils. His once-black pant legs were spotted with soot and dirt.

"I don't want to kill anyone, Vincent," Charlie said.

For a second, Charlie could have sworn he saw Vincent's eyes soften. Then something strange happened. Vincent's face contorted, revealing something that Charlie had never seen before on the bitter vampire's face: sympathy.

"I know you don't," Vincent said. "I told you. It's beyond my power. You will have to kill eventually. It's our nature to kill people. It is either—"

"We kill them or they kill us," Charlie said.

Vincent's eyes flickered in surprise. "Exactly, it's a cruel world," Vincent said. "I'm glad you're learning that."

"But why does it have to be like that?" Charlie threw a book down. "It's horrible! We look like them, we talk to them, and we love like them, but we can never live with them? It's a sick joke!"

"I understand what you're going through."

"Do you?" Charlie snapped. "You hate them!

"It's a lot more complicated than that," Vincent said.

"It's not complicated. Don't kid yourself," Charlie sneered. "Would your wife want to see you like this? So full of anger?"

"You know nothing about her, boy!"

"I know plenty. Ever since your wife was killed, you've been nothing more than a walking corpse! I'm supposed to believe you understand what I feel? You stopped feeling a long time ago!"

"Is that what you think? IS THAT WHAT YOU THINK?" Vincent boomed. "So you will have to kill someone. Man up to it, boy! It's cruel? Well, tough. I've seen and experienced a hell unlike any other, and you preach to me about suffering? You know nothing, nothing about true suffering, you worthless, naive boy!"

Vincent slammed the library door shut, shaking the room as he left. Aria followed him. Charlie began picking up some of the fallen books. How could Vincent ever know?

He silently cursed Vincent until he'd finally finished alphabetizing all the books in the library. It must have been a little past three in the morning when he was done, but Charlie didn't care.

Charlie reached over and snagged one of the bottles that Vincent had been periodically leaving for him to drink. Tears welled up in Charlie's eyes as he greedily embraced the cool red liquid that quenched his parched throat.

He staggered to the crystal room. He propped its large window open and sat with his legs hanging over the ledge, staring out at the empty town. All the lights were out. It looked so peaceful despite having a beast watching over it as it slept. Not a creature stirred that night. It was quiet, with only the faint sounds of dreams whispering in the air. He closed his eyes and let out a deep sigh.

At the sound of scurrying footsteps, his eyes shot open. He saw a shadow running across the marketplace. Charlie quickly slid down the side of the house before bolting toward the tall black gate. By the time he got to the town square, the far-off figure had rounded the corner just past the baker's shop, heading for the blacksmith's hut. As Charlie chased after the stranger, he could hear the faint sound of crying.

"Hey, wait up!" he said, but the figure ignored him. It just kept running until it came to the bridge Skat and he would always stand on, waiting for Sally. Only, the figure wasn't standing; it had climbed onto the stone railing.

The closer Charlie got, the more he saw the outlines of a dress, and the little tears that fell from the figure's face and into the stream below. As the moon shot through the parting clouds, the dress slowly lost its shadows, and Charlie could see its thin stripes. Then he saw the girl's long golden locks and the familiar red and white of her dress's fabric. Charlie was at the foot of the bridge when he realized the person silhouetted in the moonlight was Sally Maple.

"Whoever you are, stay away!" she said, not looking at her pursuer.

"I just want to talk," Charlie said.

"Go away! I just want to be alone."

"I don't think I can do that." Charlie walked closer to Sally. "Do you mind if I ask why you're doing this?"

"Why do you care?" she shouted. "I don't even know you!"

"But you do," Charlie said. "I'm not sure if you remember, but a while back I saved one of your apple tarts that had fallen out of your basket."

"Charlie?" she said, sniffling up her tears.

"I'm glad you remember me." Charlie gave a nervous laugh. "I'm honored."

"Yes, I do," Sally said. "But that doesn't mean you can save me."

"Well, hang on there. Then I ask again, why are you doing this?"

"I told you not to walk any closer!" she snapped. She glared at him as he tried to edge his way closer.

"Alright, I won't move." Charlie put his hands in the air. "This is as close as I'll stand."

"Not an inch further, or I'll jump!"

"I know," Charlie said.

The two of them stood watching each other. Nothing but crickets and the wind cooing through the empty branches filled the silence.

"Aren't you going to say anything?" Sally said.

"I figure if there were anything you wanted me to say, you'd ask," Charlie said.

"It's my grandmother." Sally sobbed. Tears streamed down her cheeks. Her voice shook, making some of her words hard to hear. "Three months ago her husband died, and in her grief . . . in her grief, she . . ."

"Hey, it's going to be alright."

"She killed herself!" Sally said.

"I'm so sorry," Charlie said.

"Well, now my grandfather and grandmother are both gone! What's worse is how they found him. My grandmother only knew it was him by the stitching of his name on his nightgown. He was barely recognizable."

"Well, you joining them isn't the answer," Charlie said quickly, not wanting to know any more details.

"And what would you know about death?"

"Quite a bit actually," Charlie said. "Trust me when I say you mustn't die."

"I just don't see the point," Sally said.

"Well, I do," Charlie said. "You are the most charming and beautiful woman in this town. You're the pride and joy of Maple Town. It just wouldn't be Maple Town without you. I also know a great amount of men who would be grieving over your loss."

"I don't know."

"How 'bout this," Charlie said. He picked up a rock. "If I can shoot this rock into that hole by the quarry, you get down. If I miss, you can jump, and I won't stop you. I'll even shoot it from right here."

"That's impossible. You could never make the shot."

"Then doesn't that benefit you?"

"Fine, it's a deal."

Sally eyed Charlie while he stared at the hole. He wound up his arm as if ready to throw the rock too far to the right. At the last minute, he changed aim, and the rock flew out of his hand and sailed straight into the hole.

"I believe we had a deal," Charlie said, taking a bow.

"I guess we do," Sally said. She stepped down, still eyeing the hole the rock had disappeared into. "I still can't believe you made that shot."

"Lots of practice," Charlie said. Then it happened with little notice. Sally threw herself onto him and kissed him, and nothing else mattered.

CHAPTER NINE

THE MAPLE ORCHARD

Alice brushed at the cinders in the large fireplace. She glanced up at the tall grandfather clock, groaned, and began sweeping more furiously than she had before.

It had to be a surprise.

For a brief second, she raised a finger and contemplated bewitching the clock to turn it back, just for her own sake of seeing that she had more time than she actually did. However, her better judgment got the best of her. She let out a short sigh and went back to her sweeping while clouds of ash and soot stained her apron and anything else unlucky enough to be around her.

"Now you look like a witch." The cat coughed and stretched his paws out. He was sitting in a nearby chair watching her clean.

"Very funny," Alice said, laying her broom to rest. She glanced over at her broomstick, shaking her head. "How do people expect us to fly on one of these things? I really don't know where the wild stories come from."

"From the same place every odd tale is born: fear," the cat said. He made his way over to his soot-covered student. "Now, what are you doing? It's a little late for spring cleaning, isn't it?"

"It's to convince Papa. It's getting to that time of year when he's so wrapped up in his ball planning that the mansion gets a little messy, so I'm taking it upon myself to clean it. I figured that it might help when I ask him if I can go to the Mad Hatter's Festival."

"You ask every year," the cat said.

Alice stopped.

"I know that," she said. "But maybe this year Papa will let me go. It's pretty much the Autumn Ball except a lot less formal, and he's not organizing it." Alice made her way to the kitchen. She rolled up her sleeves and grabbed some bread and jam from the pantry. "Maybe a bit of cleaning will help."

"I've never been much of a gambler, but I wouldn't bet any of my nine lives on it."

The cat hopped onto the kitchen counter. He walked back and forth, eyeing his young student cutting up the bread and some fresh fruit she'd added to her spread, when all of a sudden, they heard a noise in the atrium.

"Alistair! Alistair!" screamed a shrill voice.

Alice poked her head out of the kitchen, a slice of bread dangling from her mouth. At the very end of the entrance hallway stood a woman that Alice liked even less than Vincent. Elise Maple was a very cross woman with very long blonde hair. She had a protruding jawline and a sharp nose, complemented by her permanently furrowed eyebrows. The woman always reminded Alice of a weasel, especially in the way she'd always stick her nose in the air as if sniffing out her prey. The fact she also usually wore a fur coat didn't help with the comparison.

Her feet clicked and clacked with each step she took, and her eyes scanned the long entrance hallway until they spotted Alice.

"Have some respect for yourself!" the weasel woman spat. "Get that out of your mouth. Chew like you have a secret, my dear! You're filthy too, but never mind that. Where is your father? No, actually, I only wanted to speak with him to talk to you. Where is Sally?"

Alice took the bread from her mouth. "It's a pleasure to see you too, Mrs. Maple." Her mouth strained to contort itself into a polite smile. "I'm afraid I haven't seen Sally in weeks."

Alice shook her head at the sudden realization. "I haven't seen Sally in weeks," she repeated. The words coming out of her mouth seemed so foreign to her. "That's actually very strange. Now you've got me worried. Is she alright?"

"Yes, she's fine!" Mrs. Maple said. "She's just been . . . odd lately. If she caught whatever disease you're carrying, so help me! Perhaps your father knows where my darling daughter has gone. She's sneaking out, and if it's not to see you, then who?"

"My God, woman! I can only think to get away from you!" the cat said under his breath. Alice let out a quiet snicker as she took another bite of bread.

"What's so funny? You think this is a joke?"

"No, I'm sorry, Mrs. Maple," Alice lied. She led Mrs. Maple into the dining room to wait, then slumped into the chair farthest away from the real witch of Maple Town. Alice would have let Elise Maple stew in her own bitterness if it weren't for her wish to know what Sally was up to and for the annoyingly subtle hints her mother would drop.

The woman cleared her throat, tapped her fingers on the table, made passing glances at the breakfast spread Alice had laid out, and pretty much did everything other than grab herself a plate.

Alice set down her fork. "Care for some breakfast while you wait?

"Hand over a bread slice with jam," Mrs. Maple said. "I'm watching you. People don't like it when you laugh at them, dear."

"Well, we don't like you period," the cat said. He left the room with a mouthful of bread that Alice had left out for him.

Again, Alice held back her laughter. She handed Mrs. Maple a slice of bread with strawberry jam. Alice then made her deck of cards appear when Mrs. Maple wasn't looking and began shuffling them under the table while Mrs. Maple occasionally made crude remarks about Alice's attempt at cleaning.

At least, that was until the front door burst open again, to reveal yet another morning visitor.

"Alice! Atticus! Hang on, he's out on business again, that's right! Alice! Alice! Masks! It's brilliant! A masquerade—why haven't I entertained the idea before?"

Lord Autaine hobbled into the mansion holding boxes upon boxes of what looked to be masks. He set them down and paraded around holding an intricate black mask with red feathers, but stopped when he saw Mrs. Maple sitting at their table.

"Elise!" he said. "I wasn't expecting you. What a nice surprise! What do you think about a mask-themed ball for this year?"

"It's fine, Alistair," Mrs. Maple said. "Have you seen my daughter lately?"

"No, but I'm sure Alice—"

"I already asked her." Mrs. Maple rose from her chair. "And it seems you don't know either, so I think I'll make my leave."

"So soon?" Lord Autaine said. "You just got here!"

"I'm a busy woman, Alistair. We'll be in touch. Oh, and clean up your daughter, will you?"

She left with a loud thud, and Lord Autaine turned to look at his daughter, covered from head to foot with black dust. His eyes narrowed as Alice made a fan out of her cards and magically blew away all the soot and dirt from her body.

So many questions popped into Lord Autaine's head at this moment, but none really seemed possible for him to inquire. He opted for a safer line of questioning instead.

"Why are you so filthy?"

"You see," Alice began. She pocketed her cards and rushed over to her father out in the foyer. "I'm feeling fine, so fine in fact that I've cleaned a good chunk of the mansion."

"You did a marvelous job too," her father said, running his finger over the banisters. His eyes narrowed. "But why? I assume it wasn't out of the goodness of your own heart?"

"Why, Papa, I'm hurt you'd ever imagine I wouldn't," Alice said, holding a hand over her chest. "In fact, I'm so hurt, you should let me go out for a night to that—what is that thing called?"

"Out with it," her father said with his arms crossed.

"The Mad Hatter's Festival," Alice said weakly.

Her father scowled. It was as if he'd caught her killing a baby or something. He dropped the mask he was still holding and ran a hand over his forehead.

"I absolutely forbid you from going to that awful festival," he said. "No, this isn't a discussion. You are much too frail. You can get hurt. You can . . ." He trailed off. "No, I don't even allow your brother to go that festival!"

"Please, Papa! I really want to go just once," Alice said. "It's like the Autumn Ball. You let me go to that."

"That's because the event is here," Lord Autaine said. "This is different."

"I don't see the harm in it," Alice said. "It's just a festival where people throw hats."

"No. I'm your father, and I forbid it," he said, shaking his head rapidly. "You have the Autumn Ball. No, absolutely not."

"But—"

"I said no! You're never leaving this house."

The room fell quiet. Lord Autaine took a deep breath and regained his composure before smiling at his daughter. He laid a hand on her shoulder. "It's for your own good. Now clean up. Get those silly notions of this festival out of your head. It's a waste of time! Instead, tell me about the masks. Do you like them?"

Alice retreated upstairs, ignoring her papa's incessant talk of masks. She reached the landing of her room and slammed the door behind her. She collapsed onto the bed and screamed into a pillow, hating with every fiber how unreasonable her father was being.

"Well, your plan sure went swimmingly," came a voice next to her.

"Not now," she said. "Can I just be alone, please?"

"You make my company sound like a bad thing," the cat said. He strutted around her, snickering at the young girl's distress.

"Go away," came her muffled voice. She threw a pillow at the cat.

"Suit yourself, but I suggest you get used to my company because it seems your only plans involve a night alone with your cat."

"No." Alice snapped up with a determined look on her face. She reached for the rusty iron key hidden under the mattress. "I'll still go. Papa won't even know I'm gone."

Within seconds, an array of items around her room levitated in the air. Items ranging from scissors, to fabrics, to cardboard all hovered around her. She watched the objects and directed them in every which way she desired.

"What if someone in town notices you at the festival and tells your father? News travels fast; you know that."

"That's why I can't look like me," Alice whispered. She held her hair up, looking from side to side, while the cat could only ponder what his student meant.

"What's she doing here again?" Skat said. He nodded over at Sally, who sat on top of a crate beside Charlie's tailcoat and Skat's newsboy hat. Her sleeves were rolled up, and her feet in her brown knee-high boots kicked the air frivolously as she laughed with Sam about something obviously hilarious. The old blacksmith let out a booming chuckle while Charlie and Skat loaded coals into the furnace.

Sally had become somewhat of a regular at the blacksmith's hut, stopping by almost every day for the past few weeks. She'd taken a shine to Charlie ever since the night on the bridge, a secret no one knew other than Sally and him.

Sally brought new life to the crusty old blacksmith's hut. Ever since she first requested to sit in while Charlie worked, it just seemed like she belonged with them. Sam clearly enjoyed her company too, for he had even started to drink less and work more diligently in her presence. But what Charlie loved the most was when he and Sally would talk during his breaks and laugh about the most insignificant things. It was only Skat who seemed cautious of her.

"I can't help it if she likes spending time with us," Charlie whispered.

"Oh, we all know you don't mind, lover boy," Skat said, rolling his eyes. "I just don't get why she comes by here all the time."

"Beats me," Charlie said. He wiped away the beads of sweat from his forehead with one of his rolled-up sleeves. His shirt and vest were drenched in sweat.

The blood blade called for the furnace to burn at a temperature

known as "the demon's flame." As to what that meant, Charlie
had no idea. What he did know is that whatever temperature
that was, it made working in the blacksmith's hut feel like they
were on the very sun itself. At first Charlie thought the task to be
impossible; how could they keep a fire going at such a ridiculous
temperature? Then Sam pointed out that he had special coals
for just this purpose. Now, Charlie watched them burn in the
furnace's green and black flames, feeling very odd about creating
the only thing he knew that could harm him.

"Well, I don't like it. You disappear all winter, and you come
back with that, that thing." Skat spat.

"Hey, be nice!" Charlie said.

"Oh yeah, because you're in lo—"

Charlie kicked Skat in the shin, causing him to seethe silently
through the pain. He knew exactly what Skat was about to say
and didn't want to risk Sally hearing it. Charlie quickly looked
back at Sally. To his relief, she was still laughing with Sam, who
was now showing her how to hold a sword. Charlie couldn't help
but smile at the sight, even while Skat glared at him.

"What was that for? You know it's true!"

"Sorry," Charlie said. "Just, be careful okay? She can't know."

"Yeah, yeah, yeah." Skat threw water into a smelting pot.
"That's it for now, right?"

"It better be."

"Hey, are you two almost done over there?" called Sally, fanning
herself with one of her white gloves. "I have treats."

"Yeah," Charlie said. Even in the blistering heat, she seemed to
make it all worth it.

"You two," Skat said in disgust. "I swear. I'm so close to
jumping in that furnace. Don't test me, Charlie. I'll do it. I hope
you know that."

Charlie ignored Skat. The three of them left the hut and immediately raced toward the stream. Charlie and Skat splashed the cold stream water against their skins while Sally dabbed her handkerchief with water and wiped her forehead with it. Every splash felt like fresh rain and brought new life to the boys.

"God, I can't wait until the blood blade is over and done with." Skat rose to his feet and picked up a nearby stick. He began swinging it like a sword. "Those vampires need to pay for killing your grandfather, Sally."

"Yes. Yes, they do," Sally muttered.

"Hey, they'll get what's coming to them, but let's enjoy today, huh?" Charlie said quickly, giving Sally a knowing look.

"Exactly." Sally beamed at Charlie. "In the meantime, let's enjoy some of the tarts I've made."

Sally's tarts always looked so good, and Charlie always dreaded having to pretend to take a bite of his before throwing it into the stream. Watching Skat and Sally devour the sweet-looking confectionaries was almost too much to bear sometimes. The tarts smelled and looked so delicious that he often wondered what tasting their delectable flavors would do to him, but he never tested it for fear of the consequences.

Charlie closed his eyes and lay down on the grassy hillside. Skat and Sally did the same, enjoying the sparkling sun and the array of flowers that had recently begun revealing their beauty to the world once more. Everything seemed to sway in the breeze in a lazy lull that was not only comfortable but defined the moment between the three of them.

Then Charlie felt something land on his chest. He groaned and picked up the long stick Skat had put there. "What's this for?"

"Practice," Skat said, swinging his own stick. "They say vampires can't use magic, but they make up for it in the fact they can be

anywhere. The scary thing is that it's incredibly difficult to tell the difference between a vampire and a human. I have to be ready when I face one."

Charlie gave Skat a concerned look.

It wasn't until they'd started crafting the blood blade that Charlie realized how much of an obsession his friend had with killing vampires. It was something that both was alarming and made him extra cautious not to expose his secret. However, Charlie had to admit he had learned a lot of things from Skat about vampires. Whether they were true or not, though, was another question.

"I beat you the last few times," Charlie said.

"Yeah, but I'll beat you this time. I'll even do it with my eyes closed." Skat grinned. "Vampires only come out at night. It's because the sun can hurt them, so I need to practice fighting in the dark or hope I catch a vampire during the daytime."

Skat charged at Charlie, but in a few swift moves, Charlie sent Skat to the ground. Sally clapped at the spectacle. As always, Skat laughed off his loss as Charlie walked over to help his friend up.

"Why are you so good?" Skat said.

"I never touched a sword until we started sparring. I swear," Charlie said. "I guess I just get lucky."

All of them laughed and lay on the grass together. They looked at the clouds until Skat, as usual, left suddenly. Charlie always assumed Skat did this to give Sally and him time to do whatever Skat imagined they did together. However, what usually happened wasn't what Skat might have expected. Sally and Charlie would just sit and talk. Then they'd inevitably reach an awkward pause in their conversation, which was almost always broken by Sally.

"Hey, have you ever been to the orchard during this time of year?" she said.

"No, I haven't," Charlie said. "I think you forget that I haven't lived in Maple Town for that long."

"Ah, I do forget that." Sally stood up. "Well, I want to show it to you. I think you might love it."

She offered an outstretched hand to Charlie, and he took it. She led him through streets that seemed to be blurred by the bliss he felt holding her hand in his. As they hurried through the streets together, Charlie noticed things about the town he'd never seen before. They passed large homes that stood behind low white fences. They walked past shops with ivy snaking up their walls. The streets they passed held the faint scent of plants and sweets that tantalized his nostrils.

They got a few curt greetings from the few people who noticed them together. However, all seemed to be carrying objects to a particular area.

Charlie stopped. "What are they building?"

"Hm?" Sally said. "Summer is approaching, isn't it? They're preparing the town for the Mad Hatter's Festival. I heard it's amazing."

For a moment, Charlie saw a tinge of longing in her eyes.

"I've never been," she said. "It's a festival where everyone comes wearing a hat, and a cannon goes off every hour until midnight. The rule is that at every blast, you throw your hat in the air and collect a new one. And at midnight, you look for your original hat and return the one you're wearing to its original owner. There's this romantic legend behind it that says if two people have each other's hat by the end of the night, they're meant to be together. It was started way back by a man who lost his hat to a strong summer gust, as did a woman. The two of them ended up following their hats to the very spot where the festival is now held, and this is how the man met his wife. At least, that's how the legend goes. Doesn't it sound so romantic?"

"It sounds amazing," Charlie said. His head flashed with images of the man in the legend losing his hat and finding his future wife.

Sally and Charlie soon made it to the dirt pathway where he'd first seen her. The familiar "Maple Orchard" sign dangled from the small white fence guarding the hundreds of different fruit trees that seemed to stretch on for miles. Sally ran ahead, down the dirt trail leading into the orchard, and Charlie followed.

At every corner, there were trees of different colors, bearing different fruits, whose smells blended, creating a fantastic aroma of pears, bananas, apples, and many other fruits that Charlie had never seen before. Much like Sally, their scent was intoxicating. It was as if he were traveling to a different world. Occasionally, little petals and leaves would wisp past Charlie as he followed his princess to wherever it was she leading him.

Soon they arrived in the middle of a clearing with a small well in its center. All around them was a rainbow of different fruit trees and berry bushes, some ripe and ready and others playing catch-up, their flowers only just budding. However, what struck Charlie the most was that all the sounds of the townspeople had disappeared, and in their place was the chirping of birds.

"This is my favorite spot in the orchard," Sally said. "I could spend all day here."

"It's amazing," Charlie said. "You can't hear the town at all."

"That's why I love it." Sally beamed. "Remember when I told you about the Mad Hatter's Festival?" she said in a serious tone.

"Yeah, what about it?"

"Like I said, I've never gone," she said shyly. "It's a commoner's dance. Mother and Father have always looked down on it, saying that it was a silly tradition of a flamboyant fool."

"Well, Ms. Maple, I would love to escort you to the Mad Hatter's Festival," Charlie said, taking a bow in front of her.

"Don't be silly." Sally laughed. "You know you cannot keep that promise."

"Watch me," Charlie said. "If you keep a light on in your room during the night of the Mad Hatter's Festival, I'll come and take you. That is a promise."

"What makes you so sure that you can keep it?"

"Because it's for you," Charlie said.

Sally looked into his eyes. She seemed perplexed, as if the words he spoke were in a foreign language.

"I promise I will be on your balcony on that night. Do you trust me?"

"Do you mean it?"

"I promise," he said.

"Promise on this apple," Sally said, plucking an apple off one of the nearby trees. "They say if you share an apple from the Maple Orchard, your wishes will come true."

Charlie stared with hesitation at the shiny red apple in Sally's hand. He then stared at Sally's sparkling smile and took the apple and bit it. It felt like ash in his mouth and burned his throat more than anything he could imagine, but he stomached the pain for Sally.

At that moment, he knew he would follow her anywhere she wanted. He took her gloved hand in his. They danced across the orchard, with no plans of where they might go. The two of them simply danced in that enclosure and laughed together without a care in the world. Nothing else mattered, nor did they notice anything around them. In fact, they were so taken by each other that they didn't see the ominous eyes staring at them from a window nearby.

Walter Maple looked out at his daughter and her . . . He didn't dare think who this stranger might be. The boy made the man's slicked-back hairs curl. He gave a scowl as he saw the two of them laughing together. The boy was a mess—sweat stains covering his attire, black blotches from God knows what—and here he was with his daughter.

"Who is that boy?" Walter said.

"So that's who she's been with!" replied his weasel-faced wife.

Elise Maple had been sitting at the dining table sipping her tea when her husband called her attention to their daughter and the unknown boy. Unlike her husband, she smiled, knowing very well the fickle nature of her daughter. "No matter. She's brought young men to the orchard before. She will get bored of him like the others."

"I don't know, Elise," Walter said cautiously. "I have a bad feeling about this one."

"And I'm telling you, our daughter is too fickle to pick her own suitor. I say let her have her fun with this one and let it blow over. This one definitely cannot captivate her interests, nor can he support her for long. Who is he trying to kid with that tailcoat of his? His stains are obviously those of the working class."

"It's the way she looks at him, though," Mr. Maple said nervously. "I don't like it. I'm not taking any chances, not since—" He stopped himself. "We need the money. I have a bad feeling about him. I don't want him jeopardizing the future of this orchard."

"Well, why don't you tip the scales, then, dear?"

At this, Walter Maple retracted his gaze from his daughter and turned to his wife. He eyed her curiously, wondering what she may be insinuating. A million ideas buzzed through his head as he stared at his wife's weasely smile.

"What do you mean by that?"

"I only suggest picking a suitor for our daughter." The weasel-faced woman had gotten up and rested her arm against her husband's shoulder, ready to whisper her plan in his ear. "I want her to be with the best, so who better to pick him than us?"

"That is true," Walter Maple said. "It would put my mind at ease, now wouldn't it?"

"Yes, and we'd get a big endowment from the rich husband. We'd all win, dear." She laughed in his ear.

"Yes, we are to pick the richest and most powerful—for our daughter's sake."

"Anyone in mind?" his wife asked eagerly.

"I know of a man with a son of marrying age. It's perfect! I'll get right on it."

The Maples peered again at the orchard and their daughter's sickening smile. She wasn't to be this happy. She was supposed to marry rich. That boy had no place in their world.

Mr. Maple turned away from the window and his wife's weasely grin, and went to his desk to draft a letter.

CHAPTER TEN

THE MAD HATTER'S FESTIVAL

Streams of red, yellow, and orange burst in the distance. The evening glowed with a warm, hazy light, and the muted sounds of guitars, drums, fiddles, and flutes floated above the melodic yells and laughter that echoed through Maple Town. These sights and sounds of merrymaking carried so far, they drew two individuals to stare out longingly from their mansions as another blue firework shot into the sky.

Aria watched Charlie fidget as he looked up at the firework bursting into a thousand golden sparkles. He held a black top hat with a red ribbon sash at its base. It had a couple of mothballs and a single cobweb along the fringe, but any attempts Aria made to remove them were thwarted by Charlie's hand.

It was as if she wasn't even there. He continued to look out the window. Little paper lanterns were lit and rose into the sky one by one. Charlie took a deep breath and gave Aria a reassuring smile before opening the window latch and rushing down the hill.

Aria's head drooped as she watched him leave, but then her ears pricked up. She fluttered over to the tall black-haired vampire who had entered the room. She perched on his fingertips, looking

up at the vampire who stared listlessly as a red firework shot up into the sky. Then the two of them exited the room, but not before hearing the faint creak of the tall black gate opening and closing behind Charlie.

Alice marched around her room in an unfinished red outfit. Fabrics, scissors, and measuring instruments followed her, snipping and stitching at her outfit as she walked.

"I still don't get what you're doing," the cat said flatly. It was hard for him not to stare, fascinated as he was by the girl's ability not to crash into anything and keep her balance.

"You'll see," Alice said. Her eyes remained fixed on the crudely drawn picture on her vanity table.

She cocked her head at the drawing and whistled. Out from under her bed came a roll of white fabric that suddenly coiled itself around her legs. Scissors and needlework wove through her legs until a pair of white trousers came to fruition.

She stared at the trousers, muttering to herself as little embellishments on the pant legs were stitched with golden thread. "Not quite," she said, which was soon followed by "There we go, Alice!"

The excess white fabric floated away as she returned to her drawing, and came to land gently on top of the cat. He peeked his head from underneath to see Alice modeling herself in front of a mirror.

"So how is a red suit jacket and a pair of white trousers supposed to help Alice Autaine go undetected in the throng of commoners?"

"And for the final piece . . . ," she whispered, ignoring the cat's question.

The scissors and red fabric danced in midair, trimming bits of red fabric. The measuring instruments gauged the various lengths of the mysterious object that was in creation. When the floating objects were done, a silver ribbon looped its way around the bowl of the newly created hat to hold a long purple feather in place. The final piece was her playing card hairpin, which fastened itself to the ribbon and the large purple peacock feather. Then the hat gently drifted onto Alice's head, while her hair hastily styled itself into an updo.

"Done." Alice smiled and admired herself in the mirror. "I make a very dashing young man."

"Your father would be so proud," the cat said. "His little girl is finally a man!"

"Oh, hush up!" she snapped. Gold buttons began sewing themselves onto her double-breasted jacket while little white embroidery appeared on her cuff and the fringe of her red-and-gold dress coat. "I'm still a lady, thank you very much!"

"Clearly, because no man wears a hairpin on his hat," the cat said, rolling his eyes.

"Quit being a sourpuss. I could use a bit of luck tonight. I haven't left this house since I was five." She took a deep breath. "Confidence, Alice. Confidence," she told herself, and inserted the rusty key into her balcony door's lock. It clicked open. She stepped cautiously onto the balcony. A broad grin formed on her lips.

"What if your father or brother comes to check on you?"

"They won't if I do this."

She snapped her fingers.

The lights in her room were extinguished, and there came a quick click of her bedroom door. The large black cat walked out onto the balcony and hopped onto the railing, watching his master awkwardly hoist herself down a vine she'd just conjured up.

He stared at the vine Alice climbed down and eyed his paws, then looked at the vine again and back at his paws.

With a loud thud and the unmistakable sound of cursing behind him, the cat returned to the room and kicked the balcony door shut. He made his way to the head of Alice's bed and curled up in anticipation to see what misadventures this outing would yield.

Little children and their parents were moving toward the ever-growing sounds and smells of the festival ahead. Charlie, on the other hand, made a quick turn away from where the summer festivities were being held.

He sprinted down the familiar dirt path until he saw the faded white sign he knew so well by now: "Maple Orchard." However, the Maple estate would prove to be much different at night than in the daytime. The whole orchard was pitch black. If Sally didn't follow his instructions to leave a light on in her room, Charlie would probably never find her.

Luckily for him, far off in the black abyss of the Maple Orchard was a faint light, glowing several feet off the ground of what he assumed was the Maple estate.

He sneaked over the faded white gates and made his way toward the lit room. He eventually reached the ivy-covered wall of the house and began climbing it until he reached the window of the young woman with the golden locks. She sat brushing her hair at her vanity table, unaware her prince waited outside her window.

Sally's eyes almost jumped out of her body when he tapped on the glass. She covered her mouth while making her way toward him.

"What are you doing here?" Sally hissed.

"Didn't I promise to take you to the Mad Hatter Festival? I meant it."

"You did, but this is crazy!" She took a step back, catching her breath, still in disbelief of the boy at her window. "Are we honestly going?"

"I believe it's up to you. Though I would hurry up and make a decision. I'm not too sure how much longer this ivy I'm clinging on to will support me."

"Don't fall!" she said. "Oh, I don't know. This is happening so fast. Should I go?"

Charlie rolled his eyes. "Do you have a hat?"

"Yes, it's right here," Sally said.

"Do you trust me?" He offered her his hand.

"What does that have to do with anything?"

"Do you trust me?" Charlie said again, still holding out his hand.

"Yes, yes," Sally said.

Sally screamed as Charlie pulled her with him. The two of them fell off the edge and down the side of the grand house. Charlie laughed, holding her tight as they fell with a light thud onto a bush.

Sally, annoyed, removed twigs from her hair and cleaned her hat. She looked at Charlie with every intention of yelling at him, but before she could, he held a finger to his lips. She heard the chatter of voices. Within moments, what seemed like thousands of lights lit up within the previously dormant estate, and just as many people began shouting Sally's name. It was only after the voices moved to a different part of the estate that Charlie and Sally rushed to the edge of the Maple Orchard.

"I think we got away," Charlie said.

"Oh, you're terrible, you know that?" Sally said, hitting him.

"So you regret coming with me?" he said nervously.

"Of course not!"

She intertwined her hand with his, and the two of them raced toward the hazy orange glow ahead of them. Each step they took felt forbidden, which made their excursion all the more daring. Occasionally Sally would glance up at her gallant hero with a smile of disbelief, and Charlie returned her gaze with a reassuring smile, silently telling her that all of it was real.

Alice was in full sprint when she saw the trail of lanterns flying overhead. The smell of sweets, savory broths, and meats sailed through the air like little whispers calling out to the many hungry people whose mouths salivated for just a taste.

The drumbeat grew louder as she got closer. The music was so full of soul. The strumming of guitars rang through the air in tempo with the tapping of the musicians' feet, while violins and flutes roared in the wind with ferocity.

When Charlie and Sally arrived, they exchanged a look upon seeing all the different hats. There were small hats, tall hats, paper hats, bag hats.

Local artists in berets sat at different ends of the square sketching people who wanted to be drawn, and on a huge stage were many musicians that Charlie recognized, playing away. Maurice the baker, who wore his usual baker's cap, was strumming away on his banjo, while the sorrowful fabric woman, who on this night did not look so sorrowful, fiddled away on her violin, eliciting a roar from the crowd. She had chosen to wear a little purple hat with a black veil. Oscar, the tailor, wore a hat that was far too large for his head; it flopped around as he piped away on his flute. And one of the woodsmen was drumming away wearing a newsboy cap that made Charlie wonder if he'd see Skat tonight.

"Have you ever seen something so amazing?" Sally said, holding her hands to her mouth.

"Never," Charlie said.

"Oh, I'm so glad you took me here! I still can't believe it!"

"Well then, let's make this more real," Charlie said, suddenly taking her hand. "Let's dance."

"I don't know. I don't know," Sally said, shaking her head. But before she could deny him, he had already pulled her with him into the crowd. "Charlie! I don't know what to do!"

"And you think I have a clue?" he said. "Just go with it."

Charlie took her into his arms and jumped around, following the motions of the people around them, laughing without a care in the world of how silly they must have looked.

At that moment, he wasn't a vampire and Sally wasn't a human. They were two young lovers enjoying the night together in the most honest display of love there is: dance.

Many people at the festival thought Alice was a new nobleman rolling into town, and would occasionally bow to her and mumble drunken remarks. Alice laughed and tried her best to act as gentlemanly as possible as she made her way to the different tables of food. All the local shops had made an effort to put out the best they had to offer. The fruits, meats, and fish were all cooked to perfection for anyone who wanted to indulge themselves in their luscious flavors.

Alice passed a table where a crowd of people cheered on a man in a dunce cap while he arm-wrestled another man in a bowler hat. She laughed and walked past them until she felt her hand being pulled toward the dance floor. A woman in a yellow sundress pressed her head against Alice's chest.

"Donald! You came for me," the woman said. She had a glazed look on her face, and her white sunhat was practically falling off

her head.

"Ah, yes! My dear, I believe you've had enough for the night," Alice said uncomfortably in her most manly voice. "Now, let's sit down and—"

"No!" The woman shook her head. "Donald! It's been so long since I've seen you! Let me just, let me just . . . You're so warm, Donald. So warm!"

A cannon boomed in the distance, and a loud cheer followed from everyone, including the young woman in the sundress. Alice watched with wide eyes as her dance partner went from almost sleeping to screaming at the top her lungs and throwing her hat up in the air. Alice took her cue and slipped out of the young woman's arms. Now free, she tossed her hat up, and caught a large feathery hat that felt more like having a swan on her head than anything else.

Hands stretched into the air. Everyone grabbed whatever hat they could find. Charlie caught a pink bonnet while Sally snagged Maurice's baker's cap. The two laughed at each other's silly hat, but were then broken apart by a group of people who'd hoisted up a young man who had caught a crown. Charlie tried to reach for Sally's hand, but she was carried off by the sea of people.

Instead, Charlie was pulled by a large woman wearing the sorrowful lady's tiny cap and veil. The woman had an emotionless face. Her hair was tied up in two tight blonde buns. She stared stoically at Charlie and had a weird habit of flaring her nostrils every so often. Charlie couldn't even look at her for fear of laughing and offending his new dance partner, who would lumber around and then lift Charlie in whatever direction she desired instead of dancing.

The song changed to a more upbeat tune. The crowd hollered and hooted as various people in odd hats jumped onto the stage to dance the jig the musicians played. Charlie took this opportunity to escape from his large dance partner.

"That there is Charlie!" came a voice from the crowd.

Charlie turned his head to see Sam the blacksmith hobbling over to him. He held an iron goblet in his hand and would occasionally lose his balance entirely, shaking his finger as if giving a lecture to an invisible person that only he could see. When he'd reached Charlie, he put an arm around the young vampire and brought him to a group of laborers.

"See this young man? This, this young man right here is a natural with the coals!"

"Of course you'd know that, Sam! I bet he handles your coals all the time!"

The group laughed as splotches of their ale hit their clothes. Charlie tried to leave but was pulled back by a heavy arm on his shoulder.

"Have a drink with me, son," slurred the blacksmith. "Let's see how a nobleman holds his liquor!"

"I think you've had enough for a while." Charlie laughed, removing the arm from his shoulder. He helped the blacksmith over to a nearby picnic table. Sam smiled at Charlie, but soon lost focus upon finding a pint that someone had left behind.

"Sam, where's Skat?" Charlie said.

Sam raised his head, shook it, and squinted at Charlie. "Causing trouble," he said, pointing a finger at the sky. He gave a loud, booming laugh and leaned back again to take a swig of his drink, only to find that it was very much empty. "But no, he's not here. He never is. Never drinks with me. I'm his master. What kind of apprentice doesn't drink with his master? You should drink with me! Get me another, will you, peach?"

Another cannon fired, and another round of hats was flung into the air. The crowd screamed and shouted louder. Alice found herself in possession of an argyle newsboy cap and drifted around the festival, passing little boys and girls linked arm in arm and dancing to the beat of the music while their adult counterparts danced in a similar fashion.

Alice soon found Sally sitting at a table surrounded by drunken suitors. She was wearing the white sunhat that Alice's previous dance partner had worn. From a distance, Alice watched her friend blush uncomfortably while a few men proposed to her or offered her a drink. Alice grinned. She immediately rushed over to Sally's aid and cleared her throat.

"I'm afraid the lady promised me a dance." Without warning, Alice pulled Sally onto the dance floor. Alice and Sally linked arms and swayed to the ballad the musicians played.

"I can't believe how much fun this is," Alice said. "Sally, you should have told me you'd be here! We could've snuck out together!"

Sally cocked her head at her new dance partner. "You're very dashing, but do I know you?"

"Oh," said Alice, taken aback. "We haven't met. Sorry, I thought you were a different Sally. Um, you're a wonderful dancer," she added quickly.

"Oh, thank you," Sally said. She stared out at the crowd, her eyes furrowing slightly. "Have you seen my date? You can't miss him. Black hair—"

"You came with a date? Since when?"

"Are you sure we haven't met?" asked Sally again.

"I'm sure," Alice said, reverting to her fake man voice. "But who is this man you came with?"

"You've danced with her long enough, boy!" came a voice. The voice pulled Alice away from Sally. Alice was sent spinning until she was face-to-face with a young man with shaggy black hair and a matching black tailcoat. He looked quite silly in the baker's cap he'd snagged. His blue vest was slightly stained from whatever alcohol was in the iron goblet he held.

At first, Alice thought the young man was drunk, much like everyone else, but was soon corrected when she saw how he was quickly scolded by an obviously drunk man wearing a black bandana.

A crowd began to circle them. They cheered and whistled while both she and the young man stared, perplexed by what exactly was going on. Soon a large, muscular bald man wearing a big flowery hat stood before them. He handed them each a wooden sword.

"We've seen how the other half lives," slurred the bald man. "Now"—he hiccupped—"let's see how the other side fights!"

"What?" both Alice and the young man said.

"We have Red over 'ere." The bald man pointed at Alice. "And Charlie over 'ere! Place your bets!"

Alice held on to the wooden sword, knowing only what her father had taught her. Luckily for her, her opponent looked equally inexperienced; he swung the sword awkwardly, drawing a loud roar from the crowd.

"Fight! Fight! Fight!" the onlookers chanted.

The two circled each other, both hesitant to make the first move. The young man struck first with a horizontal slash and then with a vertical slice. Alice easily blocked and parried his assault, taking note how sluggish his actions seemed. She proceeded to hit him with a barrage of horizontal strikes.

The crowd nearly burst out of their skins watching the young man retreat farther and farther back, almost to the edge of the circle. He attempted to counterstrike, but Alice anticipated his movements and jumped back and dodged every blow. Knowing her chance had come, Alice pivoted and slashed at the young man's legs. He fell, and Alice quickly planted a foot on his chest and pointed her wooden blade at his neck.

"Red wins!" the bald man shouted.

Another cannon went off. Charlie threw his hat up and rolled out of the circle of people. He snagged a red plumed hat with a silver ribbon and a purple feather held together by a small hairpin shaped like a flower and made of playing cards, all hearts. He searched the crowd of people drinking and dancing until he saw Sally with a group of children. The children wore an assortment of hats much too large for their heads. Sally herself wore the sorrowful woman's tiny hat and black veil. The kids and Sally were hand in hand, dancing around in a circle.

Charlie watched Sally playing so effortlessly with the children. He pushed his way through to get a better look at the woman he adored playing like a mother would with her children.

Sally noticed Charlie and beamed at him. She whispered something to the children, and they scurried away. The two rushed toward each other and joined hands, and at that moment, Charlie could feel the stares of many eyes upon them, and the chatter of the noisy housewives and jealous men all around them, like bees buzzing in response to their queen being disturbed.

"It seems we're creating quite the stir," Charlie said.

"It seems so. Not a lot of men are happy to see you with me," Sally said, giving another one of her signature melodic laughs.

"I can imagine why. To be denied by you? I'd be heartbroken!"

"Oh stop it," Sally said. "I'm not that mean, am I?"

"There's not a mean bone in your body," he said, leaning closer to his date. More eyes followed them now, more than before. "May I have this dance, Ms. Maple?"

"Do you even have to ask?" Sally said. "Oh, this song is so romantic!"

The two began waltzing in time with the other couples around them, locked in each other's arms. Sally lay her head comfortably against Charlie's chest.

Holding her so close, Charlie could smell the sweet floral scents that had first captivated him. Their bodies would sway to the melody of the guitars and drums.

"I'm glad we came, Charlie," Sally said in a dreamlike state.

"As am I."

"I don't want this night to end."

"Maybe it doesn't have to," Charlie said.

"Don't be silly." Sally shook her head and stared up at him. "The festival is almost over."

"Not if we get a picture together. Capture the memory forever, you know?" Charlie said, nodding toward the artists. "After this song, let's get one."

"That sounds amazing," Sally said. "I'm so happy, Charlie."

Then Sally did something that she hadn't done since the night on the bridge.

She kissed him.

Her lips on his felt nothing less than blissful. Another round of red and orange fireworks burst above them. However, unbeknownst to Charlie and Sally, every eye seemed less concerned about the fireworks at that moment.

"Get your hands off my daughter!" a voice shouted.

The music and voices stopped. Charlie immediately let Sally go. The voice had come from a portly man with slicked-back brown hair. He glared at the young couple while he shoved his way toward them.

"You kidnap my daughter, take her to this silly party run by riff-raff! What nerve you have. Who gave you the right to touch my daughter? Let alone kiss her!" the portly man said. He yanked Sally's hand away from Charlie.

"Daddy, let go," Sally said. "I kissed him."

"You speak nonsense," the portly man said. "Do you know who this . . . this . . ."

"His name is Charlie, Daddy!" Sally said.

"This Charlie," he spat. "Nothing more than a commoner, I assume. You aren't fooling anyone with that coat and shirt."

"Daddy!"

"I will not tolerate some wannabe noble tainting my daughter with his filth!"

"Let her go!" Charlie shouted. "You're hurting her!"

"Mind your own business," the portly man said, though he did let go of his grip on his daughter's hand. Sally fell to the ground. "Do you know who I am?"

Charlie remained silent, watching as a few men came to Sally's aid. He moved to join them but was stopped by the portly man, who blocked his way.

"I'm talking to you, boy! Do you know who I am?"

Charlie turned away from the man's scrutinizing gaze.

"I'm Walter Maple! You're lucky I don't have you hanged! You have no right to be with my daughter. I don't even know who you are. Charlie, was it? Never heard that name in my life. Who is your father, hmm? Where do you stay? What business do you have dragging my family name to the ground?"

"He's my son!" growled a voice from the crowd.

The square became deadly quiet at the sound of the new voice. Slowly out of the crowd came a tall black-haired man in a black evening cloak. He stared down at Walter Maple with his piercing coal eyes.

"He's my son," Vincent repeated. "He is, in fact, of noble descent. What gives you the right to talk to him like that? Like a worm. Because I see only one worm here." He glared at Walter Maple. "Now, if we are done here, I will take my son and be gone."

Alice had arrived too late to see much of what had transpired, but she sure saw the ending. Vincent had a son! She had to find out who he was.

She made her way to the front of the crowd to see Vincent dragging the same black-haired young man she'd beaten earlier, of all people. Like everyone else, she watched in silent awe until the tall black gate slammed shut behind them.

"So that's Vincent's son," she whispered.

The Mad Hatter's Festival did not resume that night—partly because the clock tower had already chimed midnight and partly because everyone was too busy gossiping to one another in low and purposeful whispers.

Just as quickly as the magical festival had begun, everyone started taking off their hats and returning them to their original owners. Alice shook off the thought of Vincent having a son and looked at the hat she'd snagged. It was a black top hat with a red ribbon wrapped around it. She began looking for its owner but soon found that no one there seemed to own it. What's more, her own hat was nowhere to be seen. She looked until she was the only one left in the square.

She sighed, remembering that her mother's hairpin was on her red plumed hat. She trekked home. So many things ran through her head. So many things that she enjoyed, yet found perplexing. Because out of all the things that had happened that night, she couldn't for the love of herself shake the image of Vincent's son.

She conjured up a vine to climb back to her room. She opened the balcony door and saw her room lay exactly as she'd left it. The cat perked his head up and gave a long stretch. He looked at her and the different hat she'd brought home.

"My, my, you managed to transfigure your original hat into that atrocity. Tisk, tisk. What would your mother think?"

Alice ignored the cat. She drifted around the room, running her fingers over the edges of her bed before finally resting the hat on her vanity. She undid her hair's updo and proceeded to change in silence, her face completely blank. The cat continued to stare at his master's distracted expression.

"So, how was it?" he said. "Everything you expected it to be?"

"It was . . . interesting."

CHAPTER ELEVEN

TEATIME WITH AUTAINE

"Vincent has a son?" said the baker's wife.

"It would seem so," her husband whispered. "Keep it down. We don't want to cause a commotion."

"And Maple—"

"Yes."

"Aww, I can't believe I missed it." His wife pouted. "I was inside with Charlotte helping her watch her son when it all happened."

She and Maurice were helping the rest of the town with what was known as Cleaning Day. It happened every year after the Mad Hatter's Festival. Everyone in town would enjoy a night of free food, music, and dancing, and then join together in cleaning the town the morning after.

However, this year was different. People everywhere, from adults to children, buzzed quietly to one another. And every discussion seemed to lend itself to a head turn toward number thirteen Chiaroscuro Lane.

The mansion remained still and silent. Vincent didn't leave for work that morning, nor did anyone else leave the sprawling house.

What puzzled the townspeople most was how they had missed seeing Charlie coming and going from the mansion on the hilltop all this time. Some would swear that they had seen him, but then a sudden gust of wind had made them forget to tell anyone—or forget what they'd seen altogether. It was an odd phenomenon that was only discovered after the events of the Mad Hatter's Festival, for it was as though those who had been afflicted with it had suddenly woken up.

Although, it wasn't like anyone would have believed what they'd seen, even if they could have remembered. Not even in their wildest dreams could the people of Maple Town have imagined Charlie and Vincent as father and son. Charlie was nothing like the man in the mansion; while the young man always greeted people with smiles and offers of help, Vincent shot an icy glare at whoever approached him.

"Never saw it coming," Maurice said, shaking his head. He was helping some men take apart the wooden stage he'd preformed on the night before.

"I guess the rumors about Vincent marrying were correct," the baker's wife said in a dazed state.

"But I never saw him leave the mansion! How's he Vincent's son?" called a voice in the crowd.

"I have! I think," Maurice the baker said, rubbing his fiery red beard. "I don't know why I never brought it up."

"You too?" spoke a woman from the crowd. "It's so weird."

"He's the love child of Vincent and some woman, I hear," said a man carting the lanterns away. "Born after his wife died, of course."

"No, he's Vincent's son alright. And Vincent chopped up his wife in the attic to keep him!" said a voice from a window.

"What about Charlie, then?" the chimney sweeper said, poking his head out of a chimney. "Where was he when the mother was supposedly being butchered to death?"

"I hear he was just a baby," a woman whispered while walking with her children. She held them close to her and covered their ears before she went on. "Don't hold me to this, but someone told me that Vincent couldn't bring himself to kill Charlie and has locked him in the mansion until now."

"How many times must we go through this?" A man in a regal-looking suit gave an exasperated sigh. He was passing by when he overheard this conversation about Vincent and Charlie. "His wife left him. Must we go through this every time? My source is still reliable. He says Charlie is Vincent's son. Came to his doorstep one night after his mother died of natural causes."

"No, no, no, that can't be!" the butcher said. "They look nothing alike besides the hair."

"Still, Vincent has a son," Maurice said. He let the words linger in the air for a moment before continuing. "Hard to believe, huh? The kid is great. A very happy young man. Hard to believe he is related to that block of ice up there."

"What have I told you about being nice?" his wife said.

"I know, I know," the baker said. "Still, though, I remember seeing Charlie wandering around the marketplace. You'd swear he'd never seen a loaf of bread before."

"Yes, so full of wonder he is. I talked with him on occasions, actually," the baker's wife said. "Very nice young man. I offered him a roll and some pastries once, but he denied me, saying he didn't want to take away from our business. Very modest that man is. I can see what little Miss Maple sees in him."

"Aye, I forgot about that. The young Miss Maple came with him last night, didn't she?"

"They were in love." The sorrowful fabric woman smiled.

"Griselda, I didn't see you there!" the baker's wife said.

"No one ever does," the sorrowful fabric woman said, trailing off with a quick sigh. "They were in love, though, Charlie and Miss Maple. I saw them when I was fiddling. Real shame the night ended the way it did."

"Talking about yesterday night?" said one of the men carrying off the benches.

"Aye, we are," Maurice shouted. "What did you think of ol' Maple cussing out Vincent's son?"

"Who, Charlie? I'd say I'm jealous," the man said, giving a hearty laugh. "My brother and I had our shot trying to court Sally and didn't even get past the front door of the Maple estate. How Charlie managed to pull off a kiss . . . I bet every man in town is cursing his name, not only old Maple."

"I know I am." The man's brother laughed.

"Men!" the baker's wife said. She began walking over to help some other woman clean up the tables of leftover food. "Can't you be happy for Charlie for finally winning that girl's heart? I swear, I thought she'd die alone with all the men she's shot down."

"She's picky. No shame in that. She's the loveliest thing in this town after all," a man wiping windows said.

"Excuse me?" shouted a woman opening her window.

"I-I mean besides you, dearest," the window washer stuttered.

"Still, this is one festival people will be remembering," Maurice said, staring up again at number thirteen Chiaroscuro Lane.

Little did Maurice know that his prediction was again accurate. On the other side of town, in a magnificent white mansion, sat a man with a thousand masks at his feet. He hadn't gone to the Mad Hatter's Festival, but word of mouth of last night's festivities had spread like wildfire, eventually finding its way to his ears. He sat at his desk looking out at the town. He took a few sips of his tea, and his body gave an involuntary sigh as the warm liquid dropped down to his stomach.

On this fine morning, he sat with an agenda that was inspired by the events of the night prior. He picked up his pen and scribbled away on the parchment, forgetting about the letter Walter Maple had sent him a few days ago, for this had struck his interest! Charlie Prowl—who was he? His lips curled into an intrigued smile. The man who was able to steal young Miss Maple's heart. What he wouldn't give to meet the man!

"Fantastic!" he shouted, laying his pen down. "Phillip, can you come here this instant. This is a letter of the utmost importance!"

Within seconds a short man in a suit and tie was standing before for his master.

"As you wish, Lord Autaine," came the curt reply.

Charlie sat in the study staring at Vincent pacing back and forth around the room. Every so often, Vincent would glance at Charlie briefly, before suddenly turning away again. This constant pacing and stopping had gone on since sunup. Vincent had refused to see Charlie when they had arrived home the night before. However, Charlie could hear the sounds of breaking glass and furniture and venomous cursing exuding loudly from Vincent's private quarters for the rest of the night. For this reason, Charlie didn't dare leave his room until Vincent had called him into the study.

"I can't . . . ," Vincent began. "Out of . . . ," he said, then shook his head in disgust. At last Vincent took a deep breath and stared Charlie down. "This is why you can't leave. This happens. I give you an inch and you take a mile. Would you shut that damn bird up?"

Vincent's voice boomed through the study. Aria stopped fluttering around the two vampires and unfolded herself into Charlie's breast pocket.

"You scared her," Charlie said.

"I scared her?" Vincent said. "I scared her? What about me? You scared me quite a bit! I thought I'd look the other way last night. Some stupid nonsense about letting you have some freedom. Never again will I make that mistake! You are never leaving this mansion as long as I have a say in it! One night out and you cause a fiasco with the Maple family. Do you know how close you were to exposing your secret? And out of all the women for you to fall in love with, you chose that siren?"

"Vincent, let me explain," Charlie said calmly.

"Explain what? How you sneak out of the mansion every morning after I leave?"

"You knew?" Charlie said, his eyes wide.

"Of course I knew. Who do you think performed the charm around the gat—"

But Vincent wouldn't be able to finish his statement, for just then, the two of them heard a loud knocking on the door. Vincent left the room. Charlie could hear the faint and nervous stutters of a stranger and Vincent's usual curt replies. Then the brass double doors slammed shut and Vincent returned with a square piece of silver paper.

"What's that?"

"It seems we have been invited to tea at the Autaine mansion," Vincent said with an eyebrow raised. "Lord Autaine is expecting us at noon today."

"But that's less than an hour from now!" Charlie said.

"I guess we have no choice," Vincent said flatly. "Not going would raise even more suspicion. Go and get ready. But know this: we are not done talking about this."

Then Vincent was gone, leaving Charlie alone.

"How could this all happen, Aria?" Charlie said, running a hand through his hair.

Aria refolded herself in the air and rested on Charlie's shoulder as he petted her. She then flew in a complete circle around the small bramble bookcase full of dusty books. She zipped past the suit of armor and finally landed on Charlie's fingertip, staring at him earnestly.

"What do you think is going to happen?"

Aria crumpled herself up and fell to the ground with a light thud.

"I was afraid you might say that," Charlie said.

True to habit, Vincent and Charlie left a quarter of an hour ahead of their intended time of arrival. They were greeted by a gold-and-amber carriage outside the tall black gate. It took some heavy insisting from the driver to get Vincent anywhere near the carriage, but he reluctantly entered the velvet confines of their ride with Charlie following closely behind like a shadow.

Charlie gave an involuntary shudder.

At first, he thought it was from the sudden motion of the carriage. However, it persisted as they traveled. It grew from a shudder to a tingling sensation he felt every time he ran his fingertips against the velvet seats.

"What's wrong with you?" Vincent said.

Charlie jerked to attention. "Nothing," he said quickly. He shook his head while his mouth reached for the words that seemed just too far away. "I just feel funny."

Vincent just glared at him, and that was the most they'd talk during their ride.

Not that Charlie particularly minded it. He was more afraid of what their meeting with Lord Autaine would entail. Had he found out Charlie's secret? What would Vincent do then? Charlie's thoughts spiraled until he'd convinced himself that Lord Autaine and Vincent had conspired to form a joint punishment to lock him away forever.

The carriage doors opened.

Charlie walked out half expecting someone to drag him away, but instead saw a colossal monument in front of him. No, that's not quite right; the Autaine mansion was much grander and much gaudier than that. The structure could have been a whole new district in Maple Town. At its front were massive Doric pillars alongside a set of white stairs that led to two doors the size of some of the shops in Maple Town. To one side of the mansion was a sea of green dotted here and there with other colors. It wasn't until Charlie had made his way up the rather lengthy white steps that he realized he was looking at a large flower maze that stretched on and on and on.

The doors of the mansion opened with a rush of air and revealed a small man wearing a white suit and tie. He stood at attention inside the mansion. He beckoned them in and gave a low bow as they walked past the threshold.

"Welcome to the Autaine mansion. We are very glad you are here," the man said in a dry voice.

Autaine was a lot shorter than Charlie had expected. The rumors in town had made the lord seem larger than life, an idea Charlie had taken perhaps too literally. Nonetheless, Charlie remembered his manners and gave a bow, kissing the short man's hand as he did.

"It's a pleasure, Lord Autaine," he said.

Charlie felt a jab in his abdomen.

"Get up," Vincent barked. However, the damage had been done.

"I am not Lord Autaine," the short man said flatly. He gave a lazy sigh, shook Charlie off his hand, and proceeded to lead the two vampires into the mansion. "And please refrain from doing that to the real Lord Autaine as well. You are of noble descent, are you not?"

"He is," Vincent said. Then, peering down at Charlie's now reddened face, he added, "He just doesn't get out much. I apologize for him."

"If you say so." The short man sighed again. "Lord Autaine is expecting you on the veranda. The mansion was constructed in . . ."

Whatever it was the short man said after, Charlie didn't hear it, for he was too busy taking in the magnificent, if ostentatious, surroundings. They walked down a long, wide hallway that branched off into dining rooms, kitchens, a stairwell, and various reading rooms. It was like the mansion had started out within the long hallway but had gradually been remodeled and expanded over time. It now included a ballroom and four stories of rooms, many of which had peeling wallpaper and paint that hinted at the layers of colors and themes the lord had entertained in the past.

While Vincent's rooms were all random in style, although each had its own purchase, the décor of Autaine's rooms seemed almost like an afterthought. Each room had the same furnishings—bookshelves, suits of armor, long muted-colored sofas, and desks.

Then came the ballroom.

As Charlie walked into the ballroom, the room suddenly filled with loud dancing and sparkling bubbles. When he blinked his eyes, though, everything was as still and bare as it was a moment before. "What the . . . ?" Charlie muttered. He held his head, which had started to ache, and looked around at the empty room with his mouth agape.

"Don't embarrass me," Vincent hissed.

"I feel like I've been here before," Charlie said.

"Don't be silly. Of course you haven't," Vincent snapped. "Now take your hand off your head."

Charlie nodded and dropped his arms to his sides. His head seemed to throb less after they left the ballroom. He and Vincent continued to follow the short man until he stopped at an open door leading to a patio overlooking the garden. A man played a beautiful piece of music on a violin. There was a tea set ready and waiting beside a large spread of biscuits. To top off the scene, another man in a long purple robe sat with his long legs stretched onto the table, humming along with the violin's tune, a book in his lap. He continued with his reading before suddenly noticing Charlie and Vincent.

"Ah, I'm so glad that the two of you could join me!" the man said. He rested his book on a very intricately designed end table next to his large silver chair. Even more tea and refreshments were brought from a nearby room and set on the table in front of them, along with three plates and three cups already filled with tea. "Sit, sit! I've been eagerly waiting for you two to arrive. I hope my carriage was to your liking."

"It was," Vincent said. He took the seat farthest away from Lord Autaine. Charlie took the seat next to Vincent's.

"Well, let me start by saying welcome," Lord Autaine said, throwing his hands in the air. "This is my veranda. You have the fresh air, the view of the garden maze. It is truly an excellent spot for tea. I even called in a musician for the occasion. Wave, Daniel. He is truly a talent."

"Yes, we heard him as we came out. He plays very well," Charlie said, watching the young man play his haunting melody.

"The young master is a man of taste, I see." Lord Autaine gave an approving nod while taking one of the cups of tea.

"Well, I was taught by the best," Charlie said.

"It seems so." Autaine's eyes narrowed. "Vincent, you have done an excellent job with your son."

"I try," Vincent said.

Charlie could see Vincent was regarding Lord Autaine very carefully, making note of every subtle motion the eccentric lord made.

Lord Autaine didn't seem to take notice of Vincent's glares, and continued. "Now tell me. I hate to skirt around issues, and I am very interested in both of you, especially you, Charlie."

"What is it you wish to know, Lord Autaine?"

"Oh please, call me Allister! Lord Autaine was my father! No need for such formalities," he said, waving a hand. "I would like to know about the man who won Miss Maple's heart."

"I have won nothing, I assure you," Charlie said, giving a nervous smile. He refused to look over at Vincent.

"Oh, on the contrary, my boy!" Lord Autaine said. "I find you and Miss Maple lovely together. It is a shame Walter had to be such a spoilsport, but I do believe he and Elise will give their blessing."

"Blessing?" said Charlie, confused.

"My son is not marrying anyone at the moment," Vincent interrupted. "He's fifteen for God's sake. I don't see where you get that notion."

"My apologies. I have a bad habit of getting ahead of things, but it's never too soon to start thinking about your son's future. That's what I always say," Lord Autaine said, setting down his cup. "I'm merely looking out for your son's best interests. Please, care for a scone? Also, you haven't touched your tea."

"We ate before coming," Vincent said. "I do apologize."

Lord Autaine then gave a momentary pause. For a split second, Charlie caught a knowing glance from the eccentric man—a look that was so telling, Charlie began to have doubts about the man's true nature.

"Well then, I'll be sure to send the leftovers to my son's servants," Lord Autaine said, smiling. "I'm sorry he could not join us. He is often away."

"I know the feeling," Vincent said. He shot Charlie a look.

"Do you now?" Lord Autaine beamed. "I find a little deception and mystery make for better times. I remember in my youth my wife and I used to run all over this little town."

Charlie smiled at the man's remembrance.

"Unfortunately, that time is long behind me." Lord Autaine sighed. "She's passed away, but let's not taint our—well, my tea with such unpleasantries. I also brought the two of you here to extend a personal invitation to my Autumn Ball. Do you think you can attend?"

"We will get back to you on that," Vincent said. He had risen from his seat. "I'm afraid we must go now."

"So soon?" Lord Autaine said, cocking his head. "Well, if you must. I look forward to seeing you two soon, especially you, Charlie. I do hope we can get to know each other a bit more."

The men exchanged final pleasantries, and then the Prowls were gone.

On their silent ride home, Charlie thought about their meeting with Autaine, running the conversation over and over in his mind. It was so odd. Why did Lord Autaine have such an interest in him?

The moment they were back at Chiaroscuro Lane and the bronze double doors had slammed shut behind them, Vincent began rubbing his temples. He grabbed Charlie by the collar and slammed him against the wall.

"So, you've talked to the Maple girl on multiple occasions," Vincent said. "Have you learned nothing?"

"Vincent, let me explain!"

"I'm sorry to interrupt," spoke a soft voice from the unused dining room. "We let ourselves in. I hope that was alright."

"It's not like they gave us much of a choice."

"Right. Oh bother, where do we start?" Vera said. "Come to the dining room! I hope you don't mind we opened one of your bottles, Vincent. It's just very rare that we get to drink blood. It's usually only tea and wine, so blood is quite a treat."

Mira and Vera sat at the table, each with a teacup and saucer in her hands. Their legs dangled from the chairs that were too tall for them, and both gave a nod when Charlie and Vincent entered the room. Then the twins set their cups down and exchanged a look before sighing simultaneously.

"Why are you here?" Vincent asked.

"To give you this," Mira said, getting up from her chair. She walked over to Vincent and thrust a small note into his chest.

"It's who the boy will have to kill." Vera gave her sister an unpleasant look. "We're so sorry."

Then the two of them were gone.

Vincent read over the letter's contents, and Charlie watched the old vampire's face grow pale. He handed him the piece of paper.

On the note was a name:

Allister Autaine

CHAPTER TWELVE

SALLY'S LAMENT

True to her word, Alice checked on Sally after the Mad Hatter's Festival. Or rather, she made Sally believe that her condition had taken a turn for the worse. This resulted in a very frantic Sally rushing to the Autaine mansion. Alice was still in her morning gown when her friend arrived. She let Sally in and locked the door behind her, and that's how it started.

At first, Alice was patient, wanting to let Sally talk about who she was with at the festival in her own time. But this patience lasted only an hour, as she'd underestimated how good her friend would be at casually dodging that particular topic whenever Alice pressed her. So, Alice turned to threats about her health. That seemed to do the trick.

Sally started out all timid and shy about telling Alice anything concerning her and Charlie. However, Alice kept on prodding, probing, and coughing whenever Sally seemed to clam up, and before long she would quickly regret asking at all.

There were even times when Alice would give anything for a second chance to duel Charlie just for the sake of killing him and not having to hear any more about him.

The worst of it was the mood swings. One minute to the next, Sally could go from being blissfully happy to sobbing uncontrollably. She would moan about how her family hated her, how she was so embarrassed by her father, then quickly shift to talking about how handsome Charlie was or how fun the festival had been. It was dizzying to say the least. Alice just did her best to act surprised and suppress her urge to shoo her best friend out of the mansion like she usually did, until at last Sally left.

The next morning, Alice was in the dining room, her deck of cards stacked neatly on the table, and a knife in her hand. The cat had become more insistent on her training, and so she sat there, pricking her fingers with the knife and healing each wound under the cat's instruction. In between attempts, she'd take a bite of her bread and jam and glance up at the time. This went on until eleven o'clock, at which point Alice laid down her knife and nodded to one of the servants, who set another plate at the table. Sure enough, the front doors soon swung open and in barged the pride and joy of Maple Town.

"Alice! Alice!" Sally said. "What am I going do? What am I going to do?"

"For one," Alice said, "take a breath and perhaps a seat. We've got jam, bread, oh and even a few apple tarts you left behind yesterday. I hope you didn't want them back. We've been snacking on them. You know how Papa gets during ball-planning season."

"Of course, they're yours," Sally said, and frantically fell into the chair that the servant had so graciously pulled for her. She took a deep breath and then a napkin to wipe the bits of sweat from her brow. Alice raised an eyebrow at her, while Sally gave the butler a weak smile. She turned toward Alice.

"You look like you're doing better," she said cheerfully. "Whatever Dr. Prowl is giving you must be doing wonders. I should send him my thanks next time I see him. Even if he is a bit odd. He's not coming back today, is he?"

"Ah, he's long gone. He always shows up at a quarter to nine. You know that. Don't worry about him." Then as an afterthought Alice added, "And no need to thank him either." She couldn't imagine Vincent accepting anything, let alone thanks. "You look like you ran all the way over here. Have you even slept? What's going on?"

Sally played with the hem of her signature red-and-white dress and looked up meekly at Sally. "It's about Charlie," she said softly.

"Okay, before we start, let's just get this out of the way." Alice dropped her utensils and waved her hands. "I know how much you like him. I know your parents don't approve of it, but that doesn't deny the fact you like him." Waving a finger, she said, "I mean, so what if your parents don't approve? Chase what your heart wants! Isn't that what they always say?" Alice smiled and shook her fist in support. "There. Don't you feel better already?" She then returned to her cards and took another sip of her juice, hoping the subject of Charlie was behind them.

"Alice! This is different! I'm engaged!" Sally collapsed on the table.

Alice dropped her cards and nearly choked on her juice.

"Sally, you only just met him! It hasn't even been a year! How can this—"

"No, it's not Charlie! My parents have picked a suitor for me. I don't even know who it is. They say I can't be trusted to choose my own husband. What am I going to do?"

"Tell them no, of course!" Alice said.

"But they said if I don't get married to this man—" Sally stopped and looked intently at Alice as if her next words were a secret that had to be handled with the utmost care. "They said when Grandma killed herself, her will left nothing to my parents. Nothing."

"That's terrible," Alice said. "Why would she do that?"

Sally shook her head. She looked as if she were on the verge of tears. "She and my mother had issues with each other. Apparently, Daddy was working on warming Grandma to the idea of amending the will, but she never did, obviously."

"I don't understand," Alice said. "What does this have to do with you?"

"She left everything to me, Alice!" Sally said. "In her will, Grandma swore she wouldn't give even a single sapling to 'that she-witch who snaked her way into the family' and 'seduced' her son, so until I marry, none of the money can be claimed by anyone in the family. She had it set that I would inherit it all only after I marry. I can only assume she expected to stay in charge until I walked down the aisle, but . . . but . . . Oh, Alice, what am I going to do? We can't afford to keep the orchard unless I get married."

Alice stood up and went over to pat her friend's shoulder. She said, "There, there" and "It's going to be okay" a few times, but that was all she could do. It was only when Sally started sobbing that Alice took her friend to her room for some privacy.

"Here, take a seat," Alice said. "Start from the beginning. How did this all happen?"

"I don't know," Sally said. "I just don't know what to do. I just don't know, Alice."

"Well, isn't this what you always wanted?" Alice said softly. "You're finally going to get that wedding you always dreamed of."

"That's not funny, Alice!" Sally shouted. For once in her life, she glared at Alice with purpose and something else that Alice herself couldn't quite pinpoint. Then she stood with her long golden locks a mess, shook her head, and walked toward the window.

"Did I ever want this?" Sally said. "Alice, I'm asking as a friend. Did I really want to get married? I don't think I ever did. That's the scariest part, don't you see? I've been racking my head since Mother and Father sat me down, and I don't think I want to be married."

"Well, it is a big commitment," Alice said. "I don't blame you for feeling overwhelmed. Though I'm sure the man they matched you with isn't terrible, I think breaking the news to Charlie is going to be interesting to say the least."

Sally rushed over and shook her friend. "You don't get it, Alice! Nothing is ever right!"

"Sally—" Alice began, but Sally yelled at her before she could get the words out.

"No, listen! This isn't fun anymore!" Sally said. "I was lying in bed last night after they told me, and I got to thinking about everything. Everything, Alice! It was like my whole life flashed before my eyes, and do you know what I realized?"

Alice winced at her friend. She refused to look her in the eye, for she hoped with all her heart that Sally didn't realize the very thing that she'd always known about her best friend.

"How would you like it if you went through life only to realize that you've been groomed to be nothing more than a doll that can't do anything except laugh and make tarts?"

"Sally, you're much more than that," Alice said. "Everyone loves you."

"I'm not an idiot, Alice," Sally shouted. "Don't treat me like one! Men fall for me. They all bend over backward for me. For what? I don't even do anything! They even adore me when I reject them. That's sick! They don't love me; they see me as some sort of prize. And I'm just meant to wait for the guy that snatches me up."

Alice stared, taken aback. She had no words. Sally had just burst the bubble of her life—the bubble that made everything seem good, while quickly brushing aside the bad. Alice had always envied Sally for that bubble she lived in, but now she realized how wrong she'd been.

"I know what they call me. 'The queen of broken hearts.' I don't mean it. Don't you see? I'm not that heartless. I just . . . don't feel the way they do. I grow bored. Why? Why?" Sally said. She released Alice and held her head in her hands. "Even Charlie. I'm getting bored of him too. It's just not fun anymore. None of it is. It's too . . ." Sally stopped and shook her head, at a loss. "It's just not right, Alice. I know he likes me a lot, but I haven't seen him at all since the festival. I could've easily tried to convince Mother and Daddy to accept him as my fiancé instead of whoever they picked, but I haven't. I feel myself losing interest in him. I know it's terrible, but I am. Why does this always happen? Why does nothing ever seem just right? EVER? The relationship is too plain, too exciting, too fast, too something! I hate that I get bored of them. I'm terrible. I can never be happy with any of it! Why, Alice? Why?"

"Sally, you're not terrible." Alice opened her arms to Sally, who sank deep into her embrace, sobbing against her shoulder. "They just weren't right. There's nothing wrong with that. Charlie will understand. Don't beat yourself up about it, okay?"

"Alice," Sally said. "Can you do me a favor?"

"Sure, anything," Alice replied.

"Close your eyes. I just . . . I just . . . ," Sally said.

Alice closed her eyes. She stood, blind and feeling very silly for complying with her best friend's odd request.

Then Alice felt something against her lips. Her eyes shot open, and her arms raised in alarm. Sally's lips rested against her own. Alice gasped as she pulled away.

She blinked, feeling her lips.

"Sally . . . ," she began, but Sally had already turned away.

"I don't know why I wanted to do that. I'm sorry! I'm sorry! I must be sick!" Sally said, blushing slightly. It was the first time Alice had ever seen Sally blush at anything.

"Sally," Alice said again.

"No! I don't want to hear it!" Sally held her hands to her ears, but Alice shook her until she'd listen.

"Sally," Alice said.

"No!"

"Sally, please!"

Sally stopped struggling and looked timidly at her best friend. "No," she said softly.

The two locked eyes in quiet acknowledgment. Sally had grown so used to rejecting the men that'd fallen for her charm that she knew exactly what was coming next. However, this marked the first time she would be at the receiving end.

"Sally," Alice said. She fumbled with her words a bit. She desperately wanted to tell her friend that she'd felt some sort of spark. She willed herself with all her heart to feel something more than shock, but in the end, she looked into the eyes that had captivated so many men. For the first time, Sally's deep-brown eyes looked lost. "Perhaps this is why Charlie and every man isn't right." Alice began to tear up. "You know I care about you so much."

"I don't want to hear it!" Sally exclaimed.

They exchanged a knowing look that ended with Sally holding a hand over her own heart, as though it felt heavy in her chest. She wiped a tear from her eye and, keeping to how life had trained her, smiled at her dear friend.

"Sally, please."

"No. I already know," Sally said. "Just forget it. I don't know what came over me. I think I should get some rest."

"But, Sally!"

Sally sprinted out of Alice's room, knocking over her deck of cards in her rush. Alice watched her friend run off. She pressed a finger to her lips before kneeling down to pick up the cards that had fallen. She was shaking. Alice could have easily used magic, but at that moment, she just couldn't.

"Is she finally gone?" groaned a voice from the hallway.

"Atticus!" Alice shouted. Her face turned beet red as she hurried to pick up all the cards. When she'd finished, she rushed to follow him into the living room, hoping with all her heart that her brother hadn't heard—or God forbid, seen—what had just transpired.

He lay sprawled on the couch. He looked well enough. Alice had been sure he was long gone from Maple Town. Because in truth, she hadn't seen him in years. She silently cursed to herself that he'd chosen now of all times to come home.

"You're home? Why are you back? I thought you hated this place as much as I do. You even swore to Papa that you never wanted to come back. You two hate each other. Why is it that you're back?"

"I'm glad you missed me too. I do hate it here. And yeah, I'm sorry I left you alone with him. But I'm not back by choice. Our dear father just sent me this letter." He waved a sheet of paper

over his head, eventually dropping it over his face. He laid an arm on his forehead as he talked. "I hate him so much. God, who knew the queen of broken hearts was so complicated," he whispered. But before Alice could say anything, he continued. "So, is he home?"

"No, he's away meeting with some twins to plan for this year's ball. He said he'll be back later," Alice said quickly. She was about to leave when she turned meekly to her brother. "And, Atticus—"

"No one is going to know," he said, sitting up. He ran a hand over his face, and the letter fell to the ground. "But this just makes things more complicated. I don't want to be here longer than I need to. Do you know when Father will be back?"

"I don't know," Alice said uneasily.

"I need to know, Alice," her brother pressed. "Argh, this would be so much easier if she just loved him!"

"What are you talking about?"

"Nothing, nothing," he said. "Leave me alone, will you?"

"What's the matter with you?"

"I just need to be alone. Call me when he's back. Might as well see what the old man did to my room."

Atticus Autaine shoved past her. Alice could only stare curiously at her brother as he disappeared up the stairs. Then she shook her head, picked up the letter he'd dropped, and read the words, aghast.

CHAPTER THIRTEEN

CONTRACT OF THE DAMNED

Charlie had half expected Vincent to build a dungeon to lock him in. However, the contrary happened; almost overnight, every window and every door in the mansion had unlocked. Charlie woke the next morning to a note with the words Do what you want.

But even that was not exactly true. He couldn't do what he wanted because what he wanted was to not kill Lord Autaine. And as well as stating who Charlie would have to kill, Mira and Vera's note gave the deadline of the murder: the Autumn Ball.

Charlie lay on his bed staring at the single name on the small white sheet of paper.

A few days after the twins' visit came the invitation to the ball. Charlie toyed with the beveled gold font and smooth black border, then looked back at the note that Mira and Vera had left him. Not knowing what to do with it, Charlie had pinned it to the wall opposite his bed with a ruby-encrusted knife, as if hoping the next morning he'd wake up and not see it there. But day after day, it hung there, a reminder that this wasn't all a bad dream he'd eventually wake up from.

Every night, his eyes would dart from one sheet of paper to the next.

Even Aria was at a loss as to what to do, though she at least rested by Charlie's side. Vincent had locked himself in his room. Occasionally, he'd come out to give Charlie a bottle of blood, but otherwise, Charlie saw very little of him. Not that it mattered.

Charlie was just readying himself to slump back into bed when he felt a tapping on his forehead. He opened his eyes to see Aria pecking away. He brushed her off, but she returned and kept pecking him with her paper beak until he sat upright, ready to wring the paper bird.

"Go away," he muttered.

Aria kept pecking.

"I said go away!"

Charlie rose from the bed and glared down at a shaking Aria, now huddled in the blankets. Charlie's face softened. He took a deep breath before reaching down and taking Aria onto his finger.

"I'm sorry," Charlie said. "Let's go for a walk. You're right. I need to get away."

He crumpled up the invitation and marched out of his room. Aria followed.

Charlie wandered around the mansion until he reached the crystal room. He looked at the wide window that he'd once admired and stared down at the sleeping town. Aria soon joined him and landed on his shoulder.

"It's so pretty," Charlie said. "I hate this, Aria.

Aria slumped her head and leaned against his cheek affectionately, then she hopped up and down Charlie's arm. He carried her to the crystal end table, where he sat and picked up the dried-up rose on the table.

"This used to be Elizabeth's room," Charlie said.

Aria flew around the rose in Charlie's hand and looked up at him.

"He told me she used to practice magic here every chance she could. It's kind of weird to think that Vincent once loved someone as much as he loved Elizabeth."

Suddenly, thoughts of the baker and his wife, the sorrowful fabric woman, the laborers, Skat, and Sally flooded his mind. He dropped the flower on the floor. Aria tiptoed down Charlie's arm and up his fingers.

"I don't want everyone to die because I can't do this." He held his paper friend at arm's length. "But I'm no murderer, Aria."

Little to the young vampire's knowledge, Vincent had returned from hunting that night carrying two bottles filled with blood from a couple towns over, and now stood outside the crystal room. He looked down at the bottles he held and stared at his son resting his head on the table, still looking out at the town.

"He was so nice, Aria," Charlie said. "What am I going to do? What am I going to do?"

The young vampire began to sob. Aria looked up at Charlie. Her wings wiped away his tears when she could catch them. Vincent continued to stand at the threshold of the room. He was about to walk in to comfort the boy but retracted his foot upon realizing he had no words for him.

At least, this is what the vampire thought stopped him from comforting his son. However, what paralyzed him so from giving Charlie even an ounce of comfort and reassurance had nothing to do with knowing what to say at all. Like many fathers before and after him, Vincent didn't realize that all Charlie wanted was exactly what Aria could give. No words were needed, just Vincent's presence in that room. All Vincent had to do was be there for his son, and that would have been enough.

Vincent simply stood there until another idea occurred to him. He left the bottles outside the crystal room, grabbed his evening cloak, and hurried out of the mansion. He marched down the crooked hilltop and out the tall black gate. He moved quickly, taking long strides through the streets until he reached the outskirts of Maple Town.

He found a secluded patch of grass and began marking it up with a stick like a madman. Soon the ground was covered with symbols, each looking stranger than the last, until a large, intricate pattern lay beneath Vincent. He then bit into his thumb, releasing a single drop of blood onto his design.

Nothing happened at first, but slowly the drop of blood spread and oozed into every nook and cranny of the drawing. It began glowing a bright purple, and two blonde-haired girls wearing matching blue dresses emerged from the ground.

"Oh, Vincent, I wish you hadn't done this," Vera said. Her expression had no cheer to it. She looked at Mira, who held a hand over her face.

"We had always assumed," Mira said, "but we never wanted to know, so this better have been worth it. You know what's at stake for showing us what that witch gave you—vampires shouldn't have magic."

"I want to make a counteroffer," Vincent said. His breath sputtered out like smoke into the brisk night. "I'm willing to trade my magic for the boy's freedom. My magic will stand in for the murder of Lord Autaine."

Mira and Vera exchanged a look before shaking their heads.

"We can't do that." Mira sighed. "It doesn't work that way. When a deal is struck, it affects not only the person who made the deal but other people who've made deals with us too."

"What do you mean?"

"To put it bluntly," Vera said cautiously, "this was all a waste. Lord Autaine was also a client of ours. We gave him what he wanted, and in truth, his price was just his sight. But then he escalated the deal, and now his life is the price. Without his death, his payment is not made. You see how this works? Once the deal is made, it's out of our hands. It becomes part of an interconnected web of deals. Lord Autaine must die by Charlie's hands."

"But there has to be some way!" Vincent said frantically. "He's my son!"

The words echoed through the forest, causing a few birds to awaken and fly overhead. Mira and Vera conversed quietly, occasionally looking over at Vincent.

"We may not have shown it, but we don't hate you, Vincent," Mira said when their private conversation was finished. "At least, Vera doesn't."

"Regardless," Vera stressed, "the point is we find you fascinating. You're too good to the people you love, even if they can't see it, which is strange considering you don't have a heart."

"Though if you're acting like this now, I can only imagine what you'll do when Charlie has to kill again," Mira added.

"What do you mean?"

"Come on, Vincent!" Mira said. "Did you really think this was a one-time deal? Charlie will kill every time we ask him to. That was the bargain. We own him."

"What?"

"He's shocked, Vera," Mira said.

"You little! How could you do this? I thought you sympathized with him!" Vincent said.

"We do. How could you have turned him into a vampire without his own knowledge?" Vera said. "He didn't even have a choice. You should've just let him die."

"It was the only way to save him," Vincent said. "Please, what do I have to do? Fine, so he kills Autaine, but he can't do it again and again. That'd break him. Please."

"We may not be able to change the fact that Lord Autaine will die by Charlie's hand, but perhaps we can make it so he's the only one Charlie will have to kill," Vera said.

"If it's another damn deal—" Vincent said.

"Just listen," Mira cut him off.

"We can offer you a new start," Vera said. "Once Lord Autaine is dead, obviously you two can't live in Maple Town anymore, so we're offering you the ability to start a new life somewhere else."

"That's not a solution!" Vincent growled. "How does that help with anything? You'll make him kill again."

"Not if a new contract supersedes the previous one." Vera smiled. "You see how this works? Lord Autaine is a lost cause, yes. That deal is still in motion, but that's it. Any other death we need afterward can't be contracted by Charlie if his new deal states we can't make him kill anyone. Because at that point, the two contracts cancel each other out, right, Mira?"

"Exactly."

"You would do that?" Vincent eyed them.

"There's a catch," Mira said.

"You see," Vera said, "when we make a deal, we have to do this sort of balancing act. The price has to be equal to the size of the request."

"And what you're getting is pretty unimaginable," Mira cut in. "You exposed your magic to us, which goes very much against the natural order, and taking this deal will not only save Charlie but also free you from what would happen if we ever had to tell people that the witch Elizabeth shared her magic."

"This seems too good to be true," Vincent said. "What's the catch?"

The twins exchanged another look before looking back at Vincent's sad eyes.

"The catch," Vera said, "is that Maple Town disappears. That was another deal we made with someone, so it is bound to happen. However, if it were done by your hands, we could make this new deal to free you and your son from us."

"So, our lives for all the people in Maple Town—is that what you're saying?"

"Yes." The twins nodded.

Vincent ran a hand over his face and began pacing back and forth. He did this for some time before finally taking one look at the town behind him. He approached Mira and Vera again, who had started to analyze the little symbols that had summoned them.

"How are we going to do this?" Vincent said. "We have nothing to sign."

"With blood," Mira said curtly.

Vincent had reached to bite his fingertip when Vera stopped him.

"No, your wrist," she said. "For a deal like this, we need to take your blood."

"Why is that?" Vincent said, undoing his cufflinks.

"The consequences of a request this big need to be equal," Mira said. "Consider this collateral."

"What that means is that if you don't follow through in destroying the town, you pay the price of all those people's suffering on your own." Vera eyed Vincent. It was the most serious he'd ever seen the usually cheery girl. "You understand what that means? Do you still want to make this deal?"

"Yes," Vincent said. He offered up his wrist to the twins, who took one bite and pulled back, grimacing at the bitter taste of Vincent's blood.

"Well, that was unpleasant." Vera laughed. "But the deal is made."

"Can we go back now?" Mira said, nodding toward the symbols on the ground.

"Of course." Vincent nodded. He squeezed another drop of blood from his punctured wrist, and the ground began to glow purple again. "Thank you."

"You shouldn't thank us, Vincent," Vera said as they disappeared into the ground.

Vincent clutched his wrist and began his trek back to the mansion. He was not moving as briskly as he once had. He walked with a slow purpose, soaking up all that the little town had to offer. He looked upon all the things that he'd once enjoyed, knowing eventually he'd be the one to take it all away.

Now, something to know about Vincent is that despite hating the town as much as he did, he didn't find it easy to agree to that deal. The revenge that he'd always wanted for Elizabeth stood within reach, yet that night, he walked through the quiet town conflicted.

When he made it back to the dark mansion, Charlie didn't come down to greet him. Nor did Aria bounce around, tugging at his collar.

Vincent searched the mansion until he found his son collapsed at the crystal table in Elizabeth's room. The vampire stood over Charlie, whose eyes were puffy from crying himself to sleep. Aria rested beside him.

Again, Vincent stood paralyzed. He wanted to give the boy a reassuring hug or tell him that everything would be okay now, but he couldn't bring himself to do even that. He could only stand there, the light of the moon shining on his guilt-stricken face, and think of how he had caused all this pain.

Charlie was his responsibility from the start. So many people dead—Elizabeth, Charlie's mother and father, all gone. He ran a hand over his face and leaned against the wall. He'd killed them all. He still remembered seeing Charlie's mother. In truth, it was an accident that the boy had fallen into his care. It was an accident that his mother and her husband stumbled upon a cottage in the forest where there was rumored to be a witch that could cure any disease. It was by chance that the witch they were looking for had long since died. It was his fault that upon seeing them using the cottage, he'd lost his temper.

Vincent closed his eyes, unable to look at the boy anymore. He crouched down and buried his head in his arms. "Lieka, I'm sorry," he said. "I'm sorry. I'm trying my best to raise your son. I'm so sorry."

He'd sunk so far.

He stood and walked into the dark hallway, feeling guilty for the life the boy had been given, angry at the choices he had to make, and scared for the sweet hell that awaited him after making his most recent deal. The tall black-haired vampire rounded the corner and marched onward to his private quarters.

Once inside his room, Vincent reached into his drawers for parchment, ink, and a quill. He then sat at his desk, dipped the nib of the quill in the ink, and began writing furiously. He kept scribbling until he'd finished. He then held his fingers to his mouth and whistled. Aria soon swooped into the room and fluttered around Vincent.

"I've cast an enchantment onto this note," he said, tying the rolled-up message to her foot. "If you follow where it takes you, you'll be alright. But remember to hurry. He needs to get this tonight."

The paper bird flew out the window and on to the sleeping village. Vincent watched as she became smaller and smaller in the distance, until she was no bigger than the stars in the sky.

Maple Town's train station rested on the south edge of town, directly opposite number thirteen Chiaroscuro Lane, which sat at the far north. Not many people ever left or visited Maple Town, so the train came just twice a day—once at noon and once at midnight. Vincent checked his silver pocket watch and marched toward the station now, for there was one more meeting he had to attend that night.

He reached the station when the moon was at its highest. He sat on a wooden bench by the train tracks and again checked his silver pocket watch, then he waited, feeling the brisk air nip at his exposed face. He glanced around the empty platform and saw in the distance the gingerbread-like homes of the town. For a moment, he saw flashes of himself and a young woman running together down an alleyway.

He smiled before shaking his head.

"She loved this town," he said, closing his watch.

A red train rolled in with a loud roar. It whistled and hissed as its iron pistons and wheels came to a quick halt. Large clouds of steam blew away all the fallen leaves that had found their way onto the station platform. The compartment doors began opening one by one, from the very back to the front, each with a loud whoosh.

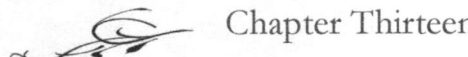 

Only one man came out of the train. He gave a nod and made his way toward Vincent. He was a very hairy man in a faded brown trench coat, and he was accompanied by a little paper swallow. Aria fluttered around him, but always at a distance.

Even from where Vincent sat, he could smell the alcohol the man reeked of. The visitor looked as if he hadn't slept for days, as there were heavy bags under his eyes. He had long, wild brown hair that branched out in every direction like greasy octopus legs, and an equally scruffy beard dotted with little pieces of food and who knew what else. As he approached, he ruffled his hair in some sad attempt to look somewhat presentable, then put his hands over his ears as the train gave another loud whistle.

"I must say I was surprised when I got your note from this little birdie here," the hairy man said once he reached Vincent.

"I wouldn't call unless it was urgent."

"Urgent, huh." The hairy man nodded his head. He pulled a crumpled piece of paper out of his pocket. The paper had large blotches from some dark liquid it had been exposed to. "Is this true?"

"Yes," Vincent said. He continued to look out at the town. "You will be paid as promised, if that's what you're worried about."

"Keep your money. It's no good to me. I know what I am, but I still have my honor. I'm repaying a debt to Elizabeth." The hairy man sighed. "It's a quaint town. It's a real shame."

His eyes narrowed on the intricate fountain, the sounds of which echoed to where the two dark figures stood. A few stray cats walked near the fountain, one of which leaned close to the water and dipped its paw in and out of the stream. The hairy man actually smiled a bit at a cottage where a light flickered on and a woman, barely conscious, walked onto her balcony to dump the contents of her chamber pot.

"You sure about this?"

"Does it matter?" Vincent said.

"I guess not," the hairy man said. "Though what you're asking is not exactly kidnapping an old man for you to interrogate and kill."

"No, but it's the only way for my son and I to be free."

"Fair enough," the hairy man said. He joined Vincent by the railing, reached in his large trench coat for a cigar, lit it, and took a long drag from it. Vincent doubted a cigar would dull either of their nerves, given what he was asking, but still cracked a grin at how human the act was.

"So we have a deal, then?" the hairy man said.

Immediately, Vincent returned to his scowl and nodded. The two stared at each other in silence. The hairy man rolled the cigar in his mouth, took another long draw, and blew out a great puff of smoke. He crossed his arms and stared at the vampire, who looked out at the town.

"I hope this kid knows you're doing all this for him." The hairy man laughed. "It's settled. The town will be ashes."

The two men stared silently into the night, unaware they were being watched from the shadows of the train station. The figure in the darkness had heard everything, had seen everything with its large amethyst eyes. It turned and left, but not without letting a large white smile spread across its face.

CHAPTER FOURTEEN

SHEEP'S CLOTHING

Charlie stared at his reflection in the wooden bucket as he crouched by the stream—Sam had sent him out to get water for the hut. He looked human. He turned his head, opening his mouth wide. Charlie remembered Skat had once told him how vampires drank blood through their fangs. He fingered every tooth, not feeling anything remotely close to a fang. He continued to look at his teeth in the water, trying to find anything about them that made him different from Skat, Sally, Sam, or anyone else he'd met in Maple Town. Finding nothing, he dropped his hands to his sides and grabbed the bucket.

"Charlie! I need that water!" called a voice from the hut.

"Coming!"

Charlie quickly rose and hurried awkwardly with the wooden bucket of water. There was no difference, he realized. He couldn't find anything that made him different from them. Then almost immediately, a group of children from the schoolhouse passed by and his throat became dry. He swallowed before continuing forward.

That was the difference.

"What took you so long?" Sam called from the furnace. He had a thick apron on and goggles that went over both eyes despite still wearing his black bandana over the right one. He held a flaming piece of metal with his tongs. It wasn't a big piece, just a thin strip of metal that supposedly would eventually be a dagger. It glowed an infernal orange until Sam plunged it into the bucket of water Charlie placed before him.

The cooling metal sent up an eruption of steam. Sam pulled it from the bucket and moved it to the anvil before giving Charlie a thumbs up, resting his tongs, and removing his goggles.

"Cut it close there," Sam said. He then cocked his head. "But I'm grateful for the help. Especially as it's my apprentice who should be here."

Charlie glanced over at the entrance to the blacksmith's hut. It was just the two of them. No Skat. No Sally.

When Charlie was given his newfound freedom to leave the mansion whenever he pleased, he thought seeing everyone at the blacksmith's hut would calm his nerves, or at least get his mind off everything.

However, somehow the mood had changed.

Sally had stopped visiting the hut. In fact, Charlie hadn't seen her since the festival. Skat would make an appearance every once in a while, but when he did, he arrived late in the morning and always seemed a bit distracted. He'd make a few wise cracks when he got in, but then would fall into a silent routine while Charlie helped him with his work. It was only when Charlie asked if his friend was alright that Skat would crack a joke or two, but every time, he'd inevitably return to his disjointed state. He went through the motions of crafting the blood blade, but he never seemed truly present. Sam even had to scold him a few times for almost burning down the whole hut.

So most of the time it was just Sam and Charlie.

"I'm sure Skat will be here soon," Charlie said. "He always is."

"But that's not why I made him my apprentice," Sam grumbled. "All I'm saying is be on time for a few days of the week. That's all! Honestly, what the hell is going on in his head these days? Blood blades are technical. He knows this. I swear, if it wasn't for you, he'd have ruined the process by now—and owe me a fortune to replace this place after he'd destroyed it in a fire. Here, pass me some polish. Did you hear me? Come on, don't tell me I'm losing you too. I can't be making everything myself."

Sam gave a throaty laugh, but Charlie remained silent. Sam had turned toward Charlie, who stared back, frozen, when he saw that Sam didn't have his bandana on for once. In his haste to take off the goggles, Sam had also pulled off the makeshift eye patch he always wore. Now Charlie could see that where Sam's right eye should have been was a thick sheet of steel.

Upon realizing how exposed he was, Sam quickly retied his signature black cloth over his face and smiled as if nothing had happened.

"You weren't supposed to see that," he said quickly. "Don't worry. It's been like that for a while."

"But your eye," Charlie said. His mind was still fixed on the empty socket covered over with metal. "What happened to it? Why cover it up? Are you okay?"

Sam's smile faded, and he slammed his hands against the work table. "Swear you'll never tell anyone about this," he said sternly. "Swear to me! You saw nothing, got it?"

Charlie nodded. He took a few steps back from the finger pointed straight at his throat. Then, almost as if coming back to reality, Sam ran a hand through his hair and shook his head.

"Sorry," he said. "I guess you can say I'm a bit sensitive about it.

Let me make it up to you. Anyway, you okay? You seem awfully quiet. I figured you had your reasons for not visiting, but you look like someone's died."

"I'm fine," Charlie said.

"Sure you are," Sam said. "Here, grab the blood blade. I'll help you out until Skat gets here. Least I can do."

Charlie scurried to the metal rack where he and Skat kept the blade. It rested in a leather scabbard that Sam had made for them. Charlie picked it up and gave Sam the blade, not daring to say a word.

The blacksmith unsheathed the blood blade and held it at arm's length, nodding and clicking his tongue as he examined it. Finally, he laid the blade on the workbench with a sigh.

"It's not bad for a first try," he said under his breath. "Here, look at your handiwork." Sam beckoned him closer, and casually reached into his pocket for a cigar and lit it.

Charlie cringed at the sight of the red blade. He felt a certain confusion that comes with seeing something so beautiful yet capable of killing you.

"Skat did a good job," he said.

"That's it? It wasn't just him. You contributed a good chunk in creating this," Sam said. "Jeez, someone really knocked the wind out of your sails." The blacksmith exhaled smoke and scuffed the bud of the cigar on his workbench before throwing it into the furnace. "You know, you should've told me you were Vincent's son."

"You'd be ashamed too if your father was a cold—"

"Hey now. We will have none of that," Sam said. "He's not all bad. He's very misunderstood, but then again, I guess the same goes for a lot of people. My point is, whatever mess you've gotten into, cheer up."

Sam hung his head and stretched his back. "You don't have to be afraid of me, Charlie."

"What? I'm not—" Charlie began.

"I can tell you are. Listen, I just got a little heated. That's all. I didn't mean to take it out on you." He nodded toward the blood blade. "Did you know that these things can kill more than just vampires? Hand me that green vial in the cupboard, will you?"

"What do you mean?" Charlie asked. He grabbed the vial and passed it to the blacksmith, who pulled at the cork cap with his teeth.

"I mean that these things can kill anything without a heart. It just so happens vampires are included."

"What do you mean they don't have hearts?"

"Most things like them don't have them. Didn't you know that?" Sam said. He dabbed a rage into the green liquid and began rubbing the blade with it.

"Does not having a heart make you bad?" Charlie said eagerly. He held a hand over his left arm, not wanting to be reminded of what he was at the one place he felt safe.

"Of course not," Sam said. "I hope not." He gave a nervous laugh. "Take werewolves for example. They don't have hearts either."

"There's werewolves?"

"There are." Sam nodded.

"So why don't they have hearts?"

Sam smiled. "You ever hear the saying 'a wolf in sheep's clothing'?"

"No."

"Well, it's a saying about how if you wear a disguise, you can get in trouble. But to werewolves it's more than that. You see, werewolves can go from human to wolf at a whim. Though, their

powers are magnified during a full moon." Sam looked down at Charlie and snapped his fingers. "You ever wonder why? Not the moon part, but why they can change their appearance? They say it's because the first werewolf was just a human who wanted to be strong enough to protect his family, so he made a deal with a demon to become stronger. However, the stronger the human got, the more animallike he became, until eventually he turned into a wolf. He'd all but forgotten about his human self until he finally realized that the family he'd sworn to protect had run away from him after he'd saved them. Eventually, he begged the demon to turn him back into a human, but all the demon could do was make him appear human for limited amounts of time. He'd still be hollow on the inside. He'd still be nothing more than an animal that knows only how to fight and kill. In that way, werewolves became half-human, so people wouldn't be scared of them all the time. Ain't that something?"

"So a wolf in sheep's clothing is really—"

"A beast who tries to look harmless even though he's a monster," Sam said solemnly. "It's only natural to hide the things about yourself that you don't like—no one wants to be feared, you know?"

"I can understand that," Charlie said quietly. He stared at his reflection in the blood blade.

"Me too," Sam added. "So please don't be afraid because of my eye. I'm not a whole man, but I'm still the same old grump."

"Yeah, you are the same," Charlie said, more to himself. "It doesn't matter what you are."

Sam nodded, then turned his head to the door. Charlie's eyes followed to see Skat entering the hut looking quite tired. He walked over to the water barrel and splashed his face before nodding back at Charlie and Sam.

"How's it looking?"

"Not bad," Sam said. "A little rough, but that can't be helped. If it keeps progressing like this, you might just become a blacksmith yet."

"Don't act so surprised," Skat spat.

"Get your head back here and only here, and then we'll talk," Sam countered.

Skat didn't respond. He only sighed and looked at the blade before turning to Charlie. "Hey, got a moment?" Skat nodded toward the outside of the hut.

Charlie followed him out to the bridge that overlooked the quarry and the hole filled with their pebbles. Charlie watched Skat ready his hand to throw another rock into the hole, if only out of habit, then stop mid-throw and pocket it instead.

"You seen Sally at all?" Skat asked.

"Why do you care?" Charlie said, perhaps a little more defensively than he'd have liked. His relationship with Sally was something he didn't want to think about.

"Look, it's weird enough for me to wonder," Skat said. "I'm just curious."

"Are you alright?" Charlie said.

"Are you?" Skat countered. "Don't think I haven't noticed how out of it you've been. Mind explaining that?"

Charlie opened his mouth. For a moment, all he wanted to do was tell Skat everything. How he was a vampire. How he had to kill an innocent man. How he was struggling with the dilemma every night to the point he cried himself to sleep. But in the end all that came out was "It's nothing. You're imagining it."

"Then it's nothing for me too," Skat replied. "It'll take it you haven't seen her, then. Though maybe that's for the best."

"Who? Sally?" Charlie said. "The second I figure out how to get her parents from locking her up, I'll—"

"You'll what?" Skat turned toward Charlie. "They're not locking her up."

"How do you know that?"

"I just do!" Skat said. Then he looked to the side. He seemed to choose his next words carefully. "Maybe she doesn't want to see you anymore. You ever think that's why she's been avoiding the hut recently?"

"Skat, that's not funny," Charlie said. "You were all for the two of us before. What's wrong with you?"

"Nothing's wrong!" Skat shouted. Then almost as an afterthought he added, "God, this would be so much easier if she actually loved you."

"She does love me," Charlie said. "She told me."

"Maybe you heard her wrong!"

"When did you become so interested in her?" Charlie said.

"I'm not," Skat said. "I'm just . . . Look, just forget I mentioned it."

"The hell I can!" Charlie said. This time he shoved Skat. "What's really going on with you? Seriously, tell me."

"Look, you love her so much, go see her already. I hate this passive stuff. You waiting like a sick puppy to hear what we already know. She's not into you, man!"

"It's her parents. I know it!"

"Sure it is, Charlie."

Charlie squinted at Skat, almost not even recognizing him. He shook his head and ran. Skat had to be wrong. He had to be. Charlie rushed down the dirt path that he'd taken so many times before. He rounded the same corner at the outskirts of town leading to the wooden sign and the clearing in the orchard.

There she was, sitting in her favorite spot. Charlie sighed at the sight of her. She wore her signature red ribbon in her hair and

a red cardigan over a white dress. Her eyes looked puffy from crying. She was leaning against the stone well in the same grove of trees where they swore they'd go to the festival together. Her fingers circled the rocks on the mouth of the well. When she noticed Charlie, she gave him a weak smile.

"Charlie," she said quietly.

"Sally, what have they done to you?" Charlie said. He rushed over to Sally's side. "Are your parents really that mad about us?"

"Us," Sally repeated. For a second, it was like she was stunned, but she regained her composure and rose to her feet. She even smiled at Charlie.

"Don't worry about them," Sally said, shaking her head. "I'm not being abused, if that's what you're wondering."

"Then why haven't you been to the blacksmith's hut? We miss you over there." Charlie paused. "I miss you. I thought you were in trouble."

"I'm not, Charlie," Sally said. "I just wanted some time to be alone. That's all." She looked back at the Maple estate. She smiled brightly and began shepherding him out of the clearing. "Well, you can go now. If you rushed all this way to check on me, I'm fine. Want to take a couple apples with you? It's been a great season."

She began to turn away when Charlie grabbed her hand. It lay in his like a dead fish until she looked up at him with a pleading look.

"Sally, can you tell me what's wrong?"

"Do you love me?"

"Of course I do. You mean more than anything to me."

"You can't be serious," she said, pulling her hand out of his grasp. "Don't say it if you don't mean it." She looked up at him with her deep-brown eyes until they sucked Charlie in as they had every time before.

"I do," he said.

"Why do you love me?"

"What do you mean?"

"It's just a question, Charlie," Sally said with a shrug. "I'm just curious. If someone were to ask you why you loved me, what would you say?"

Charlie took in and let out a deep breath. "There are too many reasons to count. You're just so amazing and wonderful. It's all the reasons and more. You know what I mean," he said.

Sally smiled and sighed. She gripped both of Charlie's hands in hers, then she just stood there, hanging her head. She remained there for a moment before finally looking up at Charlie.

"Charlie," she said slowly, "you need to know something."

"Let's run away together," he blurted out. His words surprised even him. Something in her deep-brown eyes told him it was the right thing to say, though. "Let's run away," he continued. "You and me. What's stopping us? I mean it. Tonight, let's go. We don't need Maple Town. We can start a new life. What do you say?"

Sally's mouth contorted as though she struggled to find the words to respond. He looked deep into the same brown eyes that always captivated all his senses, almost pleadingly. He couldn't breathe. He couldn't speak. He just looked at her, waiting, until at last her lips morphed into her signature smile.

"Okay," she said in that melodic voice of hers. "Where do we meet?"

"At the train station," Charlie said, so giddy he was almost shouting. "We'll leave at midnight. By tomorrow morning, we'll be long gone."

"It sounds crazy," Sally said. "But I'll go anywhere with you."

"Fantastic!" Charlie exclaimed, unable to contain his excitement and disbelief. "You run and get packed, and I'll meet you at the train station tonight."

Charlie winked at Sally and sprinted into town. He couldn't fathom what had just transpired. He had to plan. He had to think up how he'd pack everything. His heart fluttered like a million Arias dancing in his chest.

Unbeknownst to Charlie, however, Sally wouldn't pack a single piece of clothing that day. She'd sit in her room, combing her hair as each hour ticked away, staying strong in her resolve, knowing that a young man would be waiting for her at the train station all night.

CHAPTER FIFTEEN

THE AUTUMN BALL

There isn't a happy ending to this story. This tale is a tragedy. At what moment did our characters become so trapped in this web? Could all their pain have been avoided?

Their inability to communicate without a guise of sorts is frustrating. Even the slightest hint of truth from any one of them could have changed the course of their own histories.

But what was it that crippled them so?

Perhaps it was fate that compelled Charlie to fall out the window that morning, or maybe it was mere coincidence. Maybe our true female lead might've taken her rightful role if it weren't for Charlie's disobedience. We may never know. Though the final lynchpin of this tale's downfall happens on this very night.

It was a crisp, dry night, a night that made all the leaves crinkle up and crunch under one's boots. Lord Autaine stood at his balcony taking what would be his last whiffs of the cool autumn air around which his obsession revolved. He watched as his carriages came back one by one with his guests. From his perch above, he saw the people scramble out and up to the front door like rats, to see what he'd concocted this year.

As he scanned the throng of guests that hurried inside his home, he looked out at the odd mansion in the distance. If Maple Town were laid out like a compass, Vincent Prowl's manor would be due north. The Maples' orchard stood to the east, and his own mansion looked out at them from the west. He wondered if his guest of honor had arrived. How long did he have to live? The flamboyant lord shrugged off the thought. His butler, Phillip, stood nearby holding a tray and a tall glass of exactly what he needed. Lord Autaine walked back into his study and drank the dark-red liquor with great poise before throwing the glass against the wall.

He nodded at good Phillip, who left to watch over the party below. Then Allister Autaine sat down to draft two letters for two very important people. He scribbled, but being who he was, his curiosity got the better of him. He peeked again at the makeshift mansion in the distance, almost eagerly, completely unaware that his murderer had in fact just left and hadn't stopped fidgeting with the rim of his mask since passing through the tall black gates of number thirteen Chiaroscuro Lane.

Charlie stared out the carriage window with his head resting on his hand, anxiously looking out at the harvest moon overhead. It shone down on the world, calm as the sea before a storm, like a blood-red orb. How fitting, he thought.

Charlie wore a black tuxedo tailored just for him, complemented by a pair of gold cufflinks, all arranged by Vincent. It was hardly different from his usual attire, but Vincent had pointed out the wear and tear of Charlie's regular garments and put in a special order at the tailor's. When he was told of this, Charlie had no words other than to ask when he was to be fitted.

Unfortunately, Vincent had also made it clear that he'd be late in joining Charlie that night. He was very elusive as to why but gave Charlie explicit instructions to come back immediately after killing Lord Autaine.

Charlie shook the thought of Vincent from his mind and continued to play with the silver ribbon and playing card pin on the red plumed hat. He'd accidentally brought it home from the Mad Hatter's Festival. However, tonight he took it with him for good luck.

Aria emerged from the inside of his pocket and began pecking at his head before finally resting on his fingertips.

"Thanks for coming with me, Aria," Charlie said, giving a weak smile.

Aria looked up at the young vampire. She cocked her head when he returned his gaze to the window. She then flew to his shoulder and affectionately leaned against him, trying her best to calm him.

"Aria, why didn't she come?" Charlie said.

Aria shot off his shoulder and angrily pecked at his head.

"I get it," he said, shaking her off. "I'll stop bringing her up, but why?"

He'd waited until morning for Sally. He could've left, just himself, but he didn't. He got as far as the edge of the platform before he turned back toward the mansion. He couldn't bring himself to leave. Maybe it was the friends, the people he'd met here, that made him stay, or perhaps it was Vincent. He couldn't pin down why he couldn't leave Maple Town. He just knew that Sally's absence hurt him more than he would have liked to believe.

Aria flew up to him with the mask in her beak and plopped it into his hands.

"Right, I need to focus."

With that, he took the mask and hat and placed them on his head. He saw a myriad of brilliant white lights flickering like starlight in the distance. Soon the carriage pulled to the front of the mansion. Charlie took one deep breath to compose himself before taking the invitation from his pocket and flashing Aria a quick smile.

"It's showtime," he said.

In a single motion, Aria folded herself up and retreated into his coat pocket, while Charlie exited the carriage to enter the party ahead. He was walking up the long marble stairs that led inside the bright white mansion when an odd memory struck him. It was as if he'd seen the mansion lit up with these lights before, but for the life of him he couldn't remember when.

"Name?" said a short man checking people at the mansion doors. If he hadn't said anything, Charlie would have walked right past him altogether.

"Prowl," Charlie said, handing over his invitation for verification.

"Vincent?" the man asked suspiciously.

"Charlie. My father will be joining me later in the evening."

"Very well. You may enter," the small man said.

Charlie walked past the doorman and followed the other guests in a long procession to a bright ballroom. Charlie had heard stories of Lord Autaine's annual party, but seeing it was beyond anything he'd expected.

Sparkles rained down from the second story. The ceiling was enchanted to look like the night sky; thousands of stars and even a red moon hung overhead. Down below, men and women in masks danced on a floor that reflected the starry ceiling above and that was peppered with marble bridges and paths running over and around two streams with glowing flowers at their edges. These streams ran on opposite sides of the room as though

reflected in a mirror, never intersecting, and more astonishingly, never disrupting the dancers' movements. Charlie traced the streams to two identical waterfalls that seemed to come out of nowhere, raining down large amounts of water from the ceiling with barely, if any, a noise or splash.

As if all that weren't grand enough, Charlie saw a group of dining tables clustered in a corner under the shade of a large oak tree that seemed to have grown inside the mansion.

Except the colors were off.

Instead of green, yellow, orange, and red, there were black and silver leaves hanging from the oak tree. Charlie couldn't help but smile as people wrote things on the silver leaves, for once they'd plucked one from the tree and written something on it, up the leaf would float and turn into a black leaf on the tree.

Charlie walked around adjusting his mask and taking in the other guests' concealed faces. He saw every mask design one could imagine, from ones with great beaks to half masks. There were green, yellow, red, blue, and purple masks decorated with glitter, ribbons, and paint, to name only a few.

As he maneuvered his way through the ballroom, Charlie saw how the men and women would bow and curtsy to one another before a dance. It was as if that ritual initiated the dance. It was so bizarre.

A butler in a white dress shirt and black apron offered him sweets from the tray he carried. Charlie denied them and turned around to see a little boy rising higher and higher into the air on top of a bubble, until it finally burst. Charlie readied to propel himself to catch the boy, only to find little paper cranes flying around, lifting the boy up with incredible strength, and gently placing him down. At this, Aria slipped out of Charlie's pocket and flew toward the cranes as if trying to connect with her long-

lost relatives. Unfortunately, the paper cranes ignored her. Aria then proceeded to cut a few of them up with her beak before happily returning to Charlie's pocket.

Charlie retreated to one of the many dining tables, watching in amazement as more paper cranes fluttered out of the white table linen to catch anyone else who might need saving. The tables had glimmering silverware and napkins embroidered with the Autaine crest. The used silverware would disappear once a person finished eating or left, and suddenly reappear, completely clean, for the next hungry guest.

Charlie had to pinch himself just to check if this fantasy he'd stepped into was a dream or reality.

Alice saw him sitting alone.

Her nut-brown hair had been curled for the night and hung over her shoulders. She wore a sleek baby-blue gown that made her milky-white skin glow in the starlight, and a white mask with gold trimmings to conceal her identity—though she doubted it was necessary since none of the guests, barring Vincent, could pick her out from a crowd.

Neither her looks nor her anonymity at the Autumn Ball concerned her at the moment, though. She made a face at how awkwardly he sat alone. He'd occasionally try to make small talk with strangers, but it was either his lack of appetite or something he'd say that would always drive them away. It was both sad and perplexing to see the young man who, for some reason, Sally had liked. However, what struck Alice most was the red plumed hat he wore. It had the silver ribbon, the purple feather, and most importantly, her mother's playing card hairpin. She recognized it from all the way across the ballroom.

She made her way swiftly toward him. Her first instinct was to rush over and snatch the hat, but she stopped herself short. A thin smile crept across her lips, and her eyes narrowed.

"You look very dashing tonight," she said, standing over Charlie.

"Wow, you are . . ." Charlie stopped.

She noted how he blinked and fumbled his words. He's fickle, she thought. Mental note.

"I think I get it." She laughed and took a seat next to him. "Thank you."

"I'm sorry. You could say I'm a bit overwhelmed here," Charlie said nervously. "This party—"

"Oh, I know exactly what you mean," Alice said, cutting him off. She nodded her head in acknowledgment of what many had said before him. It was what everyone said about her father's parties. The two of them watched as a couple floated around in a giant bubble and danced together, blissfully unaware of their unexpected airlift. "It's a bit much. I guess it's your first time attending the Autumn Ball?"

"I'm not sure," Charlie said. The couple they had been watching were caught by a few paper cranes that continued to lift them to a safe location. "I feel like I've been here before. But I don't know how that's possible. It's kind of like a . . ."

"Dream," Alice said flatly.

"Exactly! Sorry, I probably seem very odd."

"No," Alice said, shaking her head. "Maybe that's what Sally liked in you. I've heard all about you and her," she added quickly.

"This town really can't keep a secret, can it?"

"Comes with the territory." Alice shrugged.

"Though"—Charlie paused—"I can't say I have her heart."

"You can say that again." Alice laughed. She tossed her head and took a sip from a goblet she'd snagged from a waiter who had just passed by.

"I asked her to run away with me, but she never showed up at the train station."

"She didn't tell you?" Alice gasped. She broke into a coughing fit and refused every attempt Charlie made to help her. "Um, do tell. What else happened?"

"Nothing," Charlie said. "I waited, and I haven't heard from her since. I'm hoping to see her tonight."

"I see," Alice said. "So you came to chase after a girl who clearly doesn't want to run away with you and who may be avoiding you. Am I getting that right?"

Charlie paused as though he didn't know how to answer her question. "Not quite," he said finally. "You wouldn't believe me if I told you."

"Try me," Alice said, offering her hand to dance.

Charlie blinked. He hadn't expected this sort of answer. He reluctantly took the young woman's hand and let her lead him to the dance floor full of couples swaying and moving to the melody. When they reached far enough into the crowd of dancers, she whipped around to face him, flashing a sly smile his way, and for a second, he could have sworn he saw a glint of something familiar in her different-colored eyes.

The song faded, and Charlie bowed at her curtsy and then placed his hand around her waist while their hands met. There was a moment of silence between them before the next song began.

In the brief silence, Charlie felt like he couldn't breathe. Then, upon hearing the soft plucking of the violins, he was brought back to life. The violins continued to pluck while Charlie and the masked girl slowly waltzed. The plucking was soon joined by the slow buzzing of the violas, and then, all of a sudden, a powerful strike of the cellos brought in the melody.

"So why are you really here?" the girl asked again.

"Do you always ask so many questions?"

"Only the ones that interest me," she countered.

"Well, I'm honored," Charlie said. "However, like I said, my heart belongs to Sally."

"I wasn't trying to steal your heart." She laughed as he leaned her back for a drop. "I was merely suggesting you stop chasing after Sally. She never showed up, right?"

"She must have had a reason," Charlie said firmly. "She had to."

"You've got your answer. She doesn't want to be with you. Why is it that you're expecting anything more than what she's offering?"

"Maybe it's not that simple. Ever think of that?" he said as the two of them continued to move in time. "Oh, I get it. You've never been in love."

"What? Of course I have," she snapped.

"Really? If so, you wouldn't be so skeptical. I'd give my life for her."

"I bet lines like that make her swoon," the girl said, rolling her eyes. "No wonder she couldn't say no to you!"

"You're crazy," Charlie said defensively. "What about you? What does my mysterious dance partner know about love?"

"For one, you don't have it. You're just caught in Sally's spell. If it were love, she'd have met you, and you wouldn't be here dancing with me."

Even as she spoke these harsh words, Charlie couldn't stop looking into the girl's green and turquoise eyes.

"Just move on—my honest advice."

"You don't even know me," Charlie said, giving a baffled laugh.

"Perhaps, but that doesn't make what I say any less true, does it?" said his dance partner.

"Okay, say you are right. How do I know I've actually found love the next time I think I see it?"

"Then . . . ," she said, dragging out the word, obviously stalling for time, "maybe you'll be more careful."

"Does that work for you?"

"Let's just say my dance card isn't that full to start with," she said.

"You have no idea what you're talking about, do you?"

"I'm just trying to give you good advice!"

"You're very odd," Charlie said.

"Likewise," she said. The song slowed to its final crescendo. "So what's your plan for the rest of the night?"

"I'll still take my chances finding Sally," Charlie said, maneuvering the two of them in one last rotation. "I still want to hear from her myself, you know?"

"And here I thought we were making progress." She sighed.

The music stopped. The mysterious girl looked at Charlie's confused stare and gave him her nicest curtsy.

"I mean it," she said, looking at him intently. Her eyes, he noticed, had shifted to a more serious gaze, making her appear older than she looked. All joking was aside for her. "See, right here is why love is such a silly thing. You've already lost yourself in my eyes when I'm just a girl behind a mask. Don't do this to yourself." She gave him a weak smile. "On a night when we are all hidden behind masks, just forget about Sally and about me, because in the end, does it matter?"

"I guess not," Charlie said finally.

"Good boy. Oh, and I'll be taking this by the way." She winked, taking his red plumed hat.

The whole ballroom dimmed. The music slowly faded into silence, and a tall man without a mask began walking down the main stairwell that led to the upper floors. He smiled down at all his guests with a captivating sureness. He wore a silver suit with gold trim and a black top hat. Looking like a wind-up toy, he took one of his gloved hands, grabbed his top hat, and gave an elegant bow.

"Welcome one and all!" the masked man shouted. "I am so glad you have all arrived and that we can enjoy this night of festivities. For those that don't know me, I am Lord Autaine. It is a pleasure to have you all in my home! I hope you find the festivities to be enchanting. Tonight, I am fortunate to have even more to celebrate. I would like to take this moment to acknowledge the engagement of my son and his new fiancée! So, without further ado, let me introduce the happy couple!"

Behind Lord Autaine followed a young man with a young woman on his arm. Charlie recognized the two immediately despite the masks they wore. In truth, Charlie could have picked out the man's identity even if he were wearing a sack over his head. However, the young man's brown hair was slicked back that night, and he wore a black suit, and didn't have any of his usual soot stains on him. The woman beside him wore a beautiful black dress.

"My son, Atticus Autaine, and Sally Maple!" Lord Autaine said enthusiastically. "Let us cheer to their brilliant union. And with that, I say, as the author of tonight, I hope you all have fun, be merry, and dance the night away!" He laughed at the sound of applause that followed.

CHAPTER SIXTEEN

HIS MASK, HER AID

Charlie's eyes remained fixed on the couple in black. It was hard to deny that the two seemed picturesque—Skat a tall chestnut-haired man in a black suit, and Sally in a matching midnight-black dress. She held her silver mask by a handle and carried a white fan in her other hand.

Charlie couldn't tell if she was happy or not. She didn't dare stare any higher than her feet, and she moved around as if attached to Skat's shoulder.

For a moment, the two young men locked eyes in quiet acknowledgment. Then, as if a switch had been flipped, Skat's face softened as he began grinning and shaking hands with a group of guests who had gathered at the bottom of the stairs. Sally, whose face remained hidden behind her mask and her large white fan, followed him like a shadow.

Alice was among the throng of people who had shoved their way forward to shake hands with the "happy" couple. Alice could tell Sally liked this as little as she did. She was being classic Sally and hiding behind her fan. As soon as someone had distracted her brother, Alice managed to pull Sally aside.

"Sally," Alice whispered, "what are you doing?"

"Alice," Sally said, and curtsied. It was as if she were greeting her like an old friend that she'd lost touch with over the years. "It's always a pleasure to see you. It's been so long. Thank you so much for coming—"

"Oh stop that! It's my house!" Alice said. "What in the world are you doing marrying my brother? We both know . . ." Alice looked around her, then pulled Sally up the stairs to the second story, where there were a lot fewer people. "We both know he's not right," she hissed.

"Alice, you're hysterical." Sally laughed. She fanned herself and looked below at the young man who'd grabbed her fiancé's attention. "You have a wild imagination."

"What happened to the girl who wanted to live as herself?" Alice said, shaking her dearest friend. "What happened to not wanting to be a doll anymore? I thought you were going to live for you!"

The slap happened just as quickly as the kiss they'd shared, and just as unexpectedly. Sally recoiled her hand while Alice stumbled back holding a hand to her cheek.

"Shut up!" Sally spat. "I'm doing what's right!"

"Sally, you can't mean that," Alice said.

"It's funny. You don't get it." Sally laughed, looking down at the partygoers below. "They'll hate me! I can't handle that."

"Sally, they won't hate you," Alice said.

"I was confused, Alice! That's all that was! I'm sorry. I'd rather be happy."

"How is this being happy, Sally?"

"Because it is," Sally whispered. She gave Alice a pleading look. "It's the role I was groomed to play. It's my duty to everyone, so I have to be happy with it. I don't have a choice."

"Sally," Alice said, "you don't mean that. I know you don't."

"You don't know what you're talking about," Sally whispered. She held a finger to her lips.

"Please, stop this nonsense," Alice pleaded. "I've known you all my life. You can still be so much more."

The two regarded each other, and for a moment, it seemed that Alice's words were thawing the thick layer of ice that her best friend had encased herself in.

But Alice just had to press.

"You should also tell Charlie that you have no intention of being with him. He's wandering around down there like a lost puppy looking for you."

"I can't," Sally said coolly. "He'll get the message eventually. They all do."

"Sally!"

"Just leave me alone, Alice!" she said, raising her hands. "I need to return to my fiancé."

And just like that, the queen of broken hearts regained the cold demeanor that had made her both revered and feared by all her subjects and which remained so carefully hidden under the guise of a lilting walk and wide-eyed smile. She descended the stairwell while Alice nursed the stinging heat she felt on her cheek.

"Why didn't you tell me?" Charlie said, pulling Skat by the shoulder.

Skat gave a diplomatic smile to a couple he had just been talking with before turning his attention to Charlie.

"You're embarrassing yourself, Charlie," Skat said, nodding at another couple.

"Who are you?" Charlie spat and gave Skat a shove.

A group of dancers gasped as Skat fell back on them. He politely apologized, then grabbed Charlie by the collar and dragged him to a secluded corner.

"So, Atticus," Charlie said. "That's your real name, and you want to marry the girl who I've loved ever since you've known me."

"Can we talk about this later?" Skat hastily whispered back. "Not here."

"Then when?"

"Just enjoy the party," Skat said. "And grow up! This is not a place to pick a fight. Not in my own house!"

Skat shook Charlie off, and directed his attention to the couple he'd previously been talking to. Charlie ran a hand through his hair as he watched Skat walk away. Then he looked at Lord Autaine, who continued to parade around the top of the staircase, giving bow after bow like some prized animal who had performed some impressive trick.

The reality of the act that Charlie would have to perform later that night suddenly dawned on him. He looked again at Skat and then back at Lord Autaine, and then back at Skat and then back at Lord Autaine. The room dropped out of focus as the voices reverberated in his ears. Everything was getting hazy. His hands began to quiver.

"I can't do this," Charlie said.

He rushed from the ballroom and out toward the veranda that overlooked the rose garden. He ran until he slammed his fists against the marble railing. His breathing was shallow, and he kept blinking as if this were some nightmare he'd wake up from. The guests that had retreated outside to escape the noisy ballroom quickly scattered upon hearing Charlie curse at himself. He ran one shaking hand, and then the other, through his hair before letting out a loud groan. "I can't." He paused and looked back at the party that not only had resumed but seemed even merrier than before. "I can't."

Aria unfolded herself out of Charlie's coat pocket. She gave him a pained look as she fluttered in circles, then paced back and forth on the edge of the patio railing with her little paper legs.

"Aria, I can't do this," he said, his voice quivering. "Especially not after how Skat lost his mother. Aria, what am I going to do?"

"Sir, wine?" spoke a voice.

For a second, Charlie didn't know whom the waiter was talking to, but then the waiter repeated himself and Charlie looked at him curiously.

"Wine, sir?"

"No, I don't drink, sorry," Charlie responded, signaling for the man to go away. Still, the waiter wouldn't leave.

"No, this is a glass specifically for you, courtesy of Lord Autaine," the waiter said, pressing the wine on Charlie.

Charlie eyed the waiter carefully before taking the glass. It was cold to the touch. He wasn't planning on drinking it until he realized the waiter wouldn't leave until he took a sip. Charlie slowly brought the glass to his lips and blinked. Blood. He drank the sweet red liquid and laid the empty glass on the silver tray.

"You said Lord Autaine requested I have it?" Charlie asked.

"Yes, he also requested a private conference with you."

"He did?" Charlie asked.

The waiter nodded. "He says to meet him up in the study. It's straight on up those stairs, second room to your right." He pointed in the direction of the stairs. "Would you like an escort, sir?"

"No," Charlie said, giving a cautious smile. "I'll find my way. I don't want to keep the lord waiting now, do I?

Aria returned to Charlie's breast pocket while he made his way back through the crowd of guests. He glanced around cautiously before making his ascent up the stairs.

Up on the second floor, it was a lot less noisy. A few guests who wanted to get away from some of the excitement downstairs were huddled in groups. Couples, mostly arm in arm, watched the party below, leaning on each other with a look that could only be described as love. All of it made Charlie's heart ache yet again.

He continued onward until he found the second room on the right. He could see a light emitting from inside. Charlie gently lay his hand over the doorknob and turned it quietly as a voice from inside beckoned him in.

"Come in already," a tired voice called. "Oh, and do lock the door. Interruptions would be such a bother. Well, let's not drag this out any longer than we have to. Oh, and how was the party? I'm very curious to know what a vampire thinks of my gala."

Charlie did as he was told and locked the door behind him. He slowly entered the room. The study had a window that overlooked the garden maze. The unlit fireplace was graced by a large mantelpiece with a carved stone lion at its center. Books and pictures of young children sat atop it. There was a desk with parchment and inks all scattered around, and an exotic magenta carpet adorned the middle of the room.

Despite Charlie's best efforts, he couldn't pinpoint where the voice had come from. It was Aria who flew out of Charlie's pocket and shot toward the brown chair at the desk, which was turned to face the garden maze.

Behind the chair, Charlie could see a hand extended to accommodate Aria, who happily landed on its fingers. The odd lord chuckled.

"She seems fond of you," Charlie said.

"What an impressive little creature," Lord Autaine said, rising from his chair. He turned to face the room. He still wore his silver suit but had taken off his top hat and mask. In his fancy

hat's place, he wore a faded wool cap, which Charlie found odd, even for Lord Autaine. He had a tired expression on his face as he played around with Aria, directing her movements with his finger as if he were conducting an invisible symphony that only he could hear. Humming, he picked up a cane that Charlie hadn't noticed resting against his chair and walked over to a large redwood cabinet beside a set of bookshelves. Charlie noticed this took him some effort.

"Well, I could use a drink. How about you?" He beamed at Charlie, or rather, in Charlie's direction. "Of course, you should know my bottles aren't of only wine." He gave Charlie a meaningful look, then turned back to rummage through the drinks cabinet. "I was worried for a moment that I was wrong when I asked Phillip to deliver that special glass to you. Imagine how confused you'd be if you weren't what I'd always assumed you were. Not to mention the rumors it'd cause!"

Lord Autaine gave a course laugh and produced two glasses and two dark-green bottles. Charlie rushed over to help the lord carry them to his desk. Aria rested herself on Autaine's shoulder as he poured their drinks. He then swirled each glass, taking in its scent, before offering one to his guest.

"Thank you for that," Lord Autaine said. "You can say my sight isn't what it used to be."

"You knew?" Charlie asked, taking the glass.

"Knew what? About what you are? I had my suspicions. You might want to consider taking someone's refreshments when you come over as a guest. It makes it less obvious that you don't eat. But that might be insensitive of me. Pardon me, I don't have any idea of vampire physiology."

"Why didn't you say anything?"

"Charlie, I have no intention to expose you—let me make that clear now. In fact, tonight is a night of celebration! For I have found what I've been looking for. So let me enjoy this last celebratory drink. No rush killing me just yet."

Charlie's whole body stiffened at the lord's words, delivered with such nonchalance.

"Did you know that it was because of those twins that I found the answers I've been searching for? So, cheers to that."

"Answers?"

"Ah," Lord Autaine said. He nodded and made his way toward the window. "Lovely, isn't it? I grow that maze larger and larger each year. At the center is my wife's grave." He seemed to be waiting for Charlie to respond to this, and when he didn't, he turned toward the other side of the room with his eyes narrowed.

"You didn't know that, did you?" Lord Autaine continued. "In fact, you don't know anything. The ball, my wife, what I've been tirelessly searching for?" He scoffed and took a sip of his wine. "What do you know about me, Charlie?"

"Why does it matter?" Charlie said, looking away from the man. "You seem to know exactly why I'm here."

"Just answer the question," Lord Autaine said.

"I know . . ." Charlie paused. "I know your wife died because of my kind. Your son and I are friends."

"Ah, but you know him as Skat. I swear, if he knew that I knew about this little double life of his, he'd quit pretending to be a blacksmith's apprentice on the spot. It's my little gift to him that I haven't said anything." He chuckled. "He must hate me right now, but I need to know he's in good hands after tonight. He wants to be engaged to that Maple girl as little as she wants anything to do with him, but the things you do for your child . . ."

Lord Autaine shrugged his shoulders and poured himself another glass of wine. He continued to eye Charlie, who remained speechless. Laughing to himself, Autaine laid his glass down and took off the wool hat he wore. He started playing with its fringes.

"Fate! What a fickle bitch you are," he said, shaking his head. He took another sip and looked out the window. "I truly am sorry that my deal with those twins has forced this meeting between us. I can imagine how hard it is, especially if you're close to my son."

"Is there any other way?" Charlie said weakly.

"Although, I am surprised you're wrong on one account," Lord Autaine said as if he hadn't heard Charlie at all. He continued to stare out at the garden as if the maze were his listener. "The townspeople were so close, but they got the details all wrong. Just goes to show what happens when you leave out the master of festivities. You see, long ago I was nothing more than a farmer, believe it or not. Obviously, I've struck fortune since then." Lord Autaine shrugged. "Anyway, one night I was walking toward where number thirteen Chiaroscuro Lane stands now. I wanted to see the stars. I was fascinated by them. And it was on that night my hat blew straight off my head. This one right here," he said, shaking the cap in his hand. He began to pace and play with the rim of the hat. "It flew down the hill and into town. I followed that hat until I found it next to another. And who do I find? She was a teacher who had gone on an evening stroll, only to lose her hat much like I. Oh, she was beautiful. We met every so often to look at the stars, and one day we finally married.

"She didn't die from vampires, Charlie," he said, crumpling his hat. "She died because a man kidnapped her. Right under my fingertips. I didn't know until I saw her burned at the stake. That's what happened, and here's the kicker—she was just in the wrong place at the wrong time. There's no meaning to her death.

No big elaborate story. That's it! Nothing! It could have been anyone else! So there. Now I know. I finally know." He laughed, clutching the hat close to his chest. "You ever wonder why I host these balls? It's to attract your kind, their kind, anything that can tell me why my wife died that day! I've dealt with creatures that you've only thought up in your nightmares! Ironically it took a pair of blonde demons for me to discover that it was none other than cruel coincidence that took my wife."

"And the price?"

"My life," Lord Autaine sang. He walked over to Charlie and handed him two letters. One was addressed to Atticus, and the other was to a girl named Alice. Confused, Charlie stared up at the man, who hushed him before he could ask any questions. "Give my children these letters and let them know that now, at the very end, I realize the fool I am for trading my life for the knowledge I so desperately sought."

"You can still live!" Charlie said, pushing back the letters. "This night can end differently. I walk away and—"

"But you can't," Lord Autaine said. "I know exactly the consequences you shall face if you let a foolish man go free tonight. With that said, I present myself to Death with open arms, for I've found what I spent my life searching for. There's very little else for me now. Despite what I wrote in those letters, they're no more than empty words. I've made my choice. The answer was more important in the end."

Lord Autaine began making his way closer to Charlie. He then pointed toward the fireplace. "There's a secret exit through the fireplace if you push the third brick to the right of the lion. It should give you enough time to escape. Now, shall we let an old man die?"

The lord bowed and offered up his wrist. Charlie couldn't look at the man so ready for the release of death. Charlie knelt in front of the flamboyant lord and stared up, his mouth just inches away from the man's wrist. He took a deep breath, realizing the action that would have to occur next.

"Any last words, my lord?" Charlie breathed. "You deserve better than 'let an old man die.'"

"Send my regards to Forte," he said listlessly.

Charlie bit into his wrist. There was a loud scream and then silence as Charlie drank the sweet nectar and Autaine staggered to his knees. At last, Charlie drained the life force from the author of the night. Tears streamed down Charlie's face as he lay the body down and stared at the smiling white face of the lord.

He closed the man's eyes and fell back against the wall. He held a hand to his temple and ran it down his face. He tried his best not to look back at the body, but his eyes betrayed him as he scrambled to his feet.

He followed Lord Autaine's instructions and pressed the third brick to the right of the lion carving, completely unaware that during the last few moments of Lord Autaine's life, there was a visitor at the door. Drawn by the scream, someone had kicked down the door, and he stood there now, his silver mask thrown to the ground, the only witness to Charlie's escape.

CHAPTER SEVENTEEN

THE DEATH OF SKAT

For reasons of guilt, respect, or masochism, Charlie attended the funeral service of the author of the night. Even in death, Lord Autaine would make his dramatic leave on his own terms; it was discovered not long after his demise that the deceased lord had left detailed instructions on how his own funeral would be conducted, right down to the colossal white monument he'd ordered to house his decaying corpse.

The service would take place at twilight on a day when it was still chilly but not too cold, and no words would be spoken at the service. However, despite the lord's explicit orders, there was a faint murmur that could be heard from one end of the graveyard to the other.

It was an odd phenomenon. A few brave individuals had begun to tell their fondest memories of Lord Autaine, only to stop midway. Others started to share their own stories, but one by one the same hesitation would capture all of them, which ultimately made everyone realize how little they actually knew about the deceased lord.

As much of an enigma as Lord Autaine was in life, though, there were certain facts that the townspeople discovered after his death. The first, to Charlie's dismay, was that a vampire was responsible for the lord's murder. The second was a more surprising revelation, and she had a playing card hairpin in her long brown hair.

Many of the townspeople had no idea that she'd even existed until she began to say a few words on her father's behalf. Though what she said no one remembered, as all were still wrapping their heads around the idea that Lord Autaine had a daughter that no one knew about. When she'd finished, she dropped flowers on the grave and left with her large black cat.

Charlie held the letter up to his chest, watching Alice Autaine walk away. He then felt a tug on his pant leg.

"Are you going to give that to her?"

Charlie looked down to see a small boy with a large smile looking up at him, doe-eyed. The child clearly didn't understand what a funeral was but knew enough that he had to whisper.

"I'm sorry, what?" Charlie whispered back. He knelt down and leaned his ear toward the young boy.

"The letter," the boy whispered back. "It's for her, isn't it?"

"Oh," Charlie said. His mouth remained open as his mind struggled to catch up. Then his lips formed the words that every adult has uttered at least once to a child. "It's complicated."

"Well, you still have time!" the boy said, urgently pulling on Charlie's pant leg again. "You can still catch her!"

"Listen," Charlie said slowly, "why don't you give it to her? I'm sure you must be bored standing here."

"Okay!" the boy almost shouted. He grabbed the letter and sprinted toward a very confused Alice, who would look around curiously for the origin of the mysterious note. However, her search would be in vain as its benefactor had already disappeared up the hilltop of number thirteen Chiaroscuro Lane.

Now, two characters didn't attend the funeral. You see, they were much too busy. As they did the week before the funeral and the weeks to follow it, Skat and Sally remained at the Maple Orchard picking various fixtures and going over the most finite details concerning their wedding.

"Well, of course it has to take place here!" came the shrill voice of Elise Maple. She waved her hands in the air as if what she'd said were the most sensible thing ever.

"Why, Elise, you're right, my dear!" Walter Maple said. "And what about children?"

"Excuse me?" Atticus Autaine said, coughing on his tea.

"Kids! Little slobbery bundles of joy," Elise Maple scoffed. "I'm sure you've heard of them. How many will you and my darling daughter have?"

"We haven't discussed that yet, Mother." Sally beamed as she held her fiancé's hand. "We've been engaged for a month and only made the announcement recently. It seems a bit premature for kids, don't you think?"

"How long do you two need to get acquainted?" Walter Maple shouted. "You two have practically known each other your whole lives."

"I think this is a little different, don't you?" Atticus said.

"Nonsense!" Elise said, waving her hand. "If we've learned anything from recent events it's that . . ." She paused, gave a long sigh, and looked at Atticus. "Life is too short."

"That's it!" Atticus slammed down his teacup. He rose from his seat, and his fiancée joined him. Unlike him, she gave a loving smile to her parents.

"I think what Atticus is trying to say is that perhaps we need a break," Sally said in her usual melodic voice. "Is that okay?"

Walter and Elise Maple exchanged a disapproving look before nodding toward the door.

"Make sure to be back soon!" screeched Elise Maple as the two retreated to the orchard. "We still need to talk about table linens!"

"Your mom is insufferable!" Atticus said the second they were out of earshot. He went to a nearby fountain and splashed his face. "I don't know how much of this I can take."

"Oh, so marrying me is that bad, is it?" Sally spat. She sat on a bench with her arms crossed. "Perfect! Well, I didn't expect to be marrying a liar!"

"Just because I wanted a few moments not to be an Autaine, I'm now a criminal?" Atticus rolled his eyes.

"You stole! I know you did!" Sally snapped back.

"Maybe I did." Atticus sighed and dried his face with his sleeve. "At least I'm honest with my feelings."

Sally rose to her feet. "I don't know what you think you heard, but I assure you that you are mistaken!"

"I'm not so sure," Atticus said. He turned to the Maple estate and shook his head. "That's it. I'm calling off this wedding right now."

"No!" Sally pleaded, pulling on his arm. "Please, no. We need to do this."

Atticus hung his head because despite how miserable he was, Sally was right. They had to. It was their responsibility, especially with his father's passing.

"God, I hate this," he whispered, and kicked a nearby tree. "Why did he have to die? He left me as the family head. That wasn't supposed to happen for at least another ten years!"

"We can still make it to his service if you want," Sally said affectionately.

"No," Atticus said quickly. "If I go, I might just kill someone."

He glanced down at the blood blade holstered to his belt. He'd thought about running the sword through his father's killer every day since he'd heard that scream.

This was all his fault.

"Okay." Atticus sighed. "Let's just go back in there and get all this planning over with. Let's just stick it out."

"Sounds like an excellent plan." Sally clung to his arm as they made their way inside.

A yell in the distance made them turn around. Racing toward them was a brunette blur in a dark dress waving a piece of paper in her hand.

"Atticus!" Alice called out. "You've got to see this! You can't do this!" Alice panted as she pushed the letter toward her brother.

"What's this?"

"Papa wrote it before he died," Alice said. "It has the whole truth."

"Where'd you get it?"

"I don't know," Alice said. "I just know that the letter refers to the deliverer as his 'bloody acquaintance.'"

Atticus pushed the letter back and began marching away from the two girls. "Don't trust a single thing in that letter! Go away, Alice! We need to prepare for our wedding."

"What? Atticus! What are you talking about?" Alice said, running to him and blocking his path. "What's the matter with you? Are you saying you're too busy to go to our father's funeral because you have to plan a wedding that both of you hate? Why're you going through with it?"

"You wouldn't understand!" Atticus said. "If this letter came from Papa's 'bloody friend,' I wouldn't trust any of it. And we're going to learn to be happy with each other because that's just how it is."

"Sally, say something!" Alice spat.

Sally stood glaring at her friend. Alice saw the same look Sally had had on the night of the Autumn Ball.

Chapter Seventeen

"My fiancé has spoken," Sally said, returning to his side. "He's right."

"The two of you," Alice said, taking a step back. "I can't believe either of you!"

"If you can't accept that this is how it's going to be . . . ," Sally began. She cleared her throat but didn't dare look Alice in the eye. "Perhaps this should be the last we see each other."

"Sally, it's me," Alice said. "What are you talking about? We're best friends!"

"Maybe we shouldn't be!" Sally shouted. It was a sound that even Sally didn't register at first. It was certainly something that both Atticus and Alice had never heard from Sally, for in that instance, Sally Maple's voice held a pure hatred. Then, as if her body couldn't commit to the conviction of her voice, Sally began wiping her eyes. "Just leave us alone, Alice," she sobbed.

"Here, I'll meet you inside," Atticus whispered. "I'll walk my sister off the premises."

Sally nodded and retreated into the Maple household.

"Alice, Charlie Prowl is the vampire who killed our father," Atticus said slowly.

"What?"

"You heard me," Atticus continued. "But I'll kill him. He won't get away with it."

"But vampires didn't kill Mother!" Alice shouted.

"Even if that were true, he did kill our father!" Atticus said. "Can you deny that?"

Alice was silent.

"That's what I thought," Atticus said. "Maybe Sally is right. You should just leave us be."

With that, Atticus retreated into the house, leaving Alice by herself in the Maple Orchard. She began walking back and stared up at number thirteen Chiaroscuro Lane, northwest of the orchard. She was still trying to wrap her head around the fact that her dance partner at the ball had killed her father that same night.

At that exact moment, across town, that very same vampire was toying around with a ruby-encrusted knife. It was an odd sensation to be holding a knife that he'd repeatedly stabbed his own heart with. Charlie had counted four hundred and ninety-two stabs since the Autumn Ball.

He lay on his bed playing with the outlines of the blade with his fingertips. He even pricked his fingers a few times, only to watch each wound mend itself instantly.

Charlie closed his eyes, but as had happened the last time he did so and the time before that, memories from that night sped like lightning through his head until he suddenly shot up and threw the knife across the room. It slammed with a loud thud against a piece of paper that hung across the room. It was his invitation to the Autumn Ball, though it was hardly recognizable anymore. It was so mangled by all the cuts and holes that no one could have ever recognized it as one of the lavish invitations the deceased lord had sent out.

Charlie leaned back in his bed and watched as a faint breeze blew through his room, causing the shiny bells, colorful dream catchers, and wind chimes to sway. He lifted his head, ready to trek across the room to grab the knife again, when he saw a paper bird struggling to carry the heavy blade.

"Careful with that!" Charlie said, taking the knife before it ripped her. "I appreciate it, but please, I want to be alone."

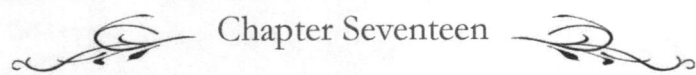

Aria began soaring around the room, flipping, spiraling, and pulling on Charlie's hair until it became too much for him.

"Leave me alone, Aria!"

His words made Aria fall to the foot of the bed. She teetered on her small paper legs, clutching her paper heart with her wing. Then she collapsed with her paper tongue sticking out. Finally, for good measure, she crumpled up into a ball.

"That's not funny. Now, if you're done, go!"

"She's not the only one worried about you," said a voice at the door.

"Go away," Charlie sobbed.

"Vampires don't cry," Vincent said, staring down at Charlie.

"I'm sorry," Charlie said, wiping his eyes on his sleeve.

Vincent's face cringed upon seeing the puffy eyes and hearing the cracked voice of the young vampire. Like any father, he couldn't stand to see his son as he was. Yet he stood there frozen, unable to provide whatever comfort the boy desired. The two remained in an uncomfortable silence for some time before Vincent's eyes narrowed.

"Just drink."

Vincent held yet another bottle of blood in his hand. Below him were at least a dozen other bottles he'd brought with him on previous visits. They had been stacking up because, along with not leaving the mansion, Charlie had refused to drink a single drop of blood since the Autumn Ball.

"If you don't, you'll only suffer. You won't die. Though, I believe you know that already," Vincent said, nodding toward the knife.

"I'll be okay."

"Drink. You'll be in extreme pain otherwise," Vincent urged. "Please."

"I'm fine with that," Charlie said passively. "I want to die, Vincent."

"That won't kill you. It'll just makes things worse."

Vincent lay the bottle on a nearby dresser. The gentle sounds of tears and weeping coincided with the rain hitting the window. The old vampire moved awkwardly around the room before finally sitting down at the foot of the bed. He raised a hand, but stopped midway and returned the hand to his side. It wasn't until Aria nudged Vincent's shoulder that the old vampire finally mustered up the courage to speak.

"I never wanted you to experience any of this. I'm sorry. I did what I did so you wouldn't grow attached to them."

"But why does it have to be that way?" Charlie shouted. "I lived among them! They were nothing other than kind to me!"

"That's because they didn't know what you are," Vincent said. "Until now, your duties as a vampire never intersected with the life you pretend to live. You're going to kill again. Sooner if you don't drink. That's a fact. What then? You struggle now for killing one man. Could you really live with yourself if you killed the loved one of another friend you've made? It's cruel, yes. But that's our life. You need to accept it and realize what you are, because you aren't human, nor will you ever be!"

"We're the same as them! I love, talk, breathe, and sleep just like them! I don't want to be this anymore! I don't want to kill anymore! I just want to be human," sobbed Charlie. "I just want to wake up, Vincent. I just want the pain to go away."

The bitter old vampire stood and stared at the rain that fell gently outside. The two remained silent for a long while, listening only to the sounds of the rain against the window.

"If we could leave, would you take that chance?"

"What do you mean?"

"I made a deal with Mira and Vera," Vincent said slowly. "We'll be free. You don't have to kill again. I'll do it all for the both of us. We will be able to leave town and live as we want."

"What's the price?" Charlie said. "They always have a price."

"The town is destroyed. Two lives in exchange for the lives of the town."

"What about all the innocent lives that will be lost?" Charlie said. "I'd rather suffer with them than torture myself knowing that I was responsible for killing them all."

"You stupid boy!" Vincent shouted. "Think this through! You know what they did to Elizabeth. Why do you still feel an attachment to them? This is our way out of all this!"

"I'll pass," Charlie said.

"And what? Letting yourself suffer will help them?" Vincent continued. "I'm talking about your happiness here! Why suffer to help a bunch of monsters who wouldn't hesitate for a second to burn you at the stake once they discovered what you are?" He nodded in contempt. "It's pathetic!"

"Even so, I wouldn't abandon them!"

"Why?" spat the old vampire. "What compels this loyalty that you don't give to me?"

"Because I still think you're wrong about them," Charlie said, thinking about Sally and Skat—or Atticus, as Charlie had to get used to calling him now. "Perhaps we can live with them. Maybe we just need to give them a chance!"

"They've had their chance. Elizabeth was proof of what they do to those they can't accept!"

"You're wrong!"

"Hear me, boy," Vincent boomed. "You want to prove me wrong, go right ahead! You know where the door is. But know this: you have sanctuary here. We can run away from this wretched town. We can be free from all this!"

"Why do you suddenly care so much? Do you think running away will solve anything? More lives will be lost! It's not a life I want."

"Fine! Go. Leave. You are no son of mine. You go to that girl and prove me wrong. Go to her and see if what I've said isn't the truth. I'm ashamed in raising such a disillusioned boy who's too blind to see the truth."

He needed to see Sally. She'd understand. She had to understand. Charlie sprinted out the doors, down the hilltop, and out the tall black gates. He bumped into a number of people who were trying to get out of the rain. He ran until his clothes were heavy with water, only stopping once he reached the familiar dirt road by the faded wooden sign. He took a quick breath before forcing himself through the grove of trees, slick with the rain that tapped on their trunks in a steady rhythm. At last, he reached the Maple estate.

"Sally! Sally! Please come out! I need to talk to you!" he shouted. He waited for a reply. However, he heard nothing but the rain beating hard against him. He stood in the downpour, searching desperately for any sign that his pleas had been heard.

The door opened.

Charlie smiled. A man stood in the doorway, talking to someone inside the house, then he walked out and shut the door behind him. He wore a double-breasted white suit with gold buttons underneath a black overcoat. He had two swords holstered at his waist. His hair was slicked back. Atticus Autaine would've been nothing more than a stranger to Charlie if it weren't for the familiar wry smile that Charlie could recognize anywhere.

"You look like a drowned rat." Atticus crossed his arms. He nodded toward the orchard. "Go home, Charlie."

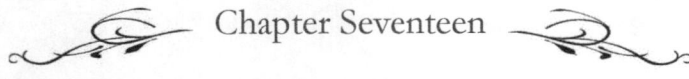

"Skat!" Charlie said. "I need to see her!"

"I told you she wasn't good for you," Atticus said. "I'm not moving aside so that you can flirt with my fiancée."

"You don't even like her." Charlie panted. "Please, it's important. I need to tell her."

"Tell her you're a vampire? Tell her that you killed my father in cold blood?" Atticus said, cocking his head. He pursed his lips before pulling a steel blade from his holster. He threw it at Charlie's feet. "She knows already. I'm warning you. Now, pick it up."

"Skat, I'm so sorry. It wasn't supposed to be like this. I . . ."

"You what? No, go on, I want to hear it," Atticus said, stepping closer to Charlie. They were practically nose to nose. Rain fell over them as they stood in silence. "Didn't mean to kill my father? Is that what you wanted to say?"

"I didn't have a choice."

"That's rich coming from you," Atticus spat. "So is he a vampire too?" He nodded in the direction of number thirteen Chiaroscuro Lane.

Charlie remained silent.

"Say something!"

"Why are you doing this?"

"Pick the sword up." Atticus nodded toward the steel blade. "I said pick it up!"

When Charlie wouldn't move, Atticus drew the blood blade that he and Charlie had been working on. He charged at Charlie. Charlie quickly reached for the blade on the ground and blocked Atticus's attack. The two boys locked eyes, and for a moment, Charlie could've sworn he saw tears among the raindrops on his friend's face. Atticus would slash and slash again at Charlie, but each time, his blow was blocked.

"Fight back!" Atticus shouted. "I know you can!" He pressed his blade against Charlie's. "You're gonna die if you don't do anything!"

"I'm not going to fight you!" Charlie screamed.

Charlie and Skat parried and blocked all around the clearing until Charlie's blade slipped out of his hand. Skat took his chance and slashed at Charlie's chest. Charlie fell backward against an apple tree, seeing trickles of his own blood taint the orchard. He closed his eyes, waiting for the final blow, but it never came. He peeked his eyes open to see Skat shaking.

"Your father was going to die anyway," Charlie breathed.

Skat raised his blade again and held it against Charlie's neck. "I'd watch your mouth," he spat. "I'll gut you. I swear I will! One more word about my father. I dare you."

"You father was dead the second he made a deal with two girls named Mira and Vera," said Charlie.

"Shut up! Shut up! He always was a fool," Skat said, shaking his head. "In this world, there's no room for fools!"

He raised his blade, but couldn't deal the final blow no matter how hard he tried. Tears erupted from his eyes. He threw aside the blood blade, punched Charlie square in the jaw, and held him by the collar.

"You're a vampire!" he shouted. "How could you? I thought . . . I thought . . ." He took a few steps back. "You threw it all away!"

"I'm sorry," Charlie said.

"No, shut up! SHUT UP! We were brothers! You're worse than dirt to me. Is this what our friendship means? Hmm? We were best mates, and you up and decided to kill my dad. I heard him before he died. I heard him SCREAM! How can you throw this all away? I don't even love this girl, and I have to marry her! It's your fault!! ALL OF IT!"

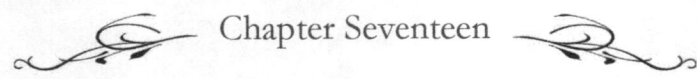

Atticus gripped Charlie again. He held his fist up, ready to strike. He was shaking with anger, but nothing happened.

"Do it yourself. I'm only doing this because we were best friends," he said. "Get out of town! Because by tomorrow, everyone will know what you are."

Charlie staggered to his feet, then stood pressing a hand over where Atticus had slashed him. He limped over to the blood blade and took it, then looked back at his former friend before scampering away as fast as he could. Atticus had begun to throw pebbles at him to make sure he'd leave.

"Get!" Charlie heard in whimpers. "Get out of here!"

CHAPTER EIGHTEEN

THE CAT WITH NO NAME

It's hard to tell what went through the young vampire's mind after that. He must have walked miles upon miles without stopping. His cerulean-blue eyes were streaked with red. The rain washed all the blood from his wound, and after that, the heat from the day dried the wetness from his clothes, leaving only a large scar across his chest. It was shallow enough that it wouldn't kill him, but deep enough that it would remain a constant reminder of how he'd lost his best friend.

However, there was no doubt that Charlie wished it would end him.

People occasionally passed by on carriages or by foot, and all would offer to help, but no one came close to him—Charlie made sure of it. The moment they came within breathing distance, he'd yell at them, curse them out, and threaten them in ways that would make even Vincent proud.

For no sooner than they left, Charlie would cough, pant, and wait for his mouth to stop salivating. The sun began to irritate him. His steps became heavier and more painful. It was like each step stuck a million needles into his skin. This continued

until Charlie was barely walking. He swayed and dragged his feet before finally collapsing on the dirt road. He gripped the soil and shivered, feeling suddenly cold and hot at the same time.

"Have you had enough?"

Charlie lifted his head. He coughed and looked around for the person who'd spoken, but found no one in sight.

"Behind you," sang the voice. There, prancing proudly toward the young vampire, was a cat.

Charlie gripped the soil, feeling the strong dryness in his throat and the convulsive shaking that possessed him to contain his bloodlust. "Shoo, go away!"

Charlie dropped his head. But the cat remained. It even pawed at the young vampire's head.

"My, what red eyes you have!"

"You can talk," Charlie growled as he looked into the amethyst eyes of the large black cat.

"Always the same." The cat shook his head. "Honestly, if I got a piece of gold for every time I heard that, I'd be a very, very rich cat."

Charlie continued to eye the cat. When he failed to say anything in response, the cat smiled and continued to chatter away.

"I'm not a normal cat, obviously," it said, rolling its eyes. "But you already knew that." Then after a pause, the cat's lips curled again. "Or perhaps you didn't," he said. The cat walked in front of Charlie and stared deep into the boy's bloodshot eyes. It rocked back and forth, its head darting as it examined different aspects of the boy's confused expression, before it finally broke into a wide smile. "You don't remember me?"

"Please leave!" Charlie screamed. "I'm begging you!"

"It's good manners to answer when spoken to." Again, the cat broke into a wide grin before repeating his initial question. "Have you had enough?"

It happened so fast. Charlie pounced without realizing it and slashed at the cat, who casually dodged the vampire's advances. Charlie snarled and growled, trying his best to grab the cat. He raced forward and finally pinned the cat down. Charlie salivated over it, while at the same time shaking and trying his best to pull himself away from his prey.

"Sit, boy," the cat said.

Immediately, Charlie froze and fell off the cat. He continued to growl, but his body remained frozen.

"I swear, where did you learn your manners? You've made me waste my magic! I've been saving it, but alas, I have a feeling you have definitely been worth the investment."

"Just kill me," Charlie managed to say.

"Kill you?" The cat burst out laughing. "Now why would I do a stupid thing like that? I need you, boy. I've invested way too much in you. Because you're going to set me free. Now, I repeat. Have. You. Had. Enough?"

Charlie snarled before shaking again.

"What sharp teeth you have! Okay, I'm going to count that as a yes. From the looks of things, you could go feral at any moment, and there's no going back from that, so I'll make this quick. What if I told you I can save you and everyone you love, and to top it off, you won't have to kill anyone again?"

"How?" Charlie croaked.

"My name," said the cat gingerly. "If there ever comes a day that you discover what my name is, you have to tell me immediately. Because the curse I'm under can only be broken if someone tells me my name. I obviously don't know it anymore, but that's the bargain. You tell me my name if you find out. And something tells me that you will. Do we have a deal?"

"Fine."

The cat came closer, to where Charlie still struggled in his invisible bindings. The cat hissed, bit at his own paw, and let a drop of blood land on Charlie's mouth.

Immediately, Charlie's whole body relaxed. But the cat wasn't finished. His tail seemed to paint the dirt as he circled Charlie. Just like that, an intricate pattern surrounded them.

"By this deal, I bind thee to this contract. From master to servant, I bind thee to my wish."

A red circle encased Charlie. It rotated and rotated like a wheel, the inscriptions on the ground becoming a blur as it tightened around him. It became smaller and smaller until finally it made its mark over where Charlie's heart would have been. Charlie glanced at the red magic circle on his chest. A moment later, the cat brushed away any traces of it with his bushy black tail.

"Let's keep this our little secret," the cat said. "Do we have that clear, servant?"

"Yes," Charlie managed to croak. "But how can you save them? How can I never drink someone's blood again?"

"Oh, I never said you'd be blood free. I said you wouldn't have to kill," the cat said.

"But you said—"

"Relax." The cat sighed. "Rejoice! Oh, Elizabeth, how can you have given me such an opening? That silly, silly Elizabeth. She knew better!" The cat returned his attention to Charlie. "Oh, when I get my paws on that woman . . ."

"Elizabeth?" said Charlie. "You know Vincent's wife?"

"Oh, you silly boy, I taught her everything she knows!" He then gave a long sigh, resting his paw underneath his chin as he lay on the ground. "But this was just careless!"

"What do you mean?"

"What exactly do you know about Elizabeth? I'm so curious now!"

"I know she's dead."

The cat gave a loud roar of laugher and practically rolled onto his back. He stared back at Charlie with his belly up. "This just keeps getting better and better!"

"You promised! Tell me how I can save everyone, cat!"

"And I keep my promises," the cat said. "You know, you and I aren't so different. You see, I can't die, so what do you do with a demon immune to death? You trap him. That was their answer. They stripped me of most of my powers and turned me into a cat. And a cat I shall forever be."

"You're not answering my question!" Charlie said. He charged at the cat, who skillfully dodged the young vampire's advances and climbed up a tree.

The cat stretched out its paws, watching Charlie down below. "Part of my punishment," he continued, "was to teach young witches and wizards for eternity. Elizabeth was one of the many students I've had. And this is my fate until the day someone tells me my name. Only then will my curse be broken. Lucky for me, I now have a servant bound to make my wish come true."

Charlie wanted to strangle the cat. But he was once again sapped of all his strength. He collapsed again on the dirt, hearing only the cat's laughter as he lost consciousness.

What happened next may or may not have been part of the cat's plan. But it so happened that someone was passing along the road where the boy and the cat lay at that exact time. It's hard to tell, but like all the actors in this tale, the witch, too, may have been playing into the cat's grand plan.

Regardless, the young vampire now lay against the witch's lap. The carriage jostled with every minor bump they passed. The witch stroked the boy's hair. She gave a slight head shake

before undoing one of her sleeves. She winced as she bit into her own skin just enough to draw blood. Carefully, much like she'd done in the past, she nursed the drops of blood into the young vampire's mouth.

"You've been busy," she said curtly. The words were so biting within the silence of the carriage, the cat couldn't help but grin.

"And you were careless," the cat said. He sat opposite the witch.

"I thought you were stripped of all your magic," the witch continued.

"Not all of it," the cat countered. "But I've made my gamble, so no more tricks. Scout's honor." The cat raised his right paw.

The witch rolled her eyes. "What have I done?" she whispered.

"You give yourself too much credit," the cat said, waving his paw, "as if all this is your fault. Most is, yes, but not all. I've grown quite fond of the girl, so my warning to you isn't completely altruistic. She may even give me what I want." The cat paused and looked up at the witch with his large amethyst eyes. "Besides, no one could have predicted that your former husband would be crazy enough to kill a whole town. But what do you plan to do? That's what I want to know. You can't go back, obviously. Last time you got that close to him, it nearly killed you, and that particular curse grows stronger over time. So what now?"

The witch remained silent as if she hadn't heard the cat. She kept nursing blood into the young vampire's mouth until he began to stir in her arms. She smiled and gave a sigh of relief.

The young vampire shook in her arms and coughed. He sat up when he realized he was lying on the witch's lap, his eyes darting from one side of the carriage to the other.

"Where am I? You need to let me go! I'm danger—" He stopped. He licked his lips, relishing the familiar taste in his mouth. He no longer hurt. He looked over at the woman next to him, who

pulled a piece of square paper from her pocket and wrapped her wrist with it before smiling at the young vampire.

"You shouldn't go that long without feeding. You could have seriously hurt someone," she said. The cat hopped onto her lap. She petted him as if she didn't realize a vampire was right next to her.

"Who are you?"

"I'm here to stop a very silly vampire from making a very silly mistake," she said. Then out of her pocket fluttered a piece of paper that did backflips and spirals in the air before resting on Charlie's shoulder. She nodded toward the paper swallow. "I've been watching you. Vincent isn't the best father, so hopefully Aria has been enough to keep you company. Honestly, how could he not know about loneliness after all he's been through? Regardless, please forgive him. He's a grieving widower, so to speak." She paused and pursed her lips before continuing. "I'm very sorry you've had to pay for the mistakes of a silly witch. I did what I thought was right, but now . . ."

"You're Elizabeth," Charlie said quietly. "You're not dead. How are you not dead?"

Elizabeth looked up at Charlie. She played with the hem of her skirt. She opened her mouth, but no words came out. She turned her gaze back down to her lap and sighed.

"She can't say," the cat said finally. "She's cursed. I imagine that she wants to tell you, but those blue runes on her left arm prevent her from doing so."

Charlie glanced at Elizabeth's arm, which had started glowing bright blue. She hid it and coughed.

"My friend here has told me what Vincent plans on doing. He made a deal to destroy the town in exchange for your lives," she said. "He's using werewolves."

"That's insane!" Charlie said.

"Exactly! He's a fool. A misguided fool twisted by his own grief. He's wrong! He's stupid! He's irrational! He'd . . . only do this if he was in great pain. And if there's anyone to blame for it, it's me." She stopped. Her nails dug into her skirt and she tilted her head up to show a weak smile. "We can't allow him to kill the town we both love."

"I don't understand. Why don't you tell him that yourself?"

"She can't, obviously," snorted the cat.

"What's he talking about?" Charlie said.

Elizabeth remained silent.

"That really is a nasty little curse you have there, my dear," the cat continued. "Honestly, how could the great Elizabeth of the Paper Cranes let herself be cursed? I must be losing my touch as a teacher."

"It's as he said," Elizabeth said. "It's impossible for me to ever see Vincent, let alone be in the same town as him anymore. It's complicated. That's why you must go back and stop him."

"Why me, though?" Charlie said. "He hates me. I'm no longer his son. He said so himself."

"He told you that?" Elizabeth said, furrowing her brow. "That dummy. He can never say what he means. Charlie, do you know why he's going so far to destroy Maple Town?"

"It's because he thinks they killed you."

"That wouldn't be enough for him to destroy the town where we had a very happy marriage. We loved everyone and everything about that town. Why do you think he's never left?" she said. "No, Charlie, he's doing it because he loves you. It's twisted and misguided, but he does love you. To him, you're the son we never had. I've seen through Aria's eyes what you've done. You've brought a certain spark back that he lost when I was taken from him. So, regardless of anything you do, Charlie, he'll always think of you as his son."

"But he said—"

"He lied," Elizabeth said. She leaned Charlie's head against her shoulder and started stroking his hair. "He was just hurt that you chose the town over him. Doesn't that sound more like him?"

"He's not going to believe me, though."

"He will if you show him this. Tell him the truth. Tell him I'm not dead. Tell him the town is not to blame. They did nothing wrong. It was all my fault," Elizabeth said. She took a locket from around her neck. It was engraved with an intricate rose design with a number of lines running through its center. The longer Charlie looked at it, the more the design's parts seemed to move like the gears of a clock, until Charlie could have sworn he saw a keyhole manifest in the middle of the rose. "Show him this. He'll believe you then."

She thrust the locket into Charlie's hands. Then Elizabeth began to wince. She hunched over herself and gripped her left arm tightly as it glowed a bright, ethereal blue.

"Stop the carriage!" she shouted. She breathed heavily before regaining her composure. She blew a strand of hair out of her face and smiled back at the young vampire.

"This is the end of the road for me. I can't get any closer to the town. Do stop him. Please. He's not a bad man."

"I'll try," Charlie said.

"Promise me!" she said pleadingly.

"I promise," Charlie said.

"Good. You'll be okay," she said.

The doors swung open, and both Charlie and the cat exited the carriage. Elizabeth waved at him, while still clutching her left arm. And with that, she left.

The cat looked up at Charlie with a wide grin. "See, I told you I can save you. Don't forget our deal."

"I won't," Charlie said. He saw the entrance to Maple Town in the distance. "That's so sad that she can never see him."

"She was forced to leave Vincent. Her ex-fiancé followed her, or something like that. Rumor has it he gave her a choice between Vincent's life or to never see him again. Guess which one she chose."

Charlie was silent.

"She's been living with that fiancé ever since. I guess I should say 'husband' now." The cat laughed. "She's miserable, as you can tell. Charlie, there are no happy endings in this world. Let me make that clear. Not for Elizabeth, or for Vincent . . . Hell, even Autaine's wife was burned at the stake just in time for Vincent to witness it. Not bad, but I take off points because it was the Autaine woman. Casting roles is such an important part. Not many people realize you can't take just anyone to be burned alive. So, heed that piece of advice before you go storming back into a town that hates you. It won't end well. It never does."

"I have to at least try," Charlie said.

"They hate you! Remember that. They know you're a vampire now. They'll kill you on the spot. You do know that?"

"Vincent needs to know that Elizabeth isn't dead. At least then he can stop hurting. Maybe he can still stop all this."

"You don't owe them anything," the cat said flatly.

"They were so good to me. I can't just let them die. I need to give them a fighting chance, at the very least. Maybe Vincent will call off the attack once I tell him they weren't responsible for Elizabeth. Maybe he'd stop the wolves if he knew Elizabeth was alive!"

"That's a lot of what-ifs," the cat said. "Well, go on! You don't have much time to waste. Tick-tock. Tick-tock. It's a big race between you and the clock—and those wolves."

CHAPTER NINETEEN

THE BOY WHO CRIED WOLF

He just had to get to number thirteen Chiaroscuro Lane. Charlie's legs ached with each step he took. They seemed to whine and anchor him down the more he tried to run, yet he did not stop until he reached the town entrance.

The sun was already setting. It shone a volcanic orange cracked with white. Traces of a pacifying blue peeked through the lava sky, but would soon vanish behind a veneer of black and a bright full moon.

He still had a bit to go. He managed to make it past the blacksmith's hut and over the bridge with the stump full of rocks. However, his trek to number thirteen Chiaroscuro Lane would prove to be far harder than he'd ever imagined as more and more eyes followed him the deeper he made it into the town.

It was only when he stepped into the marketplace that the hands clambered all over him. They dragged him. They forced him down and smothered him.

"Get the vampire!" came a voice.

"Hold him down!" came another.

The hands kept Charlie chained to the ground. He struggled to get even a few words out as the mob of people grew larger and larger until he was practically drowning under the weight of the townspeople. He kept trying to warn someone—anyone who'd listen—about the approaching werewolves.

"Wait! Please, you need to listen to me!" Charlie said.

"Shut him up! You killed Lord Autaine and Warren! You've lost any right to talk, boy!" came a rough voice in his ear.

They gagged Charlie and tied him up. They swarmed like bees. More and more people gathered, forming a circle around the young vampire.

The sunset made them all look alike. They whispered and screamed whenever he inched anywhere near the fringe of the circle they'd made around him. Charlie struggled against his bindings and tried to shake off the gag, but he was immediately forced down by someone's boot. He eventually managed to move the gag and just barely get out the word "wolves" before someone repositioned the gag and beat him.

The crowd buzzed and hollered for what felt like an eternity, until Charlie finally felt hands tug at his hair and lift his head along with it. Charlie looked up with the only eye that wasn't swollen shut. Then he was pushed back down. This time, his neck and arms landed on something wooden. Charlie heard a loud clunk as something closed around them.

He couldn't move his whole upper body. He struggled, but his arms and head remained trapped by the wood.

There was nothing but hate in the eyes of the people that once loved him. The baker was the first to throw a tomato at his face. Charlie turned his head upon impact and watched the juices dripping onto the ground. A few men broke away from the circle and proceeded to beat Charlie further. He felt their

kicks and punches bruise him repeatedly until the gag finally fell from his mouth again. Between the rotting fruit that was being thrown at him and the beating he was taking, Charlie could barely keep conscious. He heard the crowd's jeers and a man shouting, "Look at the face of the monster! Hideous! Stare in fear of the terrifying Charlie Prowl! Beat him all you like! He can't die!"

The crowd laughed. They had begun to run out of fruit and were now throwing objects from their shops at the young vampire.

"Wait! Please! Listen!" Charlie cried between the blows. "Wolves are coming!"

"Shut up, vampire!" he heard them shout, among other profanities that have no place in this tale of ours.

"The monster!" shouted one man. "It talks!"

"I'm not a monster!" Charlie shouted.

No one heard him.

Instead, some of the laborers tore at his ropes and ripped Charlie's black suit jacket. They ripped it all apart, almost dislocating his shoulders and arms. Charlie screamed as he faced the mob in nothing but his trousers.

"Wait! Please! Someone, please!" Charlie was practically begging now. Tears streamed down his cheeks. "Sally! Someone get Sally!"

"Leave her out of this," said one of the laborers holding him. "I can't believe you kissed her."

"Please, Sally!" Charlie moaned. "Where are you? You have to tell them I'm not a monster. YOU KNOW ME!"

He repeated her name over and over again. He was shouting so loud now that a few of the crowd members had quieted. They pushed him down as he continued to scream for Sally.

The mob of people hushed up, and with the little visibility Charlie had left, he saw the crowd shift to make room for a young woman with golden locks. She emerged at the front of the mob.

She stared with her arms held against her chest as if Charlie were about to attack her. Charlie smiled seeing her usual red dress with the white stripes.

"Sally," he said in barely a whisper. "You need to tell them that werewolves are coming to destroy the town! Everyone is in danger. There's no time! Sally, please tell them. Please!"

He hung his head, but he heard nothing. He raised it again, looking at her with his only good eye. She just stood there, staring back at him, and in her eyes he saw his half-naked body that oozed with rotting fruit, bruises, cuts, and shame. He breathed heavily, still looking at her.

"Did you hear me?"

The queen of broken hearts stared, obviously repulsed that she'd ever cared for the creature in front of her. In that moment Charlie realized that to her, he was the same monster that had killed her grandfather, and consequently her grandmother. He was the reason she had to marry Atticus Autaine. He was the reason for everything.

Sally's mouth quivered.

Her loyal subjects had grown deadly silent waiting for what Sally would say. Her mouth opened, shaking. She said something, but no one, at first, heard it. She said it again, but still no one heard her. Gradually, the few words grew louder and louder until the whole world heard her.

"Off with his head!"

The crowd was in an uproar. Sally returned to the mob. Out in the distance, Charlie could see the blood blade making its way toward him. He struggled to escape from the wood blocks that bound him. It was no use. Atticus emerged from the crowd and received the blood blade with a curt nod. He looked down at Charlie, shaking his head.

In that moment, Charlie read the unmistakable message in his former friend's eyes. You shouldn't have come back.

Atticus held the blade up over Charlie's head. Charlie took a deep breath and readied himself, when a loud howl echoed throughout the town.

Everyone looked around for the source of the call. The first howl was followed by several more. Atticus turned his blade toward the noise. The howls grew in number and urgency. Suddenly, racing and jumping from rooftop to rooftop were snarling beasts with gray, black, brown, and white fur. They charged at the mob that had gathered, causing a frenzy as everyone scrambled in every which direction.

Most of the women retreated to hide in their various houses as their husbands stayed behind to defend them. They huddled in closets, cupboards, and locked rooms, clutching their children if they had any. As for the unmarried women, they, like the men, grabbed whatever they could to fight off the wolves.

Charlie looked out at the carnage playing before his eyes. Cottages were on fire, people were screaming, and a wolf howled every few minutes.

Atticus had sprinted away with the blood blade while Charlie continued to struggle with his trappings. He needed to get to Vincent. It was the only way to stop it all.

To his dismay, a black wolf with a white stripe down its back had spotted him and was now inching toward him, baring its sharp teeth. It howled loudly and raced toward him. It jumped in the air and slashed at him, but hit the wood so hard that it released Charlie. Charlie rolled away and proceeded to dodge every strike the wolf made at him. He grabbed a piece of wood to defend himself with.

However, against the already weak Charlie, the wolf clawed through the wooden board as if it were paper. It then lunged, its jaws gaping, at Charlie, who quickly ducked. The wolf flew overhead, into a cottage, and gave a faint whimper when it landed.

Charlie looked out at the mansion on the hilltop and limped his way toward it. He was careful not to draw any attention to himself, but his stealth betrayed him as a small group of brown wolves eyed him hungrily over the family of four they'd just finished feasting on. They raced at Charlie with blood still dripping from their mouths. Charlie sprinted with all his might to make it to the tall black gate.

It was locked.

He slammed his fists against the metal railings. He started climbing, then he heard a faint click. The gate opened. Charlie quickly slinked in and forced the gate closed.

The wolves bashed their bodies against the tall black gate, each time whimpering, for they could not get in. In fact, as Charlie ran up the familiar hilltop, he realized that number thirteen Chiaroscuro Lane remained completely untouched.

He beat his hands against the brass double doors, which, like the gates below, opened on their own, letting Charlie in.

"Vincent!" Charlie shouted. "Vincent, where are you?"

He heard nothing.

Instead, Aria flew down the stairs to meet him. She fluttered in the air at first, happy to see Charlie, then began pecking at his head, clearly annoyed.

"I'm sorry! This is urgent. Where's Vincent? Can you lead me to him?"

Aria flew up and down quickly and gave Charlie a determined look as she swung herself up the stairs. Charlie hurried behind her, checking every room they passed.

They went through several hallways before Charlie found himself in front of the crystal room that had started it all. And inside, watching the town from the wide window, was Vincent in his usual black suit. Aria flew to Vincent's finger, and he guided her little paper legs to his shoulder. He had a bottle in his hand as he looked on, expressionless, at the burning, screaming, and howling below.

"Vincent! You have to stop this!"

Vincent turned toward Charlie as if only just realizing he was there. His narrowed eyes looked Charlie up and down. "See what they've done. Here, let me help." He walked over to his son and knelt down. He reached out his hand and began wiping the remains of rotting fruit from his son's body with a handkerchief. With each swipe of the cloth, Charlie's wounds began to heal. "Such cruelty. This only proves this is for the best. No more will they hurt my family."

Vincent returned his gaze to the window, his eyes almost vacant at the sight of all the carnage below.

"They didn't hurt anyone! Please, you have to listen to me!" Charlie pleaded.

Vincent turned on Charlie. "And here I thought you'd finally learned your lesson. You stupid boy," he said. "Regardless, we'll have our freedom soon. We can leave this wretched town."

"You don't mean that!" Charlie said. "Please listen."

"So, you've learned nothing," Vincent said, shaking his head. "I can't stop this!"

"But Elizabeth isn't dead," Charlie said frantically. "She wouldn't want this! They aren't to blame! She's not dead!"

"What are you talking about, you silly child?"

"She's alive!" Charlie said, looking down at the carnage below. "Please, stop this. She told me to tell you not to do this. They're not to blame."

It happened so fast. Vincent laid the bottle down on the crystal end table, grabbed Charlie by the throat, and pushed him hard against the wide window. It shattered, leaving Charlie hanging by Vincent's hand.

"I WATCHED HER BURN AT THE STAKE!"

"That . . . wasn't . . . her," Charlie croaked.

"And how would you know this?"

Charlie reached into his pocket and pulled out the locket.

Vincent recoiled and dropped his son back into the room. The locket fell to the floor as Charlie gasped for air. Vincent knelt down to retrieve the locket. He held it and squinted before finally looking back at Charlie. "Where did you get this?"

"Elizabeth gave it to me. She said it would convince you that I'm telling the truth."

"But why couldn't she . . ."

"A cat told me it's because of her former fiancé or something. She's cursed. Please, I don't know what it means. You need to stop this. I'm begging you! They're innocent! They didn't kill Elizabeth!"

Vincent stared out at the flames and screaming people. His face transformed into a blind rage as he threw the crystal end table out the wide window, causing shards of glass to sprinkle down the hillside.

He calmed down. His usual ponytail had broken from its hold. His long black hair hung around his shoulders as he staggered back, his hand to his forehead. Vincent looked out at the wreckage below and then back at his own quivering hands. It was as if the pieces of a puzzle he'd long been trying to figure out were slowly coming together.

"I see," Vincent said finally. "So it was him."

"Vincent, stop the attack!" Charlie said, shaking Vincent.

Vincent looked into Charlie's cerulean-blue eyes with a look that could only be described as defeat. His mouth shook as tears fell down the old vampire's cheeks. Then a few short words erupted from his mouth.

"I can't," he said. "Don't you see? I can't stop this."

Charlie stopped shaking Vincent and ran out the mansion and into the town with Aria at his heels. The two of them cut through alleyways, dodging past wolves.

Charlie needed to know that Atticus and Sally were going to be okay. The young vampire raced to the Maple Orchard, where a single man with a red blade stood defending himself against four wolves. He parried and blocked against their advances, eventually falling as one wolf struck his leg, twisting it.

Charlie sprinted up the dirt path and grabbed the blood blade the young man had dropped to nurse his leg.

"I don't need your help!" Atticus snapped.

"I beg to differ," Charlie said, pushing back each wolf that approached them.

"Why'd you come back anyway?" Skat shouted. "Aren't you supposed to be dead?"

"If you'd just listened," Charlie said, stabbing one of the wolves, "you'd have heard me trying to warn the town about these things."

"So it's my fault!" Atticus said. He threw a couple of stones at one of the wolves.

"Shut up, will you? I'm trying to save your life!"

"I never asked to be saved by a filthy—"

Charlie turned to see Atticus being held by one of the wolves. Charlie tossed the blood blade to Atticus, who caught it and slashed the head off the wolf.

Atticus fell out of the wolf's grip and began nursing his twisted leg again. He tossed the blood blade back to Charlie.

"We're even, then. Let's just call it that," Atticus said.

Then a curious thing happened.

The wolves retreated. A large cloud of black smoke emerged in the distance, covering everything in sight—even the moon. Charlie looked to see where the smoke was coming from.

He, like everyone else in town, saw that it was coming from number thirteen Chiaroscuro Lane. No matter how far away a person was—and in Charlie's case, he could barely make out the outlines of the mansion on the hilltop—they saw a great, monstrous flame engulfing the once-mysterious mansion. It shone like a beacon of hope to the townspeople as one by one, the wolves turned back into hairy men wrapped in big furs.

Charlie and Atticus coughed heavily, as did the wolves they had been fighting. However, unlike them, the wolves could not handle the smoke in their howling lungs. They hacked and hacked until they couldn't stand to be in the town anymore. They started leaving, each one turning into a speck as he sprinted away, while the smoke grew higher and higher until it blanketed the whole town.

The fire went on all night. Charlie leaned back against the Maples' front door next to Atticus, watching the mansion on the hilltop get swallowed up by the flames. The whole town, including them, was silent as all watched, mesmerized, knowing that by sunrise, the strange old house would be nothing but ash.

"You look like hell," Atticus said finally.

"Have you looked in the mirror lately?" Charlie said.

"Can't be worse than a vampire."

The two laughed, but again, the uneasy silence between them returned. The flames were beginning to die down. The two sat in silence for some time before Aria came flying toward them. She struggled and dipped in her flight for she held a letter in her paper beak.

The letter landed on Atticus's lap.

"What's this?"

"Your dad gave me this to give to you before he died," Charlie said.

"I swear, Charlie," Skat seethed. But before Skat could pick up the blood blade, Aria pecked at his head. "I get it! Just make her stop!"

Charlie nodded at Aria, who made a U-turn and landed on Charlie's head.

"I should've known that day you were looking for her," Atticus said. "I should've figured you weren't normal. I guess it doesn't matter now."

He eyed Charlie cautiously before ripping open the letter.

When he finished reading, he laid the letter down on his side and ran a hand over his mouth. He read the letter again, this time with little droplets falling from his eyes. When he was done, he passed it to Charlie.

To my dearest son,

Or perhaps I should call you Skat. I'm not a fool, and you're not as clever as you think.

Yes, I know.

Masks and secrets seem to be our family's MO. But I digress. You probably want nothing more than to bring me back alive and kill me for how I've ruined your life. Honestly, isn't that a little cliché and melodramatic? I guess the apple doesn't fall far from the tree. Knowing you, you've probably sworn revenge on Charlie. Idiot. My death was a price. You know what kind of demons I associate with. Do you honestly think I'd be killed by some timid vampire unless I wanted to?

Alas, I die knowing the truth.

Your mother wasn't killed by vampires. She was killed for no reason whatsoever. That was the answer I received. She was just in the wrong place at the wrong time.

Disappointing, isn't it?

Anticlimatic even.

Your mother, my wife, died by coincidence. How fair is that? But at least I die tonight knowing the answer. What sweet hell awaits me? I relish finding out! Maybe in death, you'll be less of a disappointment to me. Avenge me, finish your apprenticeship as a blacksmith, marry the Maple girl—I don't give a rat's ass what you do. I have no dying wish. I die tonight without any regrets. So what you do from now on is on you and you alone.

Your father,

Lord Allister Autaine

"That bastard," Atticus said, his voice quivering. "That bastard!" He wiped a sleeve against his nose and dropped his head into his hands.

"It's all here." He coughed and raised his head again. "He even admits that his death was planned and that he knew you'd take his life. It was all on his terms, but why couldn't you let me know? You bastard!"

"I'm sorry," Charlie said.

"I know."

The two watched the smoke clear in the distance as the last of the flames in town were extinguished. Only number thirteen Chiaroscuro Lane still blazed. It shone like a lighthouse, representing everything and nothing at all. Charlie laid a hand on his former friend's shoulder, and the two continued to sit in silence. Neither dared to speak. They remained at each other's side, enjoying a moment that they knew would never happen

again. Then they just sat watching the crackling of the blazing mansion on the hilltop in quiet acknowledgment that, much like our tale, their friendship had come to an end.

"Are you still going to marry her?" Charlie asked.

"Yeah."

CHAPTER TWENTY

THE WEDDING

The town had always known that Vincent was a vampire. They knew long before Atticus ever told them. It was around the time when Elizabeth was supposedly burned at the stake that they all put two and two together.

But being the incredibly brilliant woman she was, Elizabeth cast a charm similar to the one she used on Charlie, erasing all memory of her marriage to Vincent from the minds of every person in Maple Town. She encased the memory of the happy couple on number thirteen Chiaroscuro Lane in a dense fog, buried so deep that the most the villagers could do was gossip, the truth concerning her and Vincent always just beyond the reach of their recall. And as she cast this spell, she hoped with all her heart it was enough to keep her beloved safe.

So when Atticus called the town together to discuss Charlie, it was as if someone had shone a light on Elizabeth's fog. If Charlie was a vampire, could Vincent be one too? That simple thought would lead them out of the fog of their memories and remind them of the conclusions they drew all those years ago. However, they left the vampire alone—partly because Vincent had ceased leaving the mansion, and partly out of fear of what the vampire would do if they invoked his wrath.

Even so, after the fire had subsided, the people of Maple Town looked upon the ashes of number thirteen Chiaroscuro Lane with a sort of longing, as if they'd lost a close friend. The gate that had restricted them for so long was now unlocked. The baker's wife was the first to walk up the hilltop to examine the wreckage. She was soon followed by the rest of the town's survivors.

Vincent was nowhere to be found in the ruins. They found burnt paper, mountains of charred books, wooden beams snapped in half, and an old but pristine bookshelf—the only item untouched by the fire. The townspeople assumed some magic must have protected it. It took many injured men to pull the large bookshelf out of the wreckage. And what they found inside were trinkets that would have been meaningless to anyone other than them.

As a young girl, the baker's wife had given Vincent a flower wreath, which he'd kept though it had long since wilted. The sorrowful fabric woman found her favorite black ribbon, which she'd given Elizabeth after their game of hopscotch resulted in Elizabeth scraping her knee. Griselda had given Elizabeth the ribbon to wrap around her leg. Eventually, everyone came to the same realization; behind every scowl, every glare, every hate-filled remark was a man who loved them dearly.

From that moment on, great tales would be told, each more incredible than the last, of how Vincent used his vampire's knowledge of the unknown to ward off the wolves by sacrificing his mansion to block the moon. Some tales said that Vincent single-handedly burned himself alive in the fire to show his love for the people in the town. His scowl became the stuff of legends, and he was named the Vampire of Maple Town.

Unfortunately, the same night that made Vincent a legend was also the night that many of the survivors would remember as the Tragedy of Maple Town.

Many lives were lost; it took weeks to dig all the necessary graves. Of those who'd lived through the night, many remained in a state of shock, some in denial, and those who still had tears to shed would cry so much during the moments when no one could see that they'd never be the same again.

Maurice died protecting his wife and his small cottage. He had set his bakery on fire, causing a great explosion on the first floor, in the hopes of stopping the horde of wolves that surrounded him.

His wife, who hid upstairs, survived because of his heroics.

The chimney sweep stood strong with a group of laborers against an onslaught of twenty wolves at the town entrance. They succeeded in keeping many werewolves from entering the town, but sadly, none but the chimney sweep survived to tell of their great courage.

The butcher survived but was found covered in blood from head to toe, two cleavers in his hands. He'd never speak of what happened; instead, he would simply retire from being a butcher and oddly would never cut nor eat a piece of meat again.

The sorrowful fabric woman had a stub where her left arm used to be. A wolf had bitten it off as she'd tried to run away. She faked her death after that and remained still against the cobblestones until the great black cloud of smoke drove the wolves away.

She'd eventually dedicate her life to finding a method to sew and make garments with one arm.

In the battle, Sam led a ragtag team of men and women, who all managed to survive. The swords that Sam passed out helped them to get away with only a few cuts and bruises here and there. It was Sam who suffered the worst of the injuries. He lost his right leg to a wolf and would forever walk with a cane and a metal leg.

As for Sally and Atticus, they were married in a private ceremony only a few days after the Tragedy of Maple Town, in Sally's favorite spot in the Maple Orchard. There was no cake, no beautiful dress, no pews, and no arches. They had only each other.

They stood hand in hand in front of the many trees and flowers in the orchard. Their smiles concealed their resentment, for they knew that the town's future rested upon their ability to appear as happy and hopeful as they knew they could never truly be with each other. In that spot, the two of them made a silent vow to each other to return Maple Town to its former glory.

Not surprisingly, this small ceremony was completely overshadowed by their actual wedding, which took place many months later and was the focus of everyone in Maple Town. The townspeople worked tirelessly to fulfil every command the newly widowed Elise Maple shouted at them.

What happened to Walter Maple?

Elise claimed her husband had "tripped" over a rock while running from a pack of wolves. The question of whether Walter actually tripped or if Elise had tripped him was highly debated, mainly because Elise ran off and married a rich traveler a few months after her husband's demise.

Thankfully, by that point, the town didn't need her orders anymore. The wedding that had started as a means to keep busy after the tragedy transformed into something much grander than anyone expected. Everyone pitched in in some way to transform the marketplace into the setting of a lavish occasion that would represent the future of their town.

The baker's wife made a glorious cake. Laborers carved beautiful benches, arches, and pews. The sorrowful fabric lady produced a canopy using her most beautiful silk and just the one hand. All in all, it was the biggest and most beautiful wedding

the town had ever seen, and everyone was in attendance but one. The bride.

The last one to see Sally was the baker's wife, Marie, who helped the young lady with her veil. She spoke about how beautiful Sally looked in her ivory gown, how Sally regarded herself in the mirror, occasionally toying with the dress that Griselda had fashioned for her. When the wedding march began to echo in the distance, Sally turned to face Marie and flashed her signature smile.

"Can I have a moment, please?"

Marie recalled leaving to join the others, who had all gathered in the pews. There, the wedding march played on and on, until it was clear the bride would not be coming. She'd left Maple Town, and to my knowledge has never returned.

Perhaps it was for the best.

You may be wondering how Charlie felt about all this. The truth is he never learned of it.

Weeks before the wedding preparations were complete, he and his paper companion made their way to the edge of town. Charlie glanced down at the silver pocket watch in his hand. It was all he could find of Vincent in the ruins of number thirteen Chiaroscuro Lane. He soon realized that the watch was never broken at all, but just needed someone who knew how to set it.

"We should get going," Charlie said. "It's almost time."

Aria flew alongside Charlie as he walked up the steps leading to the small train station.

"Do you think Vincent survived?" Charlie asked.

Aria began flying up and down. She then tugged on Charlie's collar, urging him to keep moving.

"I know, I know. We'll find him," Charlie said. "Or at the very least, we'll finally see what's beyond the town."

Aria did a backflip when a loud roar echoed in the distance. It sounded like a giant was thundering toward them. It gradually grew louder and louder, accompanied by a low hissing sound. The train finally came to a slow halt before them. A thin layer of steam erupted in the air, and the doors to the compartments opened one by one.

Charlie made his way onto the red train. Inside, the compartments were white. All were empty. He settled into a seat by the window and waited for the train to depart, knowing that no one else waited to board it.

He'd chosen to leave during the funeral that was being held that afternoon. No one would see him depart as the whole town was gathered at number thirteen Chiaroscuro Lane. Charlie had heard rumors that at the end of the service a maple seed would be planted on the hilltop surrounded by the tall black fence, in Vincent's honor.

With Aria on his shoulder, Charlie looked out at Maple Town one last time. Perhaps Vincent had been right all along. He could never exist with the townspeople. He was foolish to think otherwise.

"Oh, now this is a surprise," said the young woman. She had long brown hair tied in a ponytail, at the base of which was a hairpin made out of playing cards, all hearts. Like Charlie, she wore black pants and a loose white shirt, except her waist had a red sash tied around it. She dragged behind her a large trunk. She took a seat in front of Charlie. "My father's bloody acquaintance."

It wasn't a question, but simply an acknowledgment of their connection. She nodded to Charlie, and a large black cat plopped himself beside her and gave Charlie a wide smile. The two exchanged a knowing look before the cat turned away. Alice, on the other hand, did not once let her green and turquoise eyes leave Charlie.

"You must think the worst of me," Charlie said.

"I don't know what I think of you," Alice replied.

The train had started to move. A pause sat uncomfortably between them for some time, until Aria began to flutter around, pestering the cat. The cat took a few swipes, each time missing the paper swallow and becoming increasingly annoyed by her inaudible laughter. Charlie and the girl couldn't help but laugh at their two companions.

With the mood lightened, Alice changed the topic of conversation. "That's a fascinating bird. Is she really made of paper?"

"As far as I know. Her name is Aria," Charlie said.

"Well, it's a pleasure to meet you, Aria," Alice said.

Aria turned at the sound of her name, flew to the girl, and landed on her fingertips.

"You know, if you ever want to ditch that lovesick vampire, you always have a place with me."

"I'm right here!" Charlie said. "And who are you calling lovesick?"

"You, obviously," Alice said. She returned her attention to Aria. "But I think we've teased him enough, don't you?" She petted Aria under her paper chest. Charlie swore he could almost hear Aria purr.

Alice stopped and began to pet the large black cat next to her. "Though not as adorable as your paper friend, this is my cat."

"He has no name," Charlie said.

"No, he doesn't, does he?" Alice said. "How would you know that?"

"Just a guess," Charlie said.

She flashed a smile at him. "You know, I'm not afraid of vampires."

"No one says you should be," Charlie countered. "But you know what I've done. What's to stop me from killing you right now?"

"Bold words," Alice said. "However, you forget that I know you too well. Someone who falls that hard for Sally must have real issues with killing humans. Besides, I knew a vampire that could've killed me for years, but he didn't, so you could say I'm pretty sure I'm safe. Besides, you don't have the scowl down just yet."

"You knew Vincent?"

"In a way," Alice said. "The question is, how well did any of us really know Vincent?" She looked out the window toward the funeral up on number thirteen Chiaroscuro Lane.

Nodding, Charlie regarded his companion's piercing eyes. They looked so familiar. And then it struck him just where he'd seen those eyes before.

"You're the girl from the Autumn Ball," Charlie said.

"Took you long enough," Alice said.

"Though that doesn't answer the question as to why you're leaving. Skat and Sally and the rest of the town could use someone like you to help them rebuild. You're going to miss their wedding," Charlie said.

"Ah well, I'm not too concerned about that." Alice rifled through her bag and pulled out a deck of playing cards. She began shuffling them in her hand. She looked as though she were thinking very carefully about how to answer his question. "Let's just say there's nothing left for me back there. And since my brother and Sally won't listen to reason, I'm not going to stand around to watch them make this huge mistake. So I'm leaving."

"At least you have a choice," Charlie said. He let his words linger, still trying to make sense of the mysterious girl before him.

"Fair enough," Alice said. "Here, pick a card."

"Why?"

"Just do it."

"No, that's silly."

"Will you just pick a card?" she snapped. "There. Now remember it and put it anywhere in the deck."

Charlie did as he was told. The girl began shuffling until Charlie was sure his card was lost. Then she waved her hands over the deck. One card shot out and began flying around the compartment.

"You're a witch!" Charlie said. He laughed, clapped, and stared in awe as the card he'd chosen did backflips in the air. Aria chased after it, but couldn't catch it.

"You like it?" Alice said.

"Of course!"

Alice gave a small smile before extending her hand. "I don't think we've been properly introduced."

"I guess we haven't. I'm Charlie."

"Alice," she said. "And I have a proposition for you."

ABOUT THE AUTHOR

Kane McLoughlin is a writer with an obsession with fairy tales. He has a degree in English from Aquinas College, too many decks of playing cards, and countless fairy tales in his bookshelf that he uses to full his passions. These fairy tales range anywhere from western classics to tales akin to his Japanese roots. *The Vampire of Maple Town* is his first novel.

CPSIA information can be obtained
at www.ICGtesting.com
Printed in the USA
FFHW021123031218
49719931-54137FF